MAKING WAVES

by

David O'Neil

W & B Publishers
USA

W & B Publishers

For information:
W & B Publishers
9001 Ridge Hill Street
Kernersville, NC 27284

www.a-argusbooks.com

ISBN: 9781942981527

Book Cover designed by Dubya

Other Books by David O'Neil

<u>Counterstroke Thriller Series</u>

Exciting, Isn't It?
Market Forces
When Needs Must

<u>Donny Weston/Abby Marshall Thriller Series</u>

A Thrill a Minute
Fatal Meeting
It's Just One Thing After Another
Lethal Complications
What Goes Around
Without Prejudice

<u>Sea & Military War Series</u>

Better The Day
Desperate Measures
Distant Gunfire
Hell is Another Place
In Dangerous Waters
Quarterdeck
Sailing Orders
Winning

Action Series

Minding the Store
The Hunted
The Mercy Run

Romance

Seasons

Chapter 1

1938

The water flooded noisily out through the drain. To Mark it sounded like a bath emptying, only on a bigger scale. As the final drops disappeared he sighed with relief. The difficult part was over. Now he could concentrate of the next stage. Only there was no next stage. He had reached an impasse. From here on in he would need back-up, and there was none.

***

In Knoxville, Tennessee, Marian Smith lifted the shot glass and downed the Jameson in one swift gulp.

***

In Cork, Eire, Ewan Fitzgerald sighed deeply and stripped the .45 colt automatic in a series of swift movements, and then assembled it almost as swiftly. Finally, he picked up the magazine and snapped it into the butt, racked back the slide cocking the gun to eject a bullet, and then lowered the hammer to the safe position. Removing the magazine once more, he inserted the ejected bullet into the magazine and replaced it in position in the butt of the pistol. He slid it into the quick draw underarm rig and rearranged his jacket.

***

Lieutenant Commander Michael Wallace RN leaned over his desk and swore under his breath. What were the Germans up to? He straightened up and looked at his watch. *Damn.* It was close to the time he when he would have to be at Northolt. There was only time for a quick wash and brush up before he would have to leave.

In the small wash room at the rear of the office he looked at himself in the mirror. He looked a little tired. His blond hair needed cutting, otherwise he was wearing quite well. He had to lean forward to use the mirror. It was set for people shorter than 6ft 2in. He grinned and, noticing his even teeth, decided a quick brush would do no harm. At thirty-two years old, having entered the Navy as a midshipman intending to become a career officer, he had progressed well. The impending war had speeded things up a bit. He still hadn't married, though it had been close on two occasions. He guessed it could be sometime before that would happen now.

***

On the Great West road the Alvis seemed to float along, passing the other traffic without effort. As he passed through Greenford the speedometer recorded 82 miles per hour. He would arrive before the aircraft landed.

***

At the airfield entrance he showed his pass to the airman on duty, drove past the raised boom and round to the apron in front of the assigned hanger. Three minutes later the De Havilland Dragon Rapide landed with little fuss, and taxied over to the hanger.

The door of the aircraft opened and a small ladder was lowered. A tall man in a navy blue suit stepped down and turned to assist a young woman descend. She was followed by two men: one a stocky man medium height, the other as tall as Michael himself. The man in the blue suit turned to Michael.

"Collected and delivered as requested, one lady, two gentlemen."

The aircrew transferred the bags of the three passengers to the trunk of the Alvis.

Michael opened the doors for the trio and slid into the driving seat. "Let's go get something to eat," he said. "We'll do the introductions over dinner." He put the car into gear and drove out to the Great West road once more, turning right toward Uxbridge and the west.

He maintained a steady sixty for the next twelve miles, finally turning off into a country lane. Marian Smith, sitting in the front seat saw a road sign, Denham Village, on the corner as they turned.

Michael Wallace drove into the driveway of a large house, only dimly seen in the darkening light. The windows were lit and there was a warm comfortable feel about the place as they were ushered into the hallway of the house. The aproned woman who received them, showed them to their rooms. Speaking is a soft Scottish voice, she invited them to join the others in the drawing room in a half-hour for a drink before dining.

***

Downstairs once more, the woman saw Michael and smiled. He smiled back at her. "Hullo, Beth," he said. "What do you think?"

She grinned. "She looks to be the best-looking one so far. Have you spoken to her yet?"

"Come on, Beth. You know I won't even look at a woman until you give the go-ahead."

"Nonsense as usual, Michael. You should really grow up. You cannot stay a wee boy all your life. I will not be here to look after you forever."

"Then marry me, Beth? Save me from myself."

"Och, away with you. I'm old enough to be your mother. Angus would spin in his grave to hear your blether."

In the drawing room a fire was warming the room from the ingle nook fireplace. The room was twenty by eighteen with a ceiling supported by timber beams, the plaster between them slightly yellowed by the smoke from the fire over the years. The room was furnished with comfortable armchairs and the stone slab floor was strewn with rugs. The side board was arrayed with drink bottles and the crystal glass glittered in the warm wall lights scattered around the walls.

Michael walked over to the side board and poured himself a scotch to which he added a splash of soda water.

He heard the door behind him open and turned to see the woman whom Beth described as the best yet.

He blessed Beth silently. She was as always right. The dark-haired woman was drop-dead gorgeous.

He stepped forward. "I'm Michael Wallace." He held out his hand, meeting her firm grip. "Marian Smith, I presume?"

She smiled and said, "Guilty," in a soft American voice.

"Drink?" He said, waving at the sideboard.

"Do you have a Jameson there?"

"We certainly do." Michael found the bottle and poured for her. "Mixer?"

"No. Thank you. Just as it comes." She received the drink and tasted it, restraining her impulse to toss it down.

The door opened once more and the two men entered. The stocky man introduced himself as Ewan Fitzgerald, from Cork. The tall man was Mark Randall, from Seattle.

Both men helped themselves to drinks: the Irishman, Jameson's, and the American a Scotch.

They sat down to dinner around a starched linen tablecloth, silverware, crystal ware and roast beef.

The conversation was light and without strain throughout the process of eating. When it was over they returned to the drawing room and, over cigars and cigarettes, coffee and brandy, the real business began.

Ewan Fitzgerald spoke, "What are we all doing here?" His soft Irish accent was warm and deceptively caring.

Michael smiled and said in German, "You may not realise that we all have one thing in common. All here speak German fluently." He paused for a moment to allow his comment to sink in. "Also, you all have reason to hate the National Socialist Party led by Herr Hitler."

The people in the room looked around at each other, showing interest for the first time.

Michael spoke again, still in his Berliner German accent. "Of course, you all realise that you have been invited here for a reason. I have the impression that what I have to tell you, and subsequently, the job I have in mind for us all, will be acceptable, as it offers a method of achieving the revenge I'm sure you all wish for. It will be damaging to the party and cause more upset than a division of troops. That is..." he added, "provided things go as planned."

Mark Randall smiled grimly. "We await the disclosure of the catch. Having seen the bait, where is the catch?"

"Knowing the Nazi party, do you really have to ask that question? The catch is of course, if things go wrong, the Gestapo will have some extra bodies to play with."

Marion Smith asked the other question. "What have you got in mind?"

Michael paused before answering. "I need to know if you are in or out? If you are out, you have the teaser I sent and a ticket home. If you are in, I will collect the tickets and hold them until the job is done. Until I have your reply, you know all you need to know."

Ewan asked, "We go to Germany?"

"German travel will be necessary." Michael replied.

Mark said, "I'm not unknown in Germany."

"That will apply to us all. We are not seeking old friends or, in fact, enemies per-se. and we will all be altered in appearance if necessary. We do understand that there are risks for us all in crossing the border. The main thing is that we have the chance to make a real impact on the enemy when the war begins."

Marion was last to speak. "Didn't I read that the British Prime Minister had made a deal with Hitler to put the whole thing off?"

"Mr Chamberlain lives in hopes. The real leaders here are well aware that Hitler will not stop now over a silly little piece of paper waved by someone whom he despises."

He looked around the trio. "Well? What will it be?"

Ewan said, "I'm in."

Mark nodded, "Me too."

They all looked at Marion. She shrugged. "I guess that means I am in as well."

Michael smiled and settled the automatic back more comfortably in his shoulder rig. That was the part he had not been looking forward to. It seemed he need worry no more about it.

"Let's drink a toast to our project." He lifted his glass. "Long life for us and death to the enemy."

***

After drinking the toast, Michael opened a small note book. We have two projects to consider. The Germans have conventional weapons in abundance. They will need more than they have at the moment to achieve their aims. They have begun work in two new fields, rockets and atomic energy."

Mark looked up at the words. "They are working on atomic energy, an atom explosive?"

"According to my sources, they are sourcing heavy water for the line of research they are currently following. You know something of this?"

"I have been involved on the fringes of the research. I am a scientist after all. It's what I do!"

"What the hell is an atomic? Is it some sort of bomb?" Ewan asked.

"That is exactly what it is. Hell in big letters." Mark replied. "Bigger than anything so far known. Think of one bomb that can wipe out New York. That big!"

"Ouch!" Marion said. "Is he kidding?"

Michael stopped the discussion there. "That big, and the rockets that could deliver it from 5000 miles away."

The three sat in silence, absorbing the enormity of the task possibly ahead of them.

Michael rose to his feet, collected the brandy bottle and went around the trio, topping up glasses.

After a short while he said, "Right now our problem is people. For this all to happen, people have to do their jobs. We have to identify those people and where they work. That is phase one."

"Phase one?" Marion asked, with raised eyebrow.

"Actually, no. It's phase two. First, we have to get you trained and toughened up and, for that purpose, we've arranged for all three of you to attend a special course. I have experienced this course and survived, so I have no doubts you will all manage. When you complete the training, you will each be allocated a team to work with you."

"Why us?" Ewan asked determinedly. I'm not even bloody English, and they are not either."

Michael sat down in his chair once more and looked at each of them one by one. "I thought I would not need to answer that question. You all hate the Nazis. You all have good reasons to. You all speak German. You all can claim to be who you are, American, Irish, and you can all prove it.

"All of you are pretty fit, athletes in the recent past, and it matters not that you dislike the British. We are the only ones to take the Nazis seriously enough to do something positive about them before it's too late.

"We will train you, and put you in the field. From then on it's up to you. If you need us we will be here. If you wish to fly solo then you can. The point is that this is the second time Britain has been forced into the front line against a quite aggressive German government. They are already better prepared for war than any other country in the world at the moment, except possibly Japan. That may be the next one we have to face. First, we have to survive this problem. Last time, it took four years for America to enter into the fight for survival. This time? Who knows? All I know is we need to win the time to hold off Hitler until the country can be prepared to put up a real defence. That is, until we have time to mobilize properly. We have to start the ball rolling now.

"I know of your cases because I was in Germany at the time your particular tragedies occurred. The payment you receive reflects your civilian status. This will be a private operation, unlinked to any other official body, subject to Naval Intelligence only, and to this department only."

Chapter Two

Munich-Berlin Express

The tramcar rattled and swayed through the centre of the city, a lowering sky causing walkers to pull their coats around them against the chill of the late autumn wind.

Albert Kessler hugged his battered briefcase to his chest, head down, avoiding eye contact with the lady opposite who seemed to be taking a special interest in him.

He was beginning to wish he had not accepted the position he had been offered in Berlin. The past years had been difficult, and with the loss of his parents, rather more lonely than he would have believed. So the offer of the research place in Berlin had been a godsend. He was surprised at the provision of the suit and accessories which came after he had accepted the position, and surprised to learn he would be met by a representative for the journey north.

When he came to his stop at the Hauptbahnhof, he left the seat and stepped down into the street, looking warily to the right to make sure there was no threat from illegal traffic, sweeping through on inside between the tram and the pavement. He hurried into the railway station and made his way to the indicator board to check the departure platform for the train to Berlin. Satisfied that his information was correct thus far, he scurried through the station to the platform indicated and waited until the announcement to board the train.

Having located the carriage, he entered the luxury of the first class end of the train for the first time in his life. The porter directed him to his private compartment. At last he was able to lock the door and sit down in the armchair to relax. The heated compartment warm and he realised he was still wearing his coat. With a sigh he rose to his feet and removed the coat and hat, revealing the suit he had been given to wear. He stood in front of the mirror admiring the cut and style of the suit. It was better than any he had worn in the entire thirty-six years of his life.

The knock at the door made him jump. "Wha---who is it?" He called.

"Porter!" Came the voice, "Tea is served. Sir."

"I did not order tea." He said, impatiently opening the door.

The lady who had been watching him on the tram stood there, a gun in hand. She pushed him into the compartment, shut and locked the door. "Sit!" She said, and pushed him manually back into the chair.

He sat and stared at the gun. The woman looked at him and at the way he was watching the gun. With an impatient toss of her head she put the gun in her handbag.

Albert's eyes moved up to the woman's face. For the first time, he really looked at a stranger without losing focus and he realised that the face he was studying was alert. The clean cut features were interesting and put together in a most pleasing manner. The woman was beautiful. What? Why? Who?

She spoke. The voice was deep and warm, like velvet. "Sorry about the gun. I needed to get out of sight as fast as possible. I did not want an argument on the doorstep."

Albert found himself speaking, "What did you want with me?"

"I am here to protect you." She sounded serious. "There are people out there who would harm you if they could. I am here to stop them, if I can!"

"Harm...who sent you?" Albert was speaking like a robot, still puzzling out the question.

"Friends from overseas," she replied minimally.

Albert thought about it, adding up the various events of the past two weeks. The message about the death threats, the train reservations, the new clothes, and the attempt by the three men to rob and hurt him yesterday. He recalled the two other men who had saved him. The swift clinical way the men had dealt with his attackers. He shuddered. At least one of the attackers would never walk again, and both others had broken arms at least. Both his rescuers spoke fluent German, but he had not known them before. Now this woman was here to protect him. "Why?" He said at last.

The woman looked at him. "You don't know?"

He shook his head.

"What do you carry in your briefcase?"

He instinctively clutched the case, making sure it was still there and undamaged. "This is just some private work I have been trying on my own. It is precious to me only. Why would people wish to hurt me for this?"

"You attempted to patent your process and the authorities would not allow it?"

"True. They said it infringed another patent."

"They lied. Your work is unique. No-one has ever attempted to do what you are doing, up to now."

"This is what it is all about? The new clothes, the train tickets with the passport in another name. You here to protect me?"

"That is what it is all about. We travel together because you are normally alone. We are now husband and wife. My name is Maria, by the way, and, as your passport says, we come from Karlsruhe."

The train was moving quickly now and the lights of the city were getting fewer as they passed through the suburbs and into the countryside.

Maria stood and took Albert's coat. "Is there anything in the pockets?" She asked.

He shook his head. "No, nothing."

"Good. It can go now. It does not go with your new identity." She opened the window and the coat disappeared out into the darkness. Then, closing the window, she turned to Albert. "Now empty your pockets, of everything."

He stood up and emptied his pockets one by one, piling the contents on the table in the compartment. He removed his jacket and Maria checked the pockets herself. She then came over to him and put her hands into his trouser pockets one by one to make sure they were completely empty, while Albert stood blushing at the intimacy the contact entailed.

Maria saw his blushes. "Please remember, I am your wife. You should not be embarrassed by my close touch." She smiled as she spoke, and kissed him on the cheek. "There, that was not so bad, was it?"

She went through everything on the table. Then, satisfied, she said, "You are meticulous. There is nothing here to link you to your past life, except that. She pointed at the briefcase. Albert grabbed it protectively.

Maria smiled and shook her head. Walking over to the wardrobe, she opened it and removed a smart executive briefcase with a combination lock. Opening it, she pointed out the various features of the case, the file compartment, the penholders, and the small incendiary device which was there to destroy the contents if the case was tampered with. Finally, she showed him how to set the combination to his own selected pattern.

Albert saw the rest of his new clothes in the wardrobe, alongside the feminine collection, presumably for Maria, his wife?

Two suitcases stood in the bottom of the wardrobe.

Maria spoke from the other side of the compartment, "Please transfer your things to the new briefcase. The old one must go! From now on you are Eric Rohm. Get used to it. Think it. Dream it. Remember it at all times!"

Albert/Eric transferred his papers to the new case and set the combination, only then did they go to the dining car for dinner.

***

Marian felt a pang as the train passed through the Bavarian countryside. Her memories of the last time she was here came flooding back. Joseph had been alive and they were discussing getting married. Their train had been stopped at some small station and men got aboard, and came through the train talking loudly, ignoring the protests of the passengers they disturbed. Having taken over a large section of the carriage they were in, the newcomers started taking an interest and making comments about the other passengers. One grabbed a young girl passing his seat and dragged her into his lap, pawing her clumsily despite her protests, while his friends gave advice. Her family came to her rescue. The fight started there. But at the end Joseph had been shot in the face by one of the group attempting to rape Marian. She shivered at the memory. That was one of her reasons for trying to join the FBI.

She felt Eric grip her hand, he said, "Are you all right?"

"Someone walked over my grave." She said, with a small smile.

***

For Eric there was something about eating dinner on a train. Watching the passing countryside while eating appealed to some inner part of him. The romance of the whole business now involving him found him sitting looking into the eyes of the beautiful woman opposite him. Unbidden his hand reached out and once more covered Maria's. He found himself saying, "You are truly beautiful and I cannot believe that I am here holding your hand on this romantic train journey to Berlin."

Maria smiled at him and said quietly, "Am I hearing correctly? Is this the timid withdrawn man I met two hours ago?"

Eric answered equally quietly, "I have hidden depths." he smiled back at her. "The comment is trite, but in fact the reason I have managed to survive thus far, is that I try to adapt to the situation I am in. When I was a boy my parents were entertainers, acting and singing in small theatres throughout Europe. Living a life out of suitcases was safer if you could blend in. The alternative was being able to look after yourself. There was little chance that the local police would show any interest in complaints from itinerant players. My father had learned to fence for his acting career, and he extended his training to rough and tumble fighting. Having found a colleague who was once a bodyguard for a Paris mobster, he practiced self-defence and, in fact, offence as well. I went through the training and practice with my father. I also was trained to act as part of the family business. When I began my proper schooling, my parents lodged me in the locality of the best school they could afford.

"My advanced schooling came with scholarship awards to university. My progress was low key because I maintained a low profile, and kept my marks to a level that I thought would keep me out of the public eye."

"Why on earth would you do that?"

"Even in my youth, there was prejudice against 'travelers', whether they were gipsy or not. The less publicity I received the better. The fact that you are here protecting me should make it obvious that the prejudice still exists. I am aware that many of my former colleagues are in camps, regardless of their talent, and their mental ability, only because they are Jewish.

"When I am in a situation, I act the part to blend in. I wear the suit so I become the man."

He leaned forward over the table toward her. "What brought you into this game?"

Maria, aka Marion Smith, was surprised to find that she had no real answer to Eric's question. "I seriously do not know. I am here because I was recruited to be here for you."

"Why were you chosen?"

"Because of my special training, I guess."

Eric lifted his eyebrow.

"Maria shrugged. "I was trained for the FBI."

Eric looked about casually. There was no one in earshot. "You were FBI?"

"No!" The flat statement allowed no further comment.

After a moment Eric smiled. "Time to go, I believe." He held his hand out to Maria. "Shall we?"

She returned his smile, accepted his hand and, clinging to it, led the way out of the dining car back to their compartment. Once within, she turned the lock and turned to her charge.

"We have things to do tomorrow. It will be best if we go to bed and get some sleep."

Eric looked at the double bed that the steward had set up. "I suppose he has us down as a married couple?"

"Of course. We'll survive. Remember when we get to Berlin we will be a married couple, and we will need to act like it. You use the bathroom first. I will follow you. Don't use all the hot water."

Chapter Three

Shadows

In London Ewan Fitzgerald and Mark Randall were meeting Michael Wallace in the Admiralty. The office was a newly constructed affair which was actually underground. As Michael explained, "The public idea that the war is not going to happen is not reflected in Service circles. All preparations are being kept out of the public eye, but in the background preparations are being made as fast as possible for the war we know will come." He indicated the office. "This is part of what will be the planning complex for the Admiralty, in wartime circumstances."

He sat behind the desk and waved the others to the other chairs. Producing two folders, he gave them out and sat back while they studied the papers inside.

When he was satisfied that they had read everything, he pulled out his pipe, stuffed tobacco into the bowl and lit up, waving to the cigarette box on the desk at the same time.

"Help yourselves." He invited them. "Now, you must be beginning to understand what we have in mind. Marion is in Germany with Eric Rohm. They are husband and wife for the purpose of the exercise. The man, Rohm, is known to very few people. All that most know is that he is a research chemist working with the team on the so-called A-Bomb project. He is actually Albert Kessler, one of the most advanced scientists in research of this nature. He is there to assess the present stage of development in their research. On receipt of that information we will be able to pace out counter-measures accordingly, without letting the Germans know what we are up to."

Mark said, "Where do I come in? This is not my field?"

"Good question. You, apart from your qualifications as a soldier, will be useful if the Germans take the heavy water route in their research. So far there is little sign that they will go that way. The fact that you were a trained Marine, alongside your scientific qualifications, makes you a perfect candidate for this work.

"Pro-tem, you and Ewan will be the security for our pair in Berlin. They will arrive in Berlin tomorrow morning. You will fly in tonight and be there when they arrive at the Hauptbahnhof. Your job will be to ensure they are safe while they establish the situation regarding the research." He looked keenly at them both through the pipe smoke. Taking the pipe from his mouth, he pointed it at them both. "There is no leeway here! We need to keep Eric and Marian safe at all costs. What we are looking at is the possible destruction of this country, followed by any other country that disagrees with Herr Hitler. Have I made myself clear?"

Mark reared back at the fierce tone of Michael's voice. Ewan did not stir. He merely said quietly, "Got the message. Where do we pick up our weapons?"

"The address for your accommodation is a small hotel on 'Unter den Linden.' There is a suite booked in your names. The cistern in the toilet will have a package taped to it with weapons and ammunition. Your clothing is all provided. As you have already seen, your identities as company executives in an associate company of the Speer organisation will stand up to scrutiny. The company secretary is one of us and will verify your credentials if needed, but that will be a last resort. I would prefer to keep him out of this. We may need him in future." He paused. "Anything else?"

Both men shook their heads.

"Well, bugger off. Don't miss your flight. Next time you see me, do not recognise me unless I recognise you. Oh! By the way, good luck! "

The two men left the office carrying the folders they had been given.

***

As the door closed behind them a second door opened. A grey-haired man came into the room. "What do you think, Michael?" The voice was quiet, almost a whisper.

"We have set up everything we can at this time. It's now in their hands. If it works, it will be because they have made it work. We will know in two weeks' time. Or they will all be dead and we start again."

The grey haired man sighed and shrugged. "When are you off?"

Michael looked at his watch. "My plane is in two hours and I have things to do. I'll meet you for a quick drink at Croydon before I go, just in case there is any last minute detail I haven't taken into account."

The grey-haired man turned to the door he had entered by, "See you at Croydon." He left the room.

Michael sighed and sat down running his hands through his hair. He rested his head on his hands for a few moments. Then he rose to his feet, picked up his briefcase and opened it to check the contents. He pressed the buzzer on the desk and his secretary came in. Sarah Manners was the daughter of an old friend, a pretty brunette 28 years old. Oxford graduate with a first in German and French, among other subjects. She was here because her secretarial skills were awesome, and she had requested work where she could use her talents.

So far, Michael had not dared use her abroad. Truth to be told, he was more interested in her as a woman, than an agent, though she was technically listed as an agent, despite her current occupation here in the office.

"I'm off, Sarah. So you are in charge in my absence. Any problems, talk to Sir Henry. I'll be in touch tonight. I'll call you at home. You'll be my bit of fluff for anyone listening. OK?"

"Go it, boss. And what do I call you, apart from 'darling'?" She smiled, as she noticed him blush.

"Ouch! Caught me out there," he said, hurriedly. I'll be Carl tonight, Carl Gerber."

"Have a good flight, Carl." Sarah smiled as she said it, knowing that Michael hated flying, but taking the opportunity to tease him just a little. He was far too serious most of the time.

***

The flight to Berlin was less troubling than usual for Michael. The woman in the next seat absorbed his attention for the entire trip. She left him at the Tempelhof Airport, in Berlin with her card and an invitation to call at any time.

While Michael had encountered many women in his lifetime, he had not really had much experience in dealing with them. His education, despite his stint at Oxford, had been a period of concentration on the more manly aspects of life, and he found this gap in his experience frustrating. He made a mental note to discuss the matter with Sarah when he got back. His first thought had been his mother, but he realised that if she had been more forthcoming he would not be in this position now. So Sarah it would have to be. Oddly, he felt warmth at the idea, and that he thought curious.

***

His taxi dropped him off at the townhouse which the firm maintained as a safe house. He was still intrigued by the new vocabulary he had been forced to learn. The firm, was the Office of Naval Intelligence. The safe house was the local accommodation maintained by the firm. It was for visiting agents, and holding and concealing fugitives. For the word safe, use secret. In truth it was a more appropriate description.

The caretaker of the house was an ex-service man named Hans Berg. He had been a member of the Life Guards until he had been wounded in Mesopotamia in 1932. His father had been the conductor of the Berlin Philharmonic, and the house had belonged to the family for over 100 years. As a Prussian the conductor had not been impressed with the result of the rise of the German people. The efforts of the Socialist elements had risen with the dissolution of the Austrian Empire and destroyed the long tradition of honour maintained through Prussian history. The English Lady he had married with her inherited title made his move to England before the birth of their first child an almost inevitable decision. They had retained the house in Berlin. It had survived the war and was maintained with discreet funding: first in the hands of the former nanny, later, when Hans had been invalided out of the army, in his capable knowing hands. Bi-lingual from a baby, Hans slotted into place in the area without raising a ripple. He had been there for a year when Michael arrived.

***

In the offices of the Bendlerblock, on Bendlerstrasse, Commander Heinrich Stolle traced a lazy line around the name he had written down on the pad on the desk in front of him. The offices occupied by the OKW Abwehr were comfortable and Heinrich had no complaints about his boss, Admiral Wilhelm Canaris.

The Abwehr offices were a sharp contrast to the offices of the SS and the Gestapo, in Prinz-Albrecht-strasse. The organisations, despite being under orders to co-operate, were in many ways rivals, and this did lead to gaps in the security field, allowing significant intelligence to be missed or misfiled.

Currently, the name on the pad on the desk, Helga Berger, was of interest only to the Abwehr, and, the commander admitted, to himself. His interest was in the fact that the lady in question regularly travelled between Berlin, London, Paris and now, New York. That made her interesting. Of course, the fact that she was beautiful gave a piquancy to his enquiries. The file, so far, was slim. It was now apparent that the lady was an actress travelling to auditions for parts in movies, but the costs involved seemed rather excessive for someone in her position.

The commander rose to his feet and walked over to the window. His wounded leg still reminded him of the last ship he had commanded. The Spanish conflict had left him unscathed until the last minute. Then, nine months ago, an odd shell from a shore battery had ricocheted from the armour of the forward gun and holed the bridge screen, wounding him in the leg and, as he pointed out afterwards, the idiot Admiral in command of the squadron in the head. The Admiral's fatal wound would make no difference, apart from removing the place for locating the Admiral's hat. On the other hand he needed the leg to maintain his equilibrium and run the ship. The six month recovery from the operations, had been painful and mentally debilitating. Another Admiral, Uncle Willie Canaris, had saved his sanity, by loading him up with information and bombarding him with questions. Extracting opinions and making judgments, that was what Intelligence was all about. He seemed to suit the Admiral and, though Heinrich told himself he would rather be on a ship, common sense told him that it was not the time.

The knock on the door reminded him of his expected visitor. The door opened and the gentle waft of perfume preceded the lady whose name he had ringed on his pad.

"Fraulein Berger." He stepped forward and took her hand. "Coffee?" He asked.

"Perfect." Helga Berger answered in a slightly American accent.

Having seated his guest, Heinrich settled behind his desk and studied the lady in front of him.

After a few moments, Helga said, "Do I pass?"

Heinrich realised he had been staring and quickly said, "In my opinion with flying colours." He shrugged sadly. "That is not the reason you are here."

The coffee arrived and was placed on the desk in front of the lady. "Would you mind?" Heinrich asked.

As she poured out the coffee, Heinrich studied the woman. She was perfect in his eyes.

As she passed the cup over he noted no tremor. *Untroubled by being here*, he thought, *interesting!*

"Why am I here?" She asked quietly.

"Because you accepted my invitation," Heinrich replied equally quietly.

"You know that in this day and age, refusing an invitation from the Abwehr or the Gestapo, is followed by the destruction of the home and the arrest of the family. Is that not so?"

"Ah! I had forgotten. My profound apologies. That was not my intention. I was so delighted to have the opportunity to meet with you that I forgot the implied threat the invitation conceals."

Helga Berger looked at him from under her lowered brow. "You do not expect me to remove my knickers?"

Heinrich looked shocked and embarrassed.

"That is good. Because of this appointment I did not wear any." She was still looking at him, and his face was red.

Eventually, she took mercy on him. "I am joking, Commander. Please, you look ready to have a heart attack."

Heinrich let out the breath he was holding. *Relief?* He was not sure. *Excitement?* Of that he was certain. *What a delightful woman this is.*

"I am relieved that you were joking. We do not conduct our business in that way in this office."

With a wicked look in her eye, Helga said, "I also am relieved. If I can be excused, I will go and put my knickers back on."

Heinrich's mouth opened to speak. Helga leaned forward and put her hand on his. "I could not resist it. You are such a perfect gentleman. My knickers are where they should be. See." She stood up and lifted her skirt, exhibiting pale blue silky underwear in its proper place with matching suspenders holding the sheer stockings in place.

Dropping her skirt, she seated herself and crossing her legs demurely. "Now, if it was not for my last suggestion, why did you call me here?"

"Why the performance?" Heinrich asked. "Though it was much appreciated, it was not really called for."

Helga Berger's face hardened. "My friend, Anna, was called to the office of the Gestapo two weeks ago to answer a few questions about a mutual friend. He had left the country for America. When she was brought through to the office of the investigating officer, they made her strip, and conducted what they called an intimate search. This was in front the four leering men, and the woman who conducted the search. She asked politely why they were doing this, and the reply was 'because they wanted to'. They continued to say that their authority within the building was total and without question. They could, in fact, do what they pleased."

Heinrich's face hardened as she told her story. He controlled the anger he felt as he listened to story he had heard before. Up to now he had not really believed it.

"We conduct our affairs in a slightly more conventional manner in this building." He said stiffly. "In fact, it is because you travel between countries on a regular basis. I wondered if you could tell me why?"

"That's easy. I am an actress. I get called to audition from time to time. I have agents in several places. Even though I do not always go for an audition, I go to be seen. It reminds people that I exist and may be available for work."

"I see. Tell me, have you been approached by anyone to carry messages or information as you travel back and forth?"

"Not up to now. Though I do believe I am about to." She said, mischievously.

"It did occur to me that we might be of assistance to each other."

"There! What did I say!" She paused thoughtfully. "You do realise that, if I do what you suggest and I get caught out, I would be shot as a spy."

"I was not suggesting you carry anything, merely word of mouth."

"How long would that last?" She said scornfully. "Just until an emergency occurs and it would be 'just this once', until the next time, and the next. Need I go on?"

Heinrich shook his head. He shrugged. "I thought I would ask. Anyway you have answered the question I needed to ask." He rose to his feet and escorted her to the door. "Perhaps I could call you and take you out to dinner one evening?" He ventured.

"You know my number." Helga answered and. with a breath of perfume, she was gone.

***

Heinrich wandered through to the Admiral's office. He poked his head round the open door. Canaris was on the telephone but he waved the Commander in, pointed to a seat and continued his conversation.

When he put the phone down me looked at his deputy and smiled. "So you got to meet the gorgeous Fraulein Berger?"

"I did, and I asked the question. I received an answer that I believe."

"And pray what was that? Dinner tonight?" The Admiral teased.

"Maybe in the future, but there is no-one using her services as a courier at the moment. I suggested she join us. She did not quite say no."

"Come, Heinrich. You can do better than that. What do you mean 'she did not quite say no'?"

"I feel there is space for negotiation, no more than that."

The Admiral smiled. "I presume the negotiations will be properly accounted for in your expenses. Is there anything else?"

"Yes. I'm afraid there is. I have suspected that our so-called colleagues in PrinzAlbrechtstrasse 8 were too big for their boots." He repeated the story told by Helga about her friend, Anna.

Canaris said nothing, but his eye grew cold as the story was told.

"As you know I can do nothing, certainly not at the moment, but keep alert. The opportunity will arise and we will act. Unfortunately many innocent people will suffer in the meantime. If they cross our path, and accidently suffer a setback as a result, I would only like to know if there is a chance of reprisal against this office. Am I clear?"

"Perfectly, sir," Heinrich left the office feeling slightly better. At least the old man was aware. If the chance arose, it would be taken.

Chapter Four

Intrigue

Helga held her breath for a few seconds as the telephone rang. Surely it was not the commander already?

She picked up and said "Hello?"

It took a moment to recognise the voice of the man she had met on the aeroplane, that morning. "Why, Carl. How nice of you to call. Can I help you?"

"Actually, you can if you will. As I mentioned I am not too familiar with Berlin and I wondered if you could recommend a restaurant, preferably with a dance floor, and …" He hesitated, then said. "And if you could accompany me to dinner there tonight?"

Helga hesitated, shrugged, *Why not?* "There is a pleasant place I know and I am getting hungry. Pick me up in an hour. Do you know where I am?"

"I certainly do; in one hour then."

He sounded pleased, she thought as she put the telephone down. Then, looking at her watch, she realised time was passing and ran, discarding her clothes on the way to the bathroom. As she turned the water on she thought of the look on the face of the Commander when she showed him her knickers. Unbidden, the giggle turned to a full laugh as she stripped the very garment off to step into the bath.

***

In the safe house, Michael stepped out of the shower. Having dried off he donned the evening dress suit, struggling slightly as he always did with the black bow tie. Finally, having done as well as he could with it, he checked his wallet, cigarette case and the slim knife strapped to his lower leg, out of sight. Then, satisfied, he called to Hans, "Don't wait up," and left the house. He went along to the main road at the end of the quiet street and hailed a cab.

He told the driver to wait when they arrived outside the apartment block where Helga Burger lived. As he entered the foyer, the elevator door opened revealing the lady herself.

They studied each other as they met, and Helga presented her cheek for Michael's peck.

All very showbiz, he thought.

In the taxi she gave the driver an address and they sat back to chat, for the twenty-minute journey.

***

In their suite at the Adlon Hotel, Maria Rohm selected her attire carefully. As the wife of a distinguished academician she had an image to maintain. The dress was elegant, showing enough to be inviting but not too much, which would have been tarty. Eric was already dressed. He was slim and elegant in his tuxedo, the black ties perfectly even and the opal studs glinting on his shirt front.

"Can I help?" he asked.

"Please do my buttons up," she said, presenting her back to him. His gentle fingers managed the small buttons easily and he followed it with the necklace which he slipped around her neck, locking the catch deftly in place. "How does that look?" He said, smiling as he spoke.

Surprised, she looked at herself in the mirror. "It is beautiful." She said touching the silver and enameled pendant surrounding the sapphire ringed with small diamonds.

"Beauty deserves beauty," he said gallantly.

Maria felt a long forgotten frission at the gesture and the comment. It had been a long time since she had experienced any reaction to another person of either sex. She could act the part, of course, but that was, what it had been now for many years, an act.

They attended a reception staged for the benefit of the industrialist, Albert Speer, at the hotel, which is the most exclusive hotel in Berlin and a regular watering hole for the glitterati of the Nazi party. Tonight was no exception. When Eric had pointed out that there may be people there who know the real Eric, Maria pointed out that it was not possible. The identity had been invented from the ground up. The people who thought they knew Rohm had only ever spoken to him, or had been persuaded they knew him at University. The photographs on record were deliberately obscured, badly taken, revealing little, and it could have been any of a number of people from the time.

So it turned out, with introductions to many of the people present, some of whom apparently knew Eric from the past, and whom he was able to introduce as old friends to others.

During that evening the couple met Dr Rittenhauser, who was the current head of the development program for the new technology. Given the opportunity to chat with the Doctor, Eric very quickly established his credentials by his conversation alone. The evening became a significant success for Herr and Frau Rohm.

***

For Michael and Helga there was a different evening, a time of flirtation and innuendo enjoyed by both of them. The restaurant chosen was discrete and friendly. Helga was obviously a favoured customer and they were treated accordingly. Carl Gerber was an excellent raconteur, his personal shyness concealed beneath the veneer of the part he was playing. The conversation between the pair was that of old friends, not newly met acquaintances. Both became aware of it simultaneously. The almost instant dropping of the act between them would, in other circumstances, have been awkward. In their case, both relaxed and ceased fighting the battle of the sexes. As friends, the need for putting on a show was no longer necessary so the dining and dancing progressed in an agreeable atmosphere throughout the evening. At the apartment building once more, Michael accepted the invitation for a nightcap and waited at the door for a moment while Helga ensured that the room was respectable, he entered and was given a glass of cognac while they sat to talk.

Helga took a sip of her drink and said, "You are not German!"

Michael looked keenly at her. "I can trust you?"

"Up to you. Whoever you are, I feel safe with you. So I believe you can."

"It's my life in your hands. Are you prepared for that?"

"I think I am. Are you a secret agent?"

"I am a British naval officer." Michael held his breath. His hand resting on his crossed leg, putting his knife under his hand.

"That is a coincidence. I was speaking to a naval commander this afternoon, a German one." Helga smiled. "There must be something about sailors. I liked him too. By the way he was an agent also: Abwehr."

Michael rubbed his hand down the length of the knife.

Helga continued, "I suppose you also wish to use me to carry messages back and forth when I travel out of Germany."

"It had not occurred to me up to now. Why? Would you be prepared to do that?"

"Do I look like a post woman?" She asked with a smile.

"Not really, an extremely desirable woman! Yes. A post woman! No."

"That was nicely put. Carl."

Michael leaned forward and kissed her. She did not pull away. She responded, her lips warm and practiced, but she did not really relax into it."

"Do you want to stay?" Helga asked.

"Would you like me to?" Michael countered.

"That tells me that we understand each other," Helga said, "I believe you and I have become friends. So, in answer to your questions, yes, you can trust me. I will never betray my friends.

"Yes. I will take messages for you if you wish me to. I do not like what that man is doing to my country. Anything I can do to stop him, I will do.

"If you wish to stay the night you are welcome, but I will not be offended if you would prefer to return to your own place. If you stay the bed is comfortable, or the settee whichever you prefer. I understand if you have a lady friend. This would be just between friends, you understand?"

***

The evening ended eventually for Eric and Maria. Together, they strolled back to their suite. There were no tensions between them. Both had relaxed into their allotted roles as husband and wife. When they were within the suite once more they shared the bathroom, and climbed into the double bed, where, when Maria shivered at the coolness of the sheets, Eric happily gathered her into his arms to warm and comfort her.

***

For the watchers Ewan and Mark, there was little to do for those first days in Berlin. So they split-up and took turns exploring the area and making contacts. Both gave the impression that they were government agents, without specifying which agency they worked for. Their task was to allow the local people to connect them with authority, albeit with a sympathetic rather than the aggressive approach of the Schutzstaffel (SS) and the Gestapo. This meant that where people suspected them, their suspicion was Abwehr, or Volkspolizei, (CID). They were thus inclined to be more co-operative. The information about the other agents within Berlin was sparse, though Mark did recognise at least one face who turned out to be an FBI agent attached to the US embassy. His details were duly noted in the event of emergency. Maria was told, just in case there was any embarrassment, though it turned out that she did not know the man personally.

During the next few days, three things happened almost at once. Ewan was recruited by the local crime lord, who had survived by making himself useful to the Gestapo. Consequently he was leading a charmed life in the underworld of Berlin. With access to the already existing Black Market, his position was probably better than most with political pull.

Ewan's qualifications as a shooter were swiftly established when he undertook a clean-up job for the mob. The neat, uncomplicated disposal looked like suicide and was accepted as such for the record. It meant that the task of security for Eric rested rather more firmly on the shoulders of Maria and Mark. As far as Michael was concerned, it entrenched an agent in Berlin, who could keep contact with Helga when needed. Michael's task, once his people were in place and active, was to return to England to co-ordinate the activities of the team. Eric was already receiving information about the research being carried out. Almost daily, he expected to be called to join the team undertaking the work. Because of the demands being made on his time by his fellow scientists, Maria was being abandoned more and more to do her own thing.

Her meeting with a charming Irishman, who was working for the mobster known only as Sigmund, was fortuitous; he, being present at the delivery of special goods for the Gestapo, arranged through the rear door of the Adlon Hotel, rather than at PrinzAlbrechtstrasse. The couple literally bumped into each other in the foyer of the hotel. Maria, having been shopping with the wife of another of the scientists, was loaded with packages and was walking, talking to her companion. She bumped into the Irishman who was talking to the concierge and passing an envelope across to him keeping the information flowing back to Sigmund his boss.

The encounter ended with Ewan carrying most of the parcels up to the suite for the lady and a consequential invitation through the door for a drink.

Once inside, Maria turned to Ewan, "We are going to have a problem. My friend, who just took me shopping, tells me that there will be an intense interrogation of both Eric and I within the week. One of the problems is that there will be an offer made to Eric to join the team researching the bomb business. There are rules dictating that the Gestapo will do an in-depth investigation into both of us. What that means is we are going to need a way out. By next week-end at the latest.

"Eric thinks he will know enough to do an assessment by Thursday. That seems to be the pivotal time for us."

Ewan thought for a moment. "Where are you dining tonight?"

"Here at the Adlon. We have been invited by the Speers."

"In that case expect the Gestapo at the most inconvenient time, possibly when you are dressing." Ewan held his hand up to stop the query on Maria's lips. "The Gestapo are a law unto themselves. They will think you will not expect them and they may even catch you naked. To them that would be best of all. It will throw you right off, making you easy to wring out, and create a certain amount of titillation, something the lads get off on."

He walked around the room and picked up the phone, got an outside line and dialed a number. He said six words, and put the telephone down. "Both of you have your silenced Walthers with you at all times, especially when you are dressing for dinner. Make sure they are handy. When the agents come in, shock! Horror! Then shoot them twice in the chest. They should fall onto their backs." He pointed at the floor. "No bloodstains," he said, succinctly.

Maria began to realise just how ruthless the charming Irishman was.

"I will be here with my men in the next room. Tap on the wall when they are down, and we will come and clear up."

***

Eric and Maria were both half-dressed, when the two men in black leather overcoats walked into the bedroom where they were dressing.

"What the blazes! How dare you just….?" One man produced an ID card proclaiming that he was Gestapo.

He looked at Maria appreciatively, as she stood there in her lacy underwear. "You are ordered to come with us to HQ for interrogation. Maria reached out for her negligee on the bed as Eric reached for his dressing gown. Both drew their Walther 9mm pistols from beneath the clothes on the bed. The attached silencers making them look unbalanced.

The two Gestapo were mesmerized. Neither managed to do more than gasp as the guns spoke. Two shots in the chest, and both dropped to the floor. Slipping the negligee on, Maria ran to the wall shared by the next suite and tapped. Ewan and his men came in. One searched the two dead agents, producing their ID and the two pass keys, one each. Pocketing the money and the other bits for later examination, they carried the two men out of the suite, and along the corridor. A door opened and closed.

Chapter Five

The end of the beginning

The three agents looked at each other. Ewan said, "Speer will not be surprised when you do not turn up. It means there will be a time-lag before they realise that you are missing. North coast is closest. Direct route may be quickest but probably blocked by the time you are halfway there. Rostock is a sailing centre. I have a friend there." He thrust the keys of his Mercedes at Maria. "This will not be missed. Take it. It is full of fuel. It should get you there."

The pair swiftly packed their bags. They only took one each.

Ewan and his men took the others and disappeared.

Maria looked at Eric, grinned and said, "That was exciting, wasn't it? Ready?"

Eric smiled back at her. "You have a way with words, my dear. By all means." He bowed her through the door and closed it behind him, hopefully on that episode of their lives.

***

Rostock sounded good. It was just over 120 miles, not too far, but as they reached the outskirts of the city an increase in the traffic on the roads north to the Baltic, caused Eric to avoid the throng and take the road west to Osnabruck.

Maria looked at him enquiringly. Eric did not slow or stop merely commented, "I'm becoming allergic to crowds, or maybe just paranoid?"

They drove almost continuously for three hours, stopping to stretch their legs and for comfort only. Eventually, as they approached Braunschweig, they pulled over and stopped outside the town proper.

"We'll need fuel and to check the water." Maria commented, yawning and stretching.

Eric admired the way Maria's blouse stretched over her upper body as she went through the process. Then, hastily, "Y...Yes I suppose we will." He stammered, embarrassed at being caught-out staring.

She laughed at him. "Why are you embarrassed at looking at my body? You have seen it all during the past few days the past few days. There did not seem to be a problem then."

Eric recovered his calm. He said simply, "That was work!"

Impressed, Maria nodded slowly, "I see what you mean. Well, let us decide what to do and get started. The sooner we are out of this particular locality the better."

The sound of heavy equipment on the move along the major highway, reinforced the suggestion, and Eric, back in the driving seat drove off once more, avoiding the major road which seemed to be full of Army tank transporters, and heavy trucks.

***

In Berlin it took time for the news to percolate down through the system. Something Ewan expected, and in fact, had planned for.

The discovery of the dead Gestapo agents was at first taken at face value, but swiftly became a cause célèbre, when it was realised they had been in the hotel to collect

Doktor Rohm and his wife. Their disappearance coincided with the two agent's deaths, clicked, and the search began. By this time the fugitives were an hour from the Dutch Border. The big Mercedes was dust and dirt covered. When they had left it in the woods outside Munster, Erich had commented, "This is not a good sign. These people make very good vehicles, and this war will start with much fighting on the ground."

"Have you noticed any other signs to support your comment?" The question quite innocently put, drew a sharp look from her companion.

"I would suggest Belgium followed by France, but also Denmark, definitely in the line of fire. From what I see, whoever drives this campaign knows where he is going, and has the force to get there."

"Eric, given we survive the return to England, and that you're no longer required for research, you could become quite a useful spy." Maria was quite genuine in her comments. Most people travelled around with their eyes open, looking but seeing, little. Eric, as did she, looked assessed and inwardly digested whatever they saw on their travels. Remembering they had been in the dark for almost the entire journey, what they had observed was unsettling, to say the least.

Both were now dressed as walkers. Each carried a rucksack and wore sensible walking boots. Eric, in shorts would have probably been a little odd in the context of scientist, but his lifestyle had always included hill-walking at weekends wherever possible. He looked a natural walker and carried a stick which he trimmed as he walked.

Maria had been surprised at the man's ability to drop into a ground-covering stride without too much effort. She shrugged into the straps of her rucksack and stepped out to keep pace with the man ahead of her.

Both had maps and, at points along their route to the border, had chosen rendezvous points, in case they got separated along the way. At this hour of the morning there was little local traffic so they walked the paved road. It seemed inevitable that they were forced to clear the way, as yet another convoy of vehicles rumbled through the area.

***

Ewan looked at his two companions, he spoke sharply! "Klaus."

Klaus snapped to attention, back rigid, shoulders back, on parade.

Ewan walked over to him. "Klaus! You idiot. Why are you standing like that?"

Klaus gingerly turned his head. Realising where he was, his tight figure relaxed bit by bit. He reverted to the six feet of indolence he had snapped out of..

The voice of Ewan stopped the progress as it whispered in his ear. "Get the car!" Accepting the keys he headed for the basement garage. Ewan waved to Alek to follow and the pair left the suite for the lobby. In the bustle of the foyer of the great Hotel, they passed through unnoticed, except, of course, by the concierge.

***

Karl Albert Curnow was an odd man. He had reached his present eminence by sheer persistence and burning ambition. He maintained it by knowing! His undoubted talent for keeping abreast of the activities of the Berlin scene was just the dedication to the job no hotel concierge could be without. It was the nod and the wink, the whisper, the quiet giggle, that made the difference. Why is that? Because it is a case of, 'what is not ever said,' that makes the position of Karl Albert Curnow inviolate.

Ewan had been aware that Curnow had observed his departure. He was also aware that the two now dead

Gestapo men were overdue to depart, and would be impatiently awaiting their reappearance. Ewan had considered putting the coats on his two men and dropping the dead men into the area behind the hotel, for retrieval. He had dismissed the idea, realising that they might have to act. A situation he could not even contemplate without a shiver up his spine.

He had kept Curnow friendly, with little gifts of information on the activities in the underworld of the capital.

***

Mark, also still in the capital, was now ensconced in an apartment in a block used almost exclusively by prostitutes. He had little to do with the girls on a day to day basis, though he met them in the elevator and in the corridor on his apartment floor. The view from his apartment window was across the city. His employer and family were quiet people who spent most evenings in the family home. It was with a certain amount of apprehension he received his first essential briefing. Ewan met him at his apartment whilst the furor over the slain Gestapo agents was still creating ripples in Berlin society.

"We have a target." Ewan said baldly, no histrionics, no emotion just the flat statement.

"Who?" Mark enquired. Anyone we know?"

There are three known Gestapo agents who have been a particular pain in the ass to my boss among others. In fact, it is nothing to do with my boss, though he will quietly be pleased.

" This is a team who work together to do snap interrogations. One pops in to say hello. The others nip round the back and break into the house. They chose Jewish targets to start with. Now it is anyone not important in the party. At least that is how it appears. Michael tells me we have a sub-plot here. The targets being chosen for these animals are intelligence subjects who are in deep cover. Their location is a closely guarded secret. It has not been every victim of this team but they have now seen off three separate members."

"So who holds the secret?" Mark enquired.

"That is the question! I believe I know who is pushing the buttons. But Michael wants to know how he got the info."

Mark nodded. "Who do we take first?"

Ewan said, "First, we have Oberstleutnant Schiller to speak with. I think he will be the top of the heap. All we need to do is get him away from his charge for long enough. Then we can perform as requested.

***

The operation base for Schiller's team was a rear facing garage, on the industrial side of the main Gestapo headquarters building. Hidden in a corner beside a garage doorway was a, single iron door. Painted grey, it looked like a service door for the garage. In fact it was the entrance to the Gestapo Special Unit, commanded by Peter Schiller.

Ewan Fitzgerald sat looking through his binoculars at the area surrounding the door. Mark sat behind him, tightening screws securing the sniper sight to the Mark IV Lee Enfield rifle, a specially calibrated model for serious shooting over distances up to 1500 yards. The specific calibration, in the opinion of the shooter, Mark Randall, was unneeded at the ranges they anticipated. His own experience with the standard model of the rifle made him confident that he could take the shot without all the extra equipment.

Ewan said, "Hello? What have we here?"

Mark thrust a loaded magazine into the Lee Enfield, and operated the bolt loading a .303 round into the breach. "What have you spotted?" Mark asked.

"Our target is climbing into a car, which will take off in this direction. He has three of his men with him."

"Who is driving?"

"A chauffeur. An SS corporal, as far as I can see. The car is a Mercedes."

"Move over!" Mark purred. Rifle raised, seeking and finding the approaching vehicle, it steadied for a moment. Then a whiplash crack. The driver of the car 800 yards away suddenly acquired a third eye, in the centre of his forehead. The rifle fired three further times. The four cartridge cases were collected. The rifle was withdrawn and the weapon, with a fresh magazine installed, went into a golfer's bag with the used cartridges alongside a set of golf clubs. The two men rose to their feet and quietly left the building. Half a mile away, the Mercedes sat with the engine running in the middle of the street. Apart from the small bullet hole in the windscreen, there was no obvious damage to the car. The other three bullets had passed through the open side window of the car. The three passengers sat sprawled leaning into each other as if they were sharing a joke. The dead driver looked surprised.

Nobody bothered with the two men carrying the golf bags to their Auto-Union saloon, sitting at the roadside outside the small coffee shop. The golf bags went into the trunk of the car. The two men went into the coffee shop, chatting and laughing together.

The man who drove the Auto Union away looked neither left of right He stepped into the car, started the engine, and drove away, leaving the place as if it had never been there. As far as the local people were concerned, it never was.

***

The Gestapo headquarters buzzed with activity, Goering was seen shouting and holding forth in general to the staff in the building. Once the stricken Mercedes had been removed, the area was swamped with mobile units and plainclothes police. Their enquiries in the area found several victims, but none involved in the shooting incident. The idea that the shooting took place from a site one half mile away was ridiculous. The man who suggested the possibility was sent off with a flea in his ear, his suggestion dismissed.

Thus the team, who had conducted their first task successfully, proceeded to examine the background of their next target.

Chapter Six

The Plan

Maria and Eric, boarded a ferry from Dunkirk and sailed across to Dover. There they were met by Michael in the Alvis and taken back to the comfortable house in Denham where a team waited to de-brief them.

The Naval Intelligence operation involving Eric and Maria also controlled Ewan and Mark, who remained in Berlin. The program for Ewan and Mark at the moment was based on a list of priority removal jobs. Mostly, their list involved far too many high profile targets who seemed to have been selected out of spite rather than logic.

Michael was discussing the list with the two returned agents. He indicated a name. "Why is this man here. I have no idea who he is?"

Eric smiled grimly. "He is in charge of security at the Weapons Research Establishment at Peenemunde."

Michael swung round to face Eric. "How do you know that? I have only just found out that there is such a place?"

Eric smiled. "One of the group I was involved with is stationed there. He said that they are using teams of Jewish scientists there, holding them under the threat to their families. The man had drunk too much and he said too much. It seems that in most cases the families have already been disposed of."

"Which man told you this?"

"Karl Planke, specialist in heavy water production. He also mentioned Norway as a target for the Reich, and how useful their heavy water plant would be when it came under German control."

"Tell me, Eric. Did you pass this information on to the people who interrogated you?"

"Certainly not! You made it quite clear that all information relating to the fission process was for our ears only. I did not consider they were ready to hear such important details. Before you ask, this is the first time we have been able to talk in private, in a secure location. "

Maria leaned forward. "I agree with Eric. You did stress that this is a secret we had to keep within our circle."

Michael dropped his head and then raised it once more. "You are right, of course. As I said at the time, this is not information that we can allow to fall into the wrong hands." He paused, then lifted his hands and dropped them, frustration at the lack of interest from his superiors. "Damn it! They never seem to learn until someone lights the bloody fuse."

Eric spoke from the depths of his easy chair. "We need photographs and written evidence which can be assessed by our own scientists. A visit to Peenemunde seems a priority and perhaps interviews with some of the scientists involved. Kidnap even?"

Maria nodded in silent agreement. "I believe the kidnap idea is a good one. But we cannot just take the fission men. We must take as many scientists as possible, across the spectrum. The fission people must be just scientists caught in the net."

Michael turned to Eric. "How important is Peenemunde?"

Eric thought for a few moments. "In my opinion the scientists being assembled there are the most important group in the German community. Among the talent being held against their will, and the pure scientists, they are probably several years of R&D ahead of the rest of the world. Don't get me wrong. This is not because they have better brains. It's purely because they have been concentrated into specific areas. And in those areas alone they have a lead on the rest of the world."

There was a period of silence, while the implications of Eric's comments sank in.

Maria stood up and walked over to the drinks table. By raising her eyebrow she received the go ahead for refills all-round. She served the drinks and then, still on her feet, she lifted her glass. "Absent friends." She said, quietly. The others repeated her words. Both men rising to their feet. "Absent friends." All three glasses were drained together.

The moment passed. All seated themselves, and the planning began.

***

Sarah Manners was in the office, after the departure of her boss, Michael. Her mind wandered back to the occasion three months ago when this episode of her life began. At home in the highlands. Her cousin had been out shooting.

Sarah Manners knew there would be game. She had heard the echo of the single shot and was therefore prepared to deal with whatever her cousin produced. She had returned to the house she had been raised in, to visit. Far from the Naval office where she was currently employed. It was as if she had never left.

The pony stopped beside the wet room where beasts could be skinned. It would be a deer, she guessed. Gralloched on the hill, it would be skinned here in the wet room.

She put the kettle on the stove. There was already soup simmering quietly, and she had made fresh bread that morning early. There would be a mug of tea for the master, and they would have soup and bread for lunch. There would be roast mutton for dinner, which was already slow cooking through the day. Beth, the housekeeper, was now more at home in the Buckinghamshire house, than here these days, so Sarah's return had been greeted with joy by the regulars in the house.

David Manners entered the kitchen in his shirt sleeves. His jacket had been discarded in the yard when he donned the overall to skin the beast.

He had washed under the cold tap in the yard and now, with his hair almost in order and a smile on his face, he breezed through the door like a breath of fresh air.

"Well, Sarah, is that my tea you are nursing?"

"What else would it be?" She said, smiling and handing over the big mug.

Sarah turned to the stove and stirred the soup. "What is it you have brought today, sir? Would it be a stag perhaps?"

"How many times have I told you not to call me sir? My name is David and I am proud of it. I have always wished to hear it from your lips, Sarah."

"One day, maybe." Sarah smiled, and carried on with the preparations for lunch. "How was the leg today?"

"You know well that it gives little bother nowadays. The new stump has a foot which moves, I hardly know it is there now." David had lost his foot during the last days of the Great War. A discarded mine had gone off. He had been lucky his foot had been the only part of his body exposed. The surgeon said that the bomb had done a better job of removing the foot cleanly than he could have done on the operating table.

David Manners would admit he had been better off than many. Over the intervening years he had learned to live with the loss of his foot, almost to the point of forgetting that it was gone.

Sarah had lost her father, killed at the same time that David had received his injury. He had been reported missing when he was flying over the lines spotting for the artillery. His aircraft just disappeared, and no trace of it was ever found.

For Sarah he was still alive somewhere. There seemed to be no way anyone could change her mind. She had became the housekeeper at the lodge because it was in these hills that she had lived with her father, so this was where she would wait for him. The lodge was owned by the Manners family. It was part of their estate spreading over several miles of the countryside, north of the great Glen.

From Loch Lochy in the south, to Clunie in the north, Sarah was at home in all the various lodges, and houses, occupied by the family. Having joined the estate as the daughter of a member of the family, her place was assured without employment. The employment was her choice and the family was grateful for it. Sarah had no other kin of her own and, though she was fond of David and her other cousins and in-laws, the work allowed her to keep them at arms' length. Having left to work in Spain during the civil war, she had returned and started work in Whitehall last year.

***

A small Bedford pick-up bumped up the track, as Sarah started to serve the soup.

David went outside to see who was calling. He returned calling out to Sarah, "Set another place for lunch, Sarah. The navy's here."

He walked into the kitchen followed by Michael Wallace, who stepped forward and swept Sarah up into his arms and kissed her on the lips. He set her down and said, "That was from, Beth. She sends her love also."

Blushing furiously, Sarah couldn't help laughing. "I don't think Beth intended you to deliver her message quite so boisterously."

Michael laughed. "I confess. That was my idea, and you may slap me if you wish, I have no regrets." He held up his face to be slapped.

Sarah laughed. It was difficult to stay annoyed with Michael, "I'll put out the soup. It will give you a chance to discuss the reason for your visit without unqualified ears around you."

She disappeared into the kitchen and began serving out the soup into bowls, and then cutting up the bread into chunks to go with the soup.

When she called out, the men arrived instantly. Sarah looked up in surprise. Pointing out their seats, she sat in her place at the head of the table, and broke a piece of bread.

"What brought you all the way up here to see David? I realised, since we met in the office last week, it was not to visit me."

Michael tried the soup and sighed in appreciation. "If I had realised that there would be soup awaiting my arrival, I would have been here sooner. But as you have already guessed, I came primarily to see David. The reason I came was that I knew this place was here, and it occurred to me that it could be of great use for special training in the event of war."

Sarah looked at him resignedly, "We all know that Mr Chamberlain has prevented that from happening." She looked sharply at Michael. "Hasn't he?"

Michael shook his head. "Anything but, I'm afraid. Basically it was 'a put off' to allow us time to prepare better for the war that is coning. And it will come." He sounded quite definite about the matter."

"What do you want from us?" David asked.

"Your expertise, and that of your gillies. Plus the use of the estate area to train special shock troops, in skills not covered by the training manuals. The idea isn't mine. It came from a former Minister of the Crown, chap called Churchill. D'ye know him?"

David smiled. "Well, I'm blessed. Somebody finally listened. Good for Winston. So he will get his commandos after all."

"So it appears," Michael said. "The main issue is whether you and your men are ready to teach these men to disappear in an open field. I ask because I was approached to ask as a personal friend."

"Of course. I still stand for King and Country. We will all pitch in to get something set-up pronto, starting with the castle. That can be available, more of less immediately."

Michael got back to the soup. When his bowl was emptied, he offered to wash-up. Both David and Sarah looked at him in astonishment.

"Don't look at me like that. We all have to pitch in at some time or other. Besides I want Sarah included in the deal."

Both Sarah and David looked at Michael disbelievingly. "Why?" David asked. "Do you need Sarah. She already works in Whitehall?"

"I have female agents, native French speaking. They have no idea how to greet a senior officer nor how to disarm an attacker. Nor do they know how to kill. These are all skills that the civilians in my group require, both male and female."

"Where would Sarah fit into all this?" David said still puzzled.

"From the Spanish civil war." Michael said. "Sarah was a nurse."

"Yes, I knew that." David said.

Sarah said, "I was not a nurse. The Germans had their fifth column working throughout Spain at the time. There was no opposition from Spain itself, but the allies used the civil war to assess how well the Germans were progressing. I was recruited to find and eliminate German agents, male and female. I speak pretty fluent Spanish, and I received training from a Shanghai Police officer and several extremely skilled British thugs, who taught me every form of personal mayhem they could get me to remember. I may say that I was rather good at what I did, and I was a successful agent throughout, which I can only verify by the fact that I am still alive." She looked at Michael.

"I work in Naval Intelligence yes, but this is a little more than that, we have a separate team, apart from the other agencies, who are setting up a joint operation to train agents to be dropped into France and the Netherlands, to organize local resistance."

"But we are not at war yet." David said.

Michael said, "We soon will be. With the way the Nazi party are operating, we estimate Germany will control most of Europe within eighteen months of the first shot being fired. By that time we hope to have agents in place in several key areas throughout Europe."

"Surely the Germans will have targeted us as well as the rest of Europe. We will not have sufficient resources to stop them invading here along with the rest of the Europe."

"We expect them to try. But we hope to be able to dissuade them, certainly in the first instance. The longer they have to put it off, the more difficult it will become. Then it will be our turn,"

David looked at the pair, shook his head, and finished the bread on his plate. "When do we start?"

Chapter Seven

The Team

Michael looked at David. "You return to the Castle tonight, talk to the gillies and prepare to meet Lord Lovat in three days."

He swung round to Sarah. "I would like you to come away with me, this afternoon. We will be going to Denham."

Sarah looked out of the window at the battered Bedford pick-up, "In that?"

"Good lord, no, The Alvis is at Northolt, but there is a Daimler at Fort William."

"Will there be room for the venison?" Sarah asked sweetly. "I will need to take Beth a little something for the larder."

David laughed, "I'll get it wrapped while you pack. I'll ride down to the Castle on the pony when I lock up after you've gone."

Sarah dashed off upstairs to pack, while David went out to the wet room followed by Michael.

"Was that necessary?" David asked.

"You have no idea how late it is already." Michael said seriously. "We have really been caught with our pants down this time. Bloody politicians! All far too busy being politicians to look beyond the end of their noses. We have been warning them about Germany for the past ten years. Apart from a few like Churchill, none would listen. The bit of paper Chamberlain has is not worth the paper it's written on. Hitler has already taken over all of Austria and Czechoslovakia, and half of the Balkans. When he turns north, it will be all hands in, I would guess."

The venison was neatly butchered by David as they talked. As soon as the selected cuts were set aside for Beth, he collected the remainder and wrapped them for the Castle kitchen. With the meat for Denham wrapped and rolled in sacking, they took it out to the pick-up and found Sarah there with her bags packed and ready to travel. Dressed in a tweed coat with a smart matching hat, she looked every inch the country lady she actually was.

***

They stopped at Manchester for the night, and boarded the chartered Airspeed Oxford at the airport, the following morning. They were at Northolt by lunchtime, and safely tucked in at Denham for tea. As Sarah commented, "There seemed little sign of the country being prepared for war, throughout that journey."

Beth was delighted to see Sarah, and to get the venison they had brought. Both had served in the Spanish war, though Beth had suffered, having been captured by Franco's men.

She had been passed to the Abwehr for questioning, and released. Only to be picked up by the Gestapo. She had been rescued by a team of partisans, who were getting revenge for the torture and death of some of their own people. Beth's rescue had not been planned and she had already been badly treated when it happened. She managed to make her way to friends who smuggled her out. She did not return to the field after that episode, but was part of the training team thereafter. Sarah had met her when she was under training, they had been friends ever since.

***

Marian Smith had completed one successful mission already. The task of close-attending bodyguard for Eric Rohm had been an urgent matter requiring her immediate dispatch into the field. Though she had been through the course at Quantico as a prospective candidate for the FBI, Michael still expected reassurance that she was fit to the standard he had set.

The FBI course had been strictly against orders. The Head of the FBI was firmly convinced that women were not physically equipped to take on the rigors involved in operating as a special agent in the FBI. While Mr Hoover remained alive no woman, officially or otherwise, was permitted to be a special agent in the organisation.

Marian went through the course with the connivance and support of Wild Bill Donavon, later to be appointed by Roosevelt to create and operate the OSS. Her course was run under the pseudonym, Alex Nichol, a special concession, as he was an actor who would be playing the part of an agent in a movie. The team which put her through was sworn to secrecy, and Hoover never knew that the course had been run by a female.[1]

Donavon, reassured that his hunch was correct, promised Marian that she would be recruited as soon as the projected OSS was created. The approach from Michael Wallace was approved by Donavon, who intended to work closely with the British Secret services when the time came, as it surely would.

---

[1] When Hoover died, his replacement Patrick Grey immediately ordered the course opened to female agents, and in 1972 the first of the official female special agents started operating.

The barn behind the house at Denham was warm, the wide floor well covered and also padded with matting for training purposes.

Sarah was currently acting as Michael's secretary, but she was now going back into the field with the team. She had already run around the extensive garden using the security track. Now, back in the barn, she was stretching and preparing for sparring practice using the punch ball. Marian was also getting ready to go through her own exercises, when the two PTI's came in.

The taller of the two men called the ladies over. "My name is Bill Murphy. Sergeant RAF. This is Peter Noble, Corporal RAF. We have been asked to coach you in unarmed combat."

Sarah exchanged looks with Marian. With a small smile, she nodded and said, "Fine, I believe it could be useful where we are going."

The two men paired off with the ladies. Bill Murphy grinned at Sarah. "Hit me anywhere as hard as you like."

Sarah smacked him hard on the jaw with a fast left. She pulled the punch, just in case.

Shocked, Bill dropped into a crouch and lashed back. Sarah caught the fist and spun round taking the arm with her. She dropped to the floor sending Bill Murphy flying over her crouched body. To her relief she saw him slap the floor and roll back up to his feet.

She was already up waiting in a half crouch for the expected attack.

Bill stood upright. He held up his hand. "Time out. I guess we are working under a misunderstanding here. I was told you needed instruction. Someone was joking, I take it?"

Sarah smiled, the other two had stopped also. "Who gave you the suggestion, that we needed instruction?"

"The Lieutenant Commander suggested it."

"Right. Let us start again. I have been through the special operation course, which included a session of the use of the Fairburn knife by a man named Fairburn. My colleague has completed the FBI, Special Agents course at Quantico, including the weapons course."

Bill Murphy grinned. "If you don't mind, we will tailor a course for you, let us work on stamina and control, starting with simple bends and stretches, then co-ordination using the punch ball."

***

Over the next two weeks both women trained daily with the two men. Finally the PTI's were satisfied that there were no men in the establishment who would be a threat to either of the lethal ladies they had shared the gym with. By that time both Sarah and Marian were judged ready to join the operating team who had moved from Berlin to the Baltic coast.

Marian's hair became dark blonde and her eyes became grey. Though she was still petite and beautiful, she was no longer the sultry wife of Eric Rohm.

For Sarah, her already fair hair and blue eyes gave her the look and her German/Dutch accent matched her papers that said she was from Bocholt on the German border with Holland.

They were established in Stralsund within easy reach of Peenemunde, the object of their current assignment. The scientist community at work in the establishment was divided between the employed and the pressed. The employed were contracted for their special qualifications and accommodation outside the site was provided, housing and pay according to status.

The pressed men were the Jewish prisoners who were blackmailed into working. Using the threat to families held hostage to ensure their cooperation.

Oddly it was Mark who made the breakthrough they needed to influence the Jewish scientists working at the site.

The male clerk was a sergeant in the records office and he fell for Mark, like a ton of bricks. The four agents accepted that these things happen, but they still pulled Mark's leg about his appeal to the homosexual Sergeant.

The takedown was simple. The question was how the Nazi's got so many Jews working willingly for the party, when, elsewhere in Europe, they were busy eliminating and evicting Jews wherever they could. To Sergeant Hochstetler the answer was simple. You take their families hostage.

There was almost a snigger behind that bland statement, which made Mark suspect that this was not the whole story. It took nearly a bottle of fine cognac to get the answer to that question. The giggle, as the admission came out, nearly cost the Sergeant his life, then and there. Of course, the answer was that the families held as hostage were no longer being fed and housed. They were all dead, and Sergeant Hochstetler held the file with the information. A record of the disposal of each and every member of the families.

***

Ewan and Mark donned their black leather overcoats. Mark found round lens glasses to wear, and both produced Gestapo paperwork to identify them as Kriminaldirektor and Kriminalkommissar, from department E, counter-intelligence.

Their visit to the Peenemunde establishment was unannounced and unrecorded. Arriving at the gate to the establishment, they were admitted without hesitation. The file was produced by Sergeant Hochstetler who trembled at the sight of his friend, now revealed as a Gestapo agent.

The inspection, conducted of the Jewish community within the compound, revealed quarters which were clean but otherwise reminiscent of the prison camps for the gypsies which Ewan had seen in eastern Germany.

The Jews were wearing their own clothing, but they were prisoners. Though Mark never saw how Ewan managed to pass the information in the file over to the Jews they interviewed, he was present when they were informed that two trucks would be outside the wire in two days, at 2100 hours, the wire would be cut and the guards absent if they cared to take the chance to escape their captors.

***

The two ladies were able to attract the attention of a group of the non Jewish scientists working on the variety of projects at the site. The weekend party, which the ladies had arranged, was for men only; the boat they provided for the promised bacchanal would be alongside the quay at 2200 hours in two days, Saturday evening. The word went round the employed scientists on site by word of mouth like wildfire. Sufficient to say the nightlife of the little town was notable by its absence. The appearance of Grafin Helene Von Klaus, the apparent owner of most of the land in the immediate area, was like a shock to the system to the scientists, who were expected to work hard without let up for any real social life. She appeared at a closed meeting with the leading members of the free scientists.

. When the Grafin spoke to the assembled scientists and staff, her suggestion that they would work better if provided with a break now and then, the wise heads nodded in agreement.

The hesitant question as to the origin of the hostesses brought a whispered hint, that the widows and wives of many of the people of the area had been without the comfort of their men folk for some months, and they were only too willing to help entertain the loyal workers who sacrificed so much for the national good. They offered their time and services without commitment.

***

When the Mercedes brought the two ladies back from their escorted visit to the Research Site, Sarah said, "We will never get away with it. Someone will talk, and everything will go down the toilet. Us first."

Ewan grinned. "I don't agree. That bunch of geeks, offered the opportunity for a dirty night out with a willing body, will be desperate to keep the secret from their wives. Most of them live in a state of permanent frustration, rationed to one night of sex per week or month or whatever. The simplicity is what is on offer will make it work; that and the Royal Marines manning the boat. Our scientists are like a bunch of schoolboys offered a fast day out to a burlesque show. And remember the staff is included. If anyone talks and buggers things up, the others will make sure their lives will be a misery.

"As far as the Jews are concerned, the trucks are already on the site. Mark and I are now accepted and feared. We will take them and place them. The cover is, we are setting a trap for what we suspect will be a seaborne raid. The raiding party who come expect an open door. What the security do not suspect is that the open door leads out, not in."

Marian looked at the smug grin on Ewan's face. "The security team does not suspect the dirty night out is some part of an escape plot?"

Mark commented, "They think it is to clear the decks, so that our response group can operate without a lot of civilians cluttering up the war zone."

"And your response group is?" Sarah asked patiently.

"A squad of Marines in SS uniforms, prepared to take on the security men if necessary." Ewan added, "The Jews have been warned. They will be ready. As for the others? We take a chance that, after your invitation, most will find a way of attending an evening of free booze, and women, without the inconvenience of wives, etc."

Marian asked the critical question, "Where did the Marines and the boat come from?"

"Dumb luck. They were sent to set up a raid on the site, but the raid was cancelled at the last moment when they received a tip-off that the enemy had guessed what was going on.

"The boat was still at Bornholm when Michael found it, and he had it re-assigned to us. As I said, 'dumb luck!' So you girls will be waiting on the quay by 2200hrs. You welcome the visitors aboard. The boat is a big white super yacht, so it looks the part. It will come in that night by 2100 and it will leave with us all together as soon as we are all aboard."

Chapter Eight

The snatch

The experimental radio detection station on Rugen Island was linked with the second unit at Oldenburg. Both Freya units were highly secret establishments known to the British Government. Permission was given for both sites to be attacked and stripped of their equipment. Raiding parties, carried in high powered motor launches, were allocated for simultaneous attacks. The timing was to coincide with the original Royal Marine raid. It had been decided to carry on with the Radar raids as the security on that aspect of the operation had not been compromised.

On the night before the Peenemunde raid, both Freya radar establishments had been raided and stripped of their equipment. When teams from the Abwehr examined the sites during the following day, they found two empty buildings, stripped clean, no casualties, no indication of who or what had carried out the raids.

Both Abwehr teams were still on location when the first moves of the Peenemunde raid were carried out.

***

The big cruise yacht *Aarhus* docked at Stralsund, at 2000. At 2030, two trucks drew alongside the fence behind the accommodation camp for the Jews at the Peenemunde site.

Ewan stepped down from the lead truck with a big pair of cutters, followed by six SS men in uniform. He commenced cutting a gap in the wire fence.

Mark looked at him cutting and said, "What happens when the guards come round and see you cutting the fence open?"

"You tell me." was the reply.

"They will shoot you."

"So there's your answer. If the guards come round and wish to shoot me, stop them, and shoot them first."

Mark looked at his partner, amazed at his sang froid. "Shoot them?"

"Yes, shoot them; using the silencer, of course. You do not want to awaken the garrison."

"What about the SS men here?"

"Window dressing, their guns are not suppressed. They are therefore the last resort."

2100 saw the cautious arrival of the first of the Jewish scientists. The sharp intake of breath signaled the sight of the first of the dead guards, near the opened section of the ring-fence that surrounding the encampment. Three other uniformed guards were lying, equally dead, at intervals around the fence. Mark had decided that waiting for the guards to appear was too risky, so he had sought them out and disposed of them where he found them. The guard room had been his final call and the figure, propped up in the Sergeant's chair, was as dead as the rest of the men under his command.

At 2130, the two trucks arrived on the quay, and the occupants were ushered aboard. The trucks were returned to the site. At 2145, A Mercedes limousine arrived. Two elegant ladies stepped out and greeted the attendants at the gangway of the yacht.

2210, a growing stream of men was welcomed on the quay by the two ladies. The men were ushered on to the big white vessel and the sounds of clinking glasses, music, and feminine laughter could be heard.

By 2220, the flow of men ceased and the two ladies boarded the yacht. The gangway was withdrawn, and the ship quietly sailed. As it reached the open sea the lights were switched off, and even the navigation lights disappeared. The vague white ship, that might have been seen on the radar, made off at high speed for the Kattegat, one of several similar cruise ships to be seen on the waters around Denmark at that time.

***

The following day, in Berlin, Heinrich Stolle studied the report of the raids on the two Radio Detection stations. As he read the conclusions of the investigation officers another report was placed on his desk.

Curious, he noted the Gestapo stamp on the paper, which also carried a 'most secret', stamp, plus a 'for Gestapo eyes only'.

The report stated that there had been a break out at the experimental establishment at Peenemunde. The 70 Jewish scientists had managed to escape, despite the threat to their families held hostage. There was a footnote. It appears that the record of the elimination of the so-called hostages had been distributed among the scientists. In addition, there seemed to have been a mass defection of the non-Jewish scientists, who had abandoned wives and families and departed without a word. There was a rumour that the scientists had been invited by Grafin Helene Von Klaus for a cruise unaccompanied by their wives, where the entertainment provided was free. Inquiry revealed that a ship had docked at Stralsund and sailed later that evening. Nothing further was known of the ship or the so-called Grafin.

Stolle picked up the Gestapo memo and knocked on the door of Admiral Canaris. As he entered he said, "We have good news, and bad news, sir…"

***

In London, at a quiet meeting in the Headquarters of M16, a group of people sat around a table and listened to a briefing by an eminent scientist.

"In the circumstances, gentlemen, it appears that, without letting the Germans know that we were targeting any particular line of research, we have managed to inhibit their efforts and thus gain time in the area of nuclear fission. The other benefits are manifest in the guided missile, and rocketry research. The Jewish scientists, particularly, have happily joined our own and our American friends' research programs.

"Though most of the other captive scientists have shown no inclination to take part in research on this side of the fence, four have, and their input so far has been valuable. It remains to be seen what will happen to the remaining uncooperative captives. Internment, I presume, in Canada and the USA, I understand.

One of the seated people spoke in a strong American accent. "Just who the hell authorized this operation. I know I knew nothing about it. I thought we had an agreement that we would share information between us?"

Michael Wallace stood up and addressed the group. "We are, at this moment, complying with the rule about sharing information. The team who undertook this operation was part of the British initial network of agents located to collect information and perform tasks to inhibit the efforts of the German Abwehr and Gestapo.

"So far we have made progress in driving the wedge between the two organisations, a process we will continue to exploit, while creating an underground network for sabotage and general resistance."

The American voice was raised once more. "But, dammit, we are not at war with Germany. You are committing crimes against a Sovereign nation. My government is dedicated to self-determination, allowing nations to go to hell in whichever way they please."

Another American voice was suddenly heard. "On behalf of the United States Government, I would like to express our sincere thanks for the efforts made on behalf of the free world. Taking a cold hard look at the situation. I cannot discount the possibility that USA may not come into the forthcoming conflict any quicker than it did last time the nations of Europe clashed. However, I can and do guarantee that our intelligence efforts will be shared with British efforts whether we join the war early or late. I have FDR's word on that."

Turning to the American who had spoken in the first place, he said, "You will place yourself at my disposal and you will do and say nothing without my approval. Is that clear?"

"Of course, Mr. Secretary." The voice was subdued and clearly the owner realised he had put his foot firmly in the mire with his earlier comments.

***

Rupert Maddox was pissed. He had spoken out as he was required to do, and he had been put down by his own boss. They had discussed the matter that morning and both had agreed that the situation as outlined by Rupert to the group was the way things were. Both had agreed that Europe should get on with its own business, leaving USA to get on with her own. Seated in the bar at the Trocadero later that evening, Rupert was working on his third drink, and the buzz was just beginning to take effect.

He hardly noticed the arrival of the person sitting next to him at the bar.

As he raised his drink a hand came across and checked the movement. The husky voice said, "Let's eat first. Then you can get a buzz on afterwards. It makes for a more survivable hangover."

He looked round. His eyes met a pair of blue eyes he could have lost himself in.

"Coming?" The voice breathed.

He shrugged. "Why not." He rose to his feet and, carrying his drink, followed his elegant companion into the dining room where they were directed to table.

The task of ordering had been undertaken elsewhere, because Rupert's full attention was taken up by the beautiful, enigmatic lady sitting opposite him.

The questions were beginning to stir somewhere south of his sternum, though up to now he was happy to leave them there until he learned more of his companion.

"Who are you?" He asked.

"I'm Sarah Manners." She said, quietly. I have just returned from Germany where I was involved in rescuing 70 Jewish scientists who were cooperating with the Nazi Government, because their families were being held hostage against their good behaviour. We discovered that the so-called hostages had all been executed. So we advised the scientists of the truth, and arranged for them to escape from Germany. We also deprived the Nazi's of the services of the team of scientists working alongside the Jews. You can depart in a high dudgeon expressing your profound disapproval of the entire business."

She sat back watching the look on Rupert's face.

The poor man did not know which way to turn. His gorgeous companion had just admitted that she had acted contrary to his own entrenched beliefs, so why was he not leaving the table as she suggested.

It occurred to him that perhaps his opinion was not as deeply held as he had once thought. After all, injustice and oppression was surely a concern for everyone, no matter where it occurred.

"You say your name is Sarah?"

"It is."

"Why do I believe you, Sarah."

"Possibly, because what I have told you is the truth."

Rupert felt that this conversation was important, and he had the urge to finish it the right way, with conclusions and opinions and possibly a seat in the cave mouth when they sheltered from the rain.

"I believe you, Sarah Manners." As he said the words he realised that it was true. He did believe her. He would also need a new job. He could no longer trust his boss.

***

In the office the following morning, Sarah reported that the dissenting American had realised the error of his ways, and was currently seeking an interview with Bill Donovan, without the permission of his current boss.

Chapter Nine

Redeployment

Michael looked at Sarah enquiringly, as she detailed her evening with Rupert Maddox.

With a small smile she set his mind at rest. "My dinner companion collapsed over his after dinner cognac. I arranged for him to be carried to his room, and put to bed. It seemed the right thing to do."

She looked at Michael steadily, her intense blue eyes holding him as she spoke. "Michael, I have the impression that you have thoughts of me other than as an operative. Am I right?"

Almost hypnotized by that stare, Michael hesitated before replying. "I am not sure I understand what you mean," he eventually got out.

Sarah stood up and turned to face him. He could feel the brush of her breath as she spoke. "What I mean is, do you fancy me, as a woman, Michael?"

"Well, that is an odd question to ask. Obviously I am aware that you are a beautiful woman, one that any red blooded man would fancy, as you put it. Do you fancy me?"

Before he could finish his little speech, he was stopped. Her lips were soft and her body was suddenly up against his, her arms around his neck. His own, he realised suddenly, were around her waist, holding her close. The kiss seemed to go on and on. Neither made any attempt to break off. Michael's hand move up stroking her back and the skin of her neck, and hers roamed across his back, holding him ever closer.

There was a knock at the door.

Reluctantly, they parted. Sarah wet her handkerchief on her tongue and scrubbed the lipstick from Michael's lips.

"Come in!" Michael called. As the door opened he was revealed, seated at his desk, Sarah was looking at the books on the bookcase against the side wall of the office.

"It's only me, old boy. I forgot to pass on this message. I received it this morning." Peter Maxwell, the Squadron Leader who had shared the office in M16 with Michael, passed over a note, took a look at Sarah, and then left them alone once more.

In a clear voice, Michael said, "The answer to your question, as I believe I just demonstrated is, yes. I am interested in you from a completely unofficial point of view, and I wish to know you better, personally."

He read the note passed on by Peter Maxwell.

"Business!" He passed the note to Sarah, who sat down to read it.

"Hitler has renounced the non-aggression pact with Poland and the Naval Agreement with Britain. Does that mean what I think it means?"

"We will be at war within the next three months, perhaps sooner. It also means that our program for the team will need to be accelerated. Take the Alvis to Denham. I'll be there for a briefing tonight. Please let Beth know. I'll be staying tonight. The others will be aware of the briefing, but be prepared to move off within the week."

He looked up at Sarah.

She was beside the desk already. She bent and kissed him. "The answer is yes," she said. Then she was gone.

***

In Denham the group sat around the lounge having dined already. There was coffee on the table, adding its odor to the cognac and mingling with the smell of the Havana cigar Ewan was quietly enjoying.

Michael started to speak. His voice quiet but clear. "We are back on the offensive, ladies and gentlemen. I would like to find a smart name other than 'the team', but at this late date I fear we are stuck with it.

"As you are aware for the past six months, information about the German high seas fleet has been sparse. We know that there are three of the so-called pocket battleships unaccounted for. All put to sea when we were blindsided for some reason. On at least one occasion, it was the direct responsibility of the US Government. I understand such a mistake will not occur again. Enough that the *Graf Spee* and the *Deutschland* are both loose, and both are powerful enough to take on any of our ships up to the battlecruisers. The Russians have got together with the Germans and they are looking at Finland. I believe we are signing a treaty with Poland. If the Germans invade then we are at war.

"I have a list with four names. All are critical. All for some reason, are pivotal in one direction or other. For this purpose we will be split into two teams. I will lead one team, Ewan and Marian will be acting independently in Frankfurt. My team will be in Austria, and will consist of Sarah and Mark, plus myself. Both teams will have back-ups provided by the regular agencies. In other words, we are to be supported by a couple of spooks, though I am informed that these particular spooks are properly trained, efficient agents of considerable experience, We have contact details so that we can get together if we need to. It could be important if we need emergency extraction.

"Any questions so far?"

He looked around at the group. No real reaction, so far.

"Good. The target in Frankfurt is Otto Gruber. He is a gangster and he is currently employed by the Gestapo to root out patriots. Of course, he is getting rid of all his enemies as part of the program. Our problem with him is that his team as closing in on one of our groups set up in the event of war. They are all anti-Nazi, and it will be bad for our side if we lose such natural allies. In the event swift action is called for. The removal of Gruber will be good news, regardless. He is a ruthless thug who has murdered many people and condemned many more to drug addiction.

"For my party, we have Generalmajor Kurt Spiegel who is in command of the SS in Vienna, and responsible for the round-up of the Jews in the area, and for their disposal. His preference for young girls is now well-known, his rank allows him to force any woman into his bed, but as said before, it is the young. untouched women he prefers.

"The other is located in Czechoslovakia. It would be good to find a very nasty way to end his career, an end that would scare the surviving members of his command. Since his best trick is to skin his victims alive, I have retained the services of an expert who will provide the same service for him personally. As you have probably gathered he is local. Havel Parnik is the name he uses, though it is not his given name. A hero of his people, he sold the country out to Hitler. We are asked to allow this man to be disposed of by local assets, so I have decided to leave it to those assets for now."

Michael stopped at that point. He looked around at his team, assessing their reaction to the bald instruction to kill people without mercy. He decided to pose the question that he had been required to answer.

"You have all accepted my orders without real argument. You have undertaken to kill people that you do not know, on my word alone. Why?"

He pointed at Sarah. "You first."

Sarah smiled. "However odd you may find it, I accept your orders because I sense that you believe them to be justified. I trust you." She sat back, her simple answer given, challenging any of the others to disagree.

Nodding to Marian, Michael, sat back waiting.

Marian said, "I am a patriot. I tried to join my country in her fight against crime on the side of law and order.

"I was turned down because I was a woman. My father fought in the great war. He swore that USA should have joined Britain on day one, and was ashamed that it took so long to become involved. I was in Germany in 1933, and I saw the way things were going. When I failed to get into the FBI, despite the efforts of the assistant director, I decided that here is where I belong. I discovered that I could kill if I felt it justified. So far it has been justified. I believe you know what you are asking of us. Like Sarah, I trust you.

She sat back, finished.

Ewan needed no urging, "I discovered that I was not too worried about killing at a young age. I could give you the excuses many other Irishmen give, but they would be just that, excuses. My father was not abused by the Black and Tans and if he had been, he would have deserved it. He treated his kids like shit. When he was killed we all sighed with relief for the sake of our mother, and ourselves. I was used to carry messages for anyone who would pay me. If I wasn't paid I shot my employer, normally in the kneecap. I acquired a reputation for fulfilling any contract I was paid to carry out. Now that the country is more or less in the hands of the Irish, who have turned out to be no better than the previous Government, I find that I have more enemies than I need. This job is useful to me. I can maintain my skills and feel virtuous while I do what I am best at. It is a no brainer."

Mark spoke up last. "I do not have a single excuse. I am what I always thought of as a failed scientist. Given that I never achieved the level of competence I aimed for, I became embittered and lost those closest to me, I see now, entirely due to my own selfish arrogance. When I was recruited for this job, I quickly learned that my function would be to perform tasks within my capacity. I am I find quite capable of killing people. I am aware that they are enemies of my country, and of humanity itself. It is excuse enough for me. Pulling the trigger becomes a virtue not a task. I'm here to stay. I'm a member of this team. You can all depend on me."

He had risen to his feet as he talked, and now, having said what he needed to say, he sat down again and returned his own private world.

Michael nodded, satisfied that he could depend on his team. "We leave tomorrow from Croydon. Get some sleep. This could be a long journey to start with."

He left the room and went through to his office, where he started sorting paperwork into some sort of order.

Chapter Ten

Maneuvers

In Berlin the offices of the Abwehr were unusually busy. Commander Heinrich Stolle walked through the offices, nodding to three of the agents who were awaiting re-assignment. In his own office, he found Frau Korder, sorting memos into some order.

"We have several matters that need attention here so I have placed them in order of priority."

"Thank you, Edith. That is most helpful."

As she left the office he looked at her trim waist and neat derriere, and sighed. It was such a waste. Edith Korder had lost her husband in 1933, six years ago, shot by mistake by the Brownshirts, during an assault on the Jewish shops in the suburbs where they lived. Edith had been there when her husband, Albert, died. As Heinrich knew, she had never forgiven the storm troopers for that particular murder. She worked for the Admiral, because she knew he was a voice of reason in the brutal regime that was modern Germany.

He eased his leg. The wound would always trouble him. The doctors had been clear about it. The alternative would have been the amputation of his leg, with the provision of prosthesis. He had decided that he would rather suffer the twinges with his useable leg, than limp about with a wooden one.

Edith came in with two cups of coffee and two biscuits each. She placed them on the desk and seated herself, carefully arranging her skirt so that it would not crease.

Heinrich smiled and sat back in his chair. "Is it to be a lecture, Frau Korder."

She smiled. Her face lit up and Heinrich felt his heart lurch. "I thought it would be a good idea to have a social moment during a busy day, and my name is Edith," she reminded him.

"Of course, Edith. I am delighted and flattered that you are ready to socialize with me in this way. You may not be aware of it but I have admired you from afar, ever since you came to work here."

He noticed her cheeks flushed at his comment. She sipped her coffee, and nibbled a biscuit. "How do you occupy your time away from the office?" She asked.

"Usually, just quietly in my apartment. Sometimes I go to a concert."

"You like music?"

"Yes, not everything, but I do enjoy much of our traditional music. Why, are you a music lover?"

"Yes, though I have not gone to a concert for a long time.."

"Would you like to go? Perhaps I can get tickets?" Heinrich said hopefully.

"That would be nice, I think. Yes, I would like to go." Edith said, quietly.

They sat in silence as they both drank their coffee, then Heinrich said, "I think there is a performance of the Pastoral on Friday evening. Would that be too soon?"

"Oh, no. That would be fine, though I wonder, what time does it begin? I live over near the River…"

"Please, I did realise it could be difficult, so I wondered if you would care to join me in that little pre-theatre restaurant on Unter-den-Linden. Then there would be no rush to get to the concert. I will have the car, so that I can make sure you get home safely afterwards."

"I think that would be very nice, if it would not be too much trouble." Edith was feeling, oddly, rather pleased at the way things were going.

"There is one thing I would appreciate, if you would not mind. In the formality of the office I am happy for you to call me Commander or Heinrich, but, in private, I wonder if you would mind calling me what my mother used to call me: Rick."

There was silence for a moment and Heinrich thought he had perhaps gone too far. He looked anxiously at Edith, who sat with her head down looking at her feet.

Then she raised her head and smiled, "I am delighted that you asked. Of course I would be happy to call you Rick, and you must call me by my other name, Sally. Then, when we are out of the office we are no longer as we are here, we will be Rick and Sally. Yes?"

"Absolutely." The word came out with a rush. He found himself up on his feet, his hand held out to take Edith's extended hand. He bent and kissed the hand, "Hullo, Sally. My name is Rick. How do you do?"

She laughed, "I am very well thank you, Rick." She retrieved her hand and sank back into the chair. "Until Friday, at five then," she said.

As he went home that evening he called at the box office of the Concert hall in Bernberger Strasse, and obtained tickets for the Friday night concert.

***

Early in the office Friday morning, he was not surprised to find the Admiral already there. He called in to see if there was anything needed.

The Admiral smiled. "You are looking very cheerful this morning. It would not have anything to do with Frau Korder, would it?"

Heinrich looked at his boss keenly. "How did you find out?" He asked.

The Admiral sighed. At my age, all I have left for me is the local gossip. I recall there was an occasion earlier this week when my plate of biscuits was short of two of my favorite Bourbons. When I enquired, I was informed that you had been the beneficiary. To a skilled interrogator such as I, it was a simple matter to discover that you had finally prevailed upon the lovely Edith to resume her social life. I am impressed and happy for you both."

As he walked into his office, Heinrich blessed the day he had accepted the posting to work with the Admiral.

***

Ewan and Marian arrived in Frankfurt during the evening, armed with papers identifying them as Horst Schwimmer and Eva Weiss. Both also had passes to allow them access to restricted areas. They kept a low profile until their local agent contacted them.

Axel Mengele was a silversmith of reputation. His current popularity, as an artist, was largely due to the fact that a nouveau class of citizens was in place through the rise of the Nazi administration. The shift in class as a result of the change of government had a dramatic effect on the status of those in positions of influence. The popularity of precious metals for ornaments and trophies had created a new market for Axel. His shop reflected the pattern of popular fashion, the collection of ultra-ornate metalware a shining example of bad taste and crude exhibitionism.

When his visitors made themselves known, he apologised for the display and pointed out that the majority of his customers did not know the difference between good taste and vulgar ostentation. "I sell them what they want, and, in taking their money, I get my revenge on the regime which put them in place.

"Now I cannot show you the target you want until later tonight. The man is bad news. It will not do to miss when you shoot him. You won't survive long otherwise.

"I will show you the man and I can give you an idea of his regular movements. The rest will be up to you."

***

In Vienna, Michael and Sarah travelled together, while Mark kept an eye open from behind them.

Their contact met them with a taxi at the railway station and took them off to his home on the banks of the river Danube.

The retired naval captain was still a fit, healthy-looking man despite his 60 years, and his house was the hub of the vineyard surrounding it. Manfred von Lutzlow, was the latest in the line of a family who had been growing wine for three hundred years. The modern estate had survived storm and war, and was still producing a fine white wine known throughout the country.

At the estate house they were greeted by Frau von Lutzlow, a statuesque blond lady who allowed the encroaching grey hair to grow unchecked, blending with the blond in a sensibly designed style which kept her from looking anything less that the natural beauty that she was.

Connie introduced herself as the old man's slave, but the look, she exchanged with him and the atmosphere at their meeting, made it clear that this was a couple who had no secrets, and shared a bond that Sarah envied.

Settled in, the four sat together in the comfortable lounge chatting like old friends. Mark had stayed clear by arrangement. Keeping his options open, was the way he put it. In fact he went and found the target, the Generalmajor, himself, so that he had a real idea of who the man was.

He found him in a café on St Stephens Platz, in the centre. There, he was able to observe their quarry eating torte and chatting to a pretty girl, who looked to Mark as if she would be happier elsewhere. The General was in uniform, looking very dapper, but, though he was smiling and laughing, as far as Mark was concerned, the ratty eyes did not smile, nor did they cease their continued examination of the curvaceous body of the young woman. Mark commented to the old lady sitting at the next table. "He looks as if he was ready to eat that pretty girl. Who is she? His girlfriend, perhaps?"

The old woman snorted. "Poor girl came in for a coffee, and now she is too scared to move. The man is a snake. He knows he terrifies people. He will force the girl to accompany him and rape her when he gets to his quarters." The woman suddenly realised that she had got carried away with her disgust. After all she did not know who this man was. Perhaps he was Gestapo? She picked up her bag and moved off.

Mark looked at the girl again, made up his mind and stood up. He walked over to the table where the General was sitting, and leaned down to the girl.

She looked up, startled at his approach. Mark smiled at her. "Come, honey. It is time to return to your hotel. The Admiral will not be pleased to be kept waiting. He turned to the Generalmajor who was looking at him, astonished that anyone would dare interrupt his campaign with the pretty girl. Mark said firmly. "Thank you, sir, for befriending the young lady. She does not normally wander in town without her escort. I will see that the Admiral contacts you personally for looking after his granddaughter."

Without waiting for a reply, he took the girl's hand in his, lifted her shopping and handbag with his other hand

and took her away from the table and the tea room. Leaving the general with his mouth half full of torte, and an angry expression on his face.

Mark swiftly led the bemused girl around the corner out of sight of the tea room. Turning to her, he said, "I presume you were not interested in being handled, perhaps raped by that pig in uniform. Does he know who you are?"

"I..I don't think so. He just appeared. But who are you? Why did you do that. That man is a bad man for an enemy."

"I got the impression that you were not enjoying his attention?"

"Well, no. I was dreading what might happen."

"Well, I did the right thing then. Can I drop you anywhere. I have a car nearby?"

"The railway station is not far. I live outside the city. I can get a train easily."

"I can understand if you don't trust me." Mark said. "After all, I am a stranger, just like the General."

"I think not, sir." By the way my name is Margarethe Froehlich, and you are?"

Mark answered almost too soon, but caught himself in time. "Hans Richter, visiting from the country myself, near the border with Czechoslovakia."

"See, we are now no longer strangers. That is the direction of my home. I would be happy to accept your offer of a lift." She had no idea why she had changed her mind, except there was something reassuring about this man, Hans Richter.

The car was an Auto Union saloon. Margarethe had been staying at a friend's house in Aspern. Mark drove her there, she collected her overnight bag and said farewell to her friend. Her home was in Fischamend on the south side of the river. They crossed at Donauinsel, with Margarethe sitting low in the seat, just in case she was spotted.

They followed the road south of the river, all the way to her village. It was dark by the time they reached her home. Her mother was happy to see her home safe and sound. Frau Froehlich was a widow. Her husband had died of wounds he had received in the Great War, although he had survived until 1927. To Mark, the lady and her daughter were obviously very close and it was, with some reluctance that he found himself standing on the doorstep with Margarethe saying goodbye, which he guessed could be forever.

He was aware that there was some reluctance from the lady also, and it was not too much of a shock when he found her in his arms while they kissed.

The dry voice of Frau Froelich brought them back to Earth.

"I think you two should come indoors while I prepare food. This could take some time. I will require an explanation for this behaviour."

Chapter Eleven

It's still murder

Mark contacted Michael the following day and advised him that, having seen the Generalmajor and studied him to some extent, he would be willing to shoot him whenever Michael decided would be a good time.

Michael looked at Mark shrewdly. "I think it might be an idea if you explained just what you got up to yesterday, while we lazed around drinking wine.

Mark smiled. "You found me out!"

"Hang on. Perhaps we should wait for Sarah. She'll be here in a minute."

Sarah arrived, pulling a small cart behind her. "Hi, Mark. Guess what I have here?"

Mark smiled. "I have no idea. What have you got there?"

"You're no fun. I have here our weapons, at least a pile that we can choose from. She flung back the cover and revealed MP3s, Walther pistols and a professional-looking sawed-off shotgun.

Mark took an MP3 and a triple pouch of loaded magazines. He also took a Walther automatic and two spare magazines.

Michael took the shotgun and bandolier, and an MP3 plus magazines. Sarah took an MP3 plus magazines, and a Walther pistol with spare magazines.

All three then proceeded to check out the guns, checking firing pins and magazine springs.

Eventually, Michael said, "Right, it's story-time." He turned to Mark. "What happened yesterday?"

Mystified. Sarah looked and listened while Mark related the events of the day before. When he finished, Michael said, "You stayed the night in the village with the girl and her mother?"

"Yes. I pointed out the problems it might cause but Frau Froelich was adamant. I believe she was worried that the General would somehow know where Margarethe lived, and he would turn up in the middle of the night to drag them off to one of their summer camps."

The other two looked at each other.

Michael said, "How long will it take to get back to the village?"

"About half an hour. From here I guess it is only just along the river road." Mark said.

"Get rolling now and take the guns with you. We'll follow just behind. Get the women out of the house pronto and off into the blue. Do not hang about to pack a bag. Have they a telephone?"

"No." I don't think so at least." Mark was unsure.

"Well, go now!" Michael said. We are right behind you.

Mark jumped into the Auto Union and flung his guns on the seat beside him. He left the estate road and joined the river road with the speed up to sixty miles per hour. The car rocked and bounced on the rather uneven surface and he found himself gaining on the Mercedes in front of him. He swung out and overtook the car, spotting the SS uniforms of the men hanging on in the speeding car. Without thinking, he picked up the MP3 pushed the switch to auto, then concentrated on making distance ahead of the heavier Mercedes. As he approached the village he saw the other car drawing up in front of the cottage. Without hesitation, he came up behind the slowing car and rammed it from behind, bracing himself against the wheel. The Mercedes shot forward suddenly as the driver groped to reapply the brake. His passenger rammed his head into the windscreen. Mark was out of the car, gun in hand, firing into the back seat of the rammed Mercedes. Then he swung round and sprayed the second car splattering blood across the seats in both front and back. There was a solitary shot from the rear car, then nothing.

Mark ran to the house. The door opened and Margarethe stood there looking at the wreckage of the cars and the blood and bodies strewn about.

Michael and Sarah arrived and slewed to a stop. Michael ran to the second car and checked on the bodies within. He turned shaking his head, and made for the first car. The passenger who had put his head through the windscreen was wearing the rank insignia of Generalmajor. Sarah went to the door of the cottage and took Margarethe inside.

Mark went to the General's body and examined it. He looked at Michael. "This job has been done!" He said, quietly. "I think we will have to move the ladies for their own protection. Don't you?"

Michael nodded. "I'll get started. You keep the locals away."

Mark went to the Auto Union and retrieved the magazine pouch for the MP3 and the Walther pistol, the pistol went into his waist band, the first magazine replaced with a fresh one.

A man approached Mark as he stood beside the wrecked cars. "What had happened here?" He spoke hesitantly.

Mark said, "These people came here to arrest a lady who had refused to sleep with the General. I am a friend of the lady. So I shot the General. And because they interfered, I shot his escort as well." Mark looked at the man. "What else should I do?"

The stranger shook his head, gloomily. "This could be trouble, with a capital T."

"Only if they are all found here. Suppose they were found just over the border?"

The man thought about that, but not for long. I'll fetch the breakdown truck and get some men together."

"Make it fast," Mark suggested. I'll keep watch.

Half an hour later, the three cars were no longer there. Six women were out with brushes sweeping up the area where the action had occurred. When they finished, there was no sign of anything out of the way to be seen.

With all the activity going on outside, there was no movement from the people of the house. Mark had put his guns away out of sight in Michael's car.

Michael appeared and strolled over to Mark. "What is going on? Why were all those people suddenly involved."

Mark grinned, "I pointed out that this would be less embarrassing if the entire incident happened over the border. So that is just what has happened. The entire scene is now over the border. All the evidence here is now gone. The men have set it out like an ambush. They have used the opportunity to dispose of one of the locals who had been pointing the finger at several people he disliked. He paid the price today because the timing was right. He is now the driver of my car."

"Sounds reasonable. Do they know who we are?"

"They do not wish to. What they do not know, they needn't lie about."

"OK, Mark. Luck is useful, but we cannot depend on it. The ladies are going to England, whatever you may say, understood!"

Mark shrugged his shoulders. Margarethe and her mother could not stay here. They would be a continual reminder of this incident and that would not allow the local people to forget the whole affair. Since that made the difference between living and dying under the new regime, the ladies had to go. The difference was that now they had time to do it properly, taking their possessions with them.

Michael went back into the house, leaving Mark to continue to keep his eyes open outside.

***

The removal of the household from the village was accomplished with minimal fuss. There were no drawn-out arrangements to be made. The collection of furniture and fittings from the house seemed to occupy little space in the six-ton truck that was used. The wine estate provided the truck and a place for the storage of the heavy furnishings. The two ladies managed with three suitcases between them. For convenience they ladies crossed the border into France and were flown to London by private aircraft.

Frau Froelich, was taken on to assist Beth in the running of Denham, Margarethe volunteered to join the service, but was persuaded to join the team instead.

Mark accompanied the ladies back to London, and saw to their settling in, leaving Margarethe undergoing training. He returned to the field to re-join Michael and Sarah.

For both teams there were secondary targets assigned, in the event of the premature demise of the first choice targets.

As was demonstrated in the case of the Generalmajor, an unplanned incident can make all the difference in the world. Now Michael and Sarah were involved in the planning for the removal of the secondary target.

***

Ewan and Marian saw little activity apart from a visit to a nightclub to identify the target positively. Staying in the house was beginning to drive Ewan nuts. He expressed himself forcibly, as he strode back and forth on the blue carpet.

"For Pete's sake, sit down for five minutes and give us all a rest. You know we cannot afford to be identified. There must be no suspicion that we are involved in anything. The only way we can do that is make sure none of our people become profiled here.

Axel Mengele came home that night. He had news.

"Your target is moving to Munchen (Munich) overnight. You will need to get packed and ready for the 20:30 train. You need to be aboard before Gruber arrives. You will share a compartment. It will minimise the risk of getting split up at the wrong moment. So now get packed. We will go out on the town tonight, and leave you with a better impression of Frankfurt perhaps."

***

The nightclub was all that could be expected of a place like that in a city like Frankfurt.

Picture an American movie, in black and white, with Harry James band playing, and Lynn Bari singing a song no one has heard of. The women are in long dresses, the men in tuxedos and black tie. Tables scattered around the dance floor, with waiters dashing back and forth, trays balancing glasses and bottles.

Add the cigar and cigarette smoke and the amalgam of perfume, cologne and sweat, and, thought Marian, *you could be anywhere in the western world, where the influence of Hollywood was felt.*

They bribed their way to a table where they could survey the scene. It was not long before Axel was able to point out Gruber and his party.

The target was a sharp-looking man, trim, fit-looking and handsome. The clothes fitted as they should and his easy manner reflected his self-confidence.

Six foot maybe plus a little, he stood tall in the group he arrived with. The girl on his arm looked as if she belonged on a catwalk. Axel was quick to point out that she was an actress, Helga Berger, also a model, and she had just returned from America. Marian noted the name for future reference.

Axel then commented, "She will be here as window dressing only, since Helga has her own life and reputation, and she lives it in her own way."

Both Marian and Ewan were pleased to leave early from the nightclub. The weather had reverted to light rain and the air outside was fresh and almost clean after the close conditions inside.

They boarded their train for Munchen, in plenty of time. Once Marian had convinced Ewan that his services were not required for the rest of the night, by the time the train left she was fast asleep.

***

Ewan and Marian followed the Gruber party from the train to a private house on the banks of the Danube.

The owner of the house was old money, and Marian questioned the reason for Gruber to be there. She also questioned why, when they had the chance, they had not killed him.

Ewan had an answer. "When I worked with the local boss man in Berlin, this man's name came up on several occasions. Despite being a low man on the scale of importance within the Mafia, his activities were highlighting his ruthless application to his work. The result was that be became a marked man in the organisation."

***

The call to Munchen had been the next stage in his upward climb in the hierarchy. The interviews with the organisation in the local HQ were vital to his career, and there was no way of avoiding it. When you are called, you go, full stop!

Gruber's meeting in Munchen was an important milestone in his career. The independent work he had undertaken for the Gestapo had all been recorded and overseen by his superiors. His efficiency had been noted and. what was much more important, his background had stood up to examination.

Sitting facing his inquisitors, he was relaxed and careful with his answers, keeping his objectives firmly in mind, power and reward.

They granted the power almost casually. By the way, as it were, offhand.

"You will now become responsible for the Frankfurt/ Dusseldorf areas. Take over the reins as soon as possible. The current incumbent has become an embarrassment. Deal with the matter and assume control of the area. It has become sloppy and income has dropped off accordingly.

"Whatever new dispositions will be fully your responsibility. So think about it and act, but make it soon."

***

In the car returning to the Hauptbahnhof in Munchen, Otto Gruber was unaware that the car was being followed, and that the trailing car was also being followed.

The first car was Gestapo, and the man in charge of that operation was no friend of Otto Gruber.

During his last clean-up for the Gestapo, Gruber had actually crossed the path of an existing Gestapo scam. His interference had cost Gruppenfuhrer Karl Schumann, not only four men, but many thousands of Reichmarks, from an operation which had virtually run itself. There was no way the operation could be restarted while Gruber was about, so he had to go.

***

Ewan and Marian followed the Gestapo car. Having identified one of the operatives, it was clear that Gruber had enemies within the system raising possibilities for the final solution of the problem.

Having once more booked themselves on the night train to Berlin, they were no longer so concerned about boarding in advance, and it was with a certain amount of amusement that they watched the activities of Gruber's men and the watchers from the Gestapo.

Marian observed and commented, "It rather looks like a shootout scenario, to me. If one of them got an itchy finger, they would all go down."

Ewan said smiling, "You've forgotten Gruber is already in his cabin."

"I haven't. I thought he would be the first to go!" Marian said innocently.

Ewan frowned, "How are you going to arrange that?"

"I thought if we should drag one of the men to the compartment, with our Gestapo ID, to accuse him of attempting to assassinate Gruber, I could shoot him then and there, while you shot the two men on the platform, The Gestapo men, I mean, of course. While the gun battle goes on, I thought we could go back to our cabin and wait until the shooting stops."

They boarded the train and found their compartment, and Marian continued.

"As long as Gruber is dead, the collateral number of Gestapo and Gruber men involved is immaterial. As long as we are not linked to the shooting, we will be home free."

"No! That's too chancy. I think the old fashioned way this time. He nodded at the stove in the corner of the compartment. All the compartments have these. I think two grenades down the chimney should do the trick, It will probably blow the side of the coach out at the same time. I'll wait until we are away from the town and climb onto the roof. When I drop them in. I'll be in a hurry, so you will need to lean right out of our window so that I make no mistake, drop over the wrong place and give the game away."

Marian grinned, "Or, miss the open window, and drop off the train? Well, we'll try it your way. If it works, good. If not we'll need to think again. If you are still with us, that is!"

Ewan had to remove his jacket to get the cowl from the chimney in Gruber's compartment. It was too hot to handle with his bare hands, He dropped the primed grenades down the pipe and ran along the roof to the end of the carriage, then ducked down below the rim of the roof. The grenades went off with a satisfying bang. Ewan was back on his feet, racing to the blown compartment, to look down through the blown out roof. There was a man on the floor, squirming. Ewan shot him twice with his silenced pistol. Then, as he watched, the toilet door opened and the bloody figure of Gruber appeared, wounded in several places where shrapnel from the grenades had gone through the wooden door.. He stood there in the howling gale of blown litter and looked at the mess. Ewan shot him twice in the head from point blank range. Gruber toppled to the floor, and lay still.

Ewan turned and ran back to where he guessed the compartment was and peered over the edge of the carriage. The smiling face of Marian looked up at him. He dropped to his knees and slid over the edge of the carriage feeling his feet guided through the open window.

As he hung at full stretch from the lip of the carriage roof the bed sheet was passed around his back and Marian leaned back with her feet braced against the window ledge hauling his upper body through the window. They collapsed together on the bunk.

Marian laughed, as they tumbled over the edge of the bunk and down on to the floor. Ewan was also laughing, with relief at his survival.

Marian was up and closing the window while Ewan got his breath back.

As he watched, Marian stripped off her clothes. "Hurry up. Strip off. "They'll be banging on the door in a minute. He ripped off his things and flung them onto the facing seat and joined Marian under the sheets of the bunk, his cold body wrapped in her warm embrace.

The door of the compartment shook as somebody hammered on it, shouting. The key turned and the porter's face appeared with an armed man behind him. The man yanked the sheet back from the couple in bed, revealing their naked state.

The porter apologised and Ewan tore the sheet away from the man and covered Marian. "How dare you!" He shouted at the man with the gun. "Get out of here, before I stuff that gun up your arse on full automatic."

The man stepped back and Ewan slammed the door shut, and turned the lock.

He turned to Marian. "That was inspired." He grinned. "I am bloody cold."

Marian reached out and wrapped her arms around him sharing her warmth. They woke in the morning still cuddled close together, though no longer cold. Neither mentioned the incident ever again.

The mangled remains of Gruber were not carried off the train. In fact the blasted carriage was unlinked and shunted into a siding, where the incident and its result would not be paraded in front of the public.

In Berlin Hauptbahnhof, the confusion of people awaiting passengers who were over an hour late, was exacerbated by the group of Gestapo and uniformed police, plus the mass of travelers leaving both the Munich train and the Paris express which had arrived on time, at the same time.

In the confusion, the two agents passed out of the station without creating a ripple in the bedlam of the moment.

***

Having a rendezvous point in the Tiergarten, they made their way there, having dropped their suitcases in the luggage deposit at the station.

The two young lovers wandered through the gardens to the café, where they settled down to coffee and cake while they awaited the arrival of their contact.

When the familiar face of Aleck appeared, Marian smiled. The leather coat of the Gestapo was gone, and the shirt and shorts worn by the agent displayed a sturdy pair of knees which would have done justice to a schuhplatten dancer from the Alps.

Aleck sat at the next table and ordered chocolate. While the waiter collected the drink, he spoke quietly giving an address in Potsdam for them to find. They finished their coffee and left the café, a couple with no eyes for anyone but each other.

***

In the office of the Abwehr, Heinrich Stolle was puzzled. The death of Generalmajor Kurt Spiegel could possibly have been an incident involving partisans, The Czechs were always quick to take offence and their reactions were likely to be violent. But there were things about the entire incident that did not really add up.

Why just there? Just over the border. Were they lured there for some purpose or was it opportunism. There was no record of the reason for the expedition, and, in the case of Kurt Spiegel, that normally indicated a woman was involved. Perhaps at the village just over the border, maybe the one this side in Austria.

Glancing at his watch, he realised the puzzle would have to wait. He had a date with Edith Korder. There was a Strauss concert in the park that he had asked her to. She had accepted his invitation, and invited him for the first time to her home for coffee afterwards. They had attended several concerts together, and the relationship between them was now relaxed. While Heinrich would not admit it, his anticipation of these meetings reflected his increasing regard for the lady.

He hoped that she returned his feelings but, up to now, he had only the fact that she was always ready to go out with him, to reassure him of her friendship. Further than that, he did not try to go.

At the concert he was interested to see Helga Berger the actress. She was accompanied by a tall fair-haired fellow, who looked more like a movie lead than the usual greasy looking executive normally hanging around her.

It was in this thoughtful mood at the end of the concert that he realised Edith was speaking to him. "If you have other things to do, I will quite understand. I noticed the actress who called at the office here at the concert. If there is something you need to do, we can continue on another occasion."

Heinrich put his finger to her lips touching her lightly. "Please, Edith, forgive me. I was, I admit, a little distracted, but it was strictly business. I would not interrupt our evening together for anything less than the declaration of war, and, in that case, I would demand a delay so that we are not interrupted."

She giggled. Heinrich smiled, then laughed. Both walked off toward her house arm in arm, in complete accord.

Chapter Twelve

Death and Taxes

Despite being a person who put himself before all others, Gruppenfuhrer Schumann was not a fool, nor was he so self absorbed that he could not accept that there were things that sometimes got past him. The death of Otto Gruber had been convenient, but the people who had accomplished it were uncaught, and apparently unknown. This had preoccupied Kurt Schumann from the moment he had recovered from the satisfaction of getting a pest removed from his district. Whoever had committed the murder – for that was what it was – may have done him a favour. But it revealed that there was someone else in the vicinity who might be a danger to the Gruppenfuhrer, and his back-door operations.

He called in his aide, Ascher Jung. When the man appeared, he studied him still thinking for a few minutes.

Jung stood patiently, accustomed to his superior's ways. He was a medium-sized man, fit but not bulky. His short fair hair was like a cap on his round skull. The clothes he wore were nondescript, not tatty, just not particularly memorable. He could disappear in a crowd without a problem. He was also, Kurt Schumann knew, lethal if called for. He had learned several ways to kill without the need of a weapon. In addition he was skilled in the use of most weapons.

Finally. Kurt looked directly at his man. "I need to know who killed Gruber."

Jung nodded and turned and left the office.

Schumann returned to the building paperwork on his desk.

***

Ewan and Marian found the house in Potsdam without difficulty. It was just a house in an avenue of other houses. All were detached, surrounded by lawns, trees, shrubs and flowers, to the taste of the owners.

The safe house was no different. It was also surrounded by lawns with trees here and there. Remarkably the trees obscured any direct view of the windows. This despite the haphazard way they had been sited. It was a comfortable enough place to stay. As soon as the two agents settled in, they began planning their next assignment. The news was, that Mark and Sarah had been tasked with the removal of several of the key people in the Nazi hierarchy.

All four agents anticipated the imminent invasion of Poland, which they understood would be the moment for the declaration of war with Germany by Britain and France.

The problem they would all face would be that the senior members of the Party would all be consequently energized, and take a public stance if war was declared. It would make it difficult to get near them. They would be in the public eye much of the time. The Team's instructions were to preserve their anonymity at all costs. Rather than be exposed, they should cancel an operation. Placed as they were at present, they were an asset in short supply.

***

Ascher Jung found the task of locating the killer of Otto Gruber impossible, mainly due to the cover-up operation carried out by the local Gestapo office, who had been intent on concealing the relationship between the mob and the Gestapo.

Finding the list of passengers on the train at the time should have been easy. It was not. The cover-up by the Gestapo had been quite comprehensive. When he found the porter for the sleeping compartments he thought he would make progress, but the description of the passengers on the train that night was not as helpful as he would have liked. Even the description of the interruption of the activities of the Gestapo man and woman caught naked, did not really give him a clue. Since both were members of the Gestapo on posting to Berlin, he decided to check with Berlin.

The Berlin HQ knew nothing of the two people involved. Jung thought he had found the killers. His only problem was working out who they were and how they had managed it.

The carriage offered no clue. It had burned out in the siding where it had been discarded when removed from the train. No forensic evidence was available, just two bullet holes in a remaining piece of the flooring. Examination suggested that the bullets were 9mm. Both had gone through the floor completely, and without having an accurate fix on where the bullets were fired, there was no chance of recovering them.

The description of the two people he now knew were masquerading as Gestapo agents was duly recorded, for what it was worth, and the word was sent out.

***

Oddly enough, Kurt Schumann did not suspect the killers to be enemy agents, rather hit men from the Mob. The relationship between the criminal organisations and the

Gestapo was mostly symbiotic, a 'you scratch my back, and I'll scratch yours' sort of deal. Nothing too overt, and no strings.

Gruppenfuhrer Schumann did not forget things. But he was capable of placing this sort of case on the back burner, until something came up to add information or a result to the file. In this case it was evident that, unless the killers surfaced once more, there was little chance of catching them.

He accepted the report from Ascher Jung and got on with the other work on his desk.

***

For Ewan and Marian there was time to wind down a little. Marian's return to her natural eye colour was a relief, if only to get rid of the contact lens.

As the political climate reflected the rising tensions between the countries of Europe, the movements of traffic on rail and road became more and more obvious.

For Ewan the temptation to indulge in sabotage was too much to endure. With the help of Marian and the cooperation of Aleck, he assembled a kit of explosives and time-fuses and set out on an orgy of annoyances for the Germans. Starting with the Ruhr, he placed charges at choke points wherever he could find one.

In each case he concealed the charge and never allowed less than 24 hours between explosions.

By concentrating on a single line to start with, he expected to cause the maximum damage and keep the security forces hopping. As soon as he laid his first trail he started on another line at random.

When the first of his local packages exploded, they were back at the house enjoying a glass of wine.

There was an explosion close by. Ewan was immediately on his feet at the sound. “Get your bags together!” He said tersely. “We have trouble.”

Marian did not wait to discuss the matter. She raced up to her room and grabbed the bag that was always packed and ready for emergencies. From the cupboard she hauled out her gun with its holster and spare magazines.

She could hear Ewan doing the same things in his own room. They met in the downstairs passageway and turned through the kitchen to the walk-in pantry.

The light fitting turned and the back wall slid back to reveal a passage to the house next door. Both stepped through carefully, and Marian pressed the release for the wall to return to its place. They waited for the door to close fully, before walking down the passage and through to the next door house, where they entered the lobby through the bathroom.

Before going further Ewan raised his head and peered through a crack in the window frame, where it did not quite close.

The raiding party arrived at the door of the house they had vacated. There was no genteel knock at the door. It was smash and rush as the raiding party poured into the house, guns up and ready. Ewan waited until all were inside, then pressed a button on the remote control in his hand. This explosion was disappointingly quiet. A sort of whump as the house caved in, the walls fell in, and the roof fell, still virtually complete, to cap the ruin.

There was no sign of anyone getting out of the wreckage. The vehicle drivers ran over and stood looking on helplessly at the collapsed house. The first flickers of flame fed by the gas supply started. By the time the fire service arrived, the house was burning, the roof timbers well alight. Satisfied, Ewan turned to Marian and said. “I have the feeling that we are no longer welcome here. Let's go to Essen. The fireworks will start tonight if I have done my sums right."

Marian nodded approvingly. "Why not. I rather prefer the transatlantic menus that most of the restaurants there offer.

The car in the garage started without fuss, and, as Marian opened the doors, Ewan rolled the big tourer out into the drive. Marian climbed in beside him, and together they drove off.

Leaving the scene well behind, they drove to Berlin once more and exchanged the car for an Auto Union saloon. Only then did they take the road to Essen and the Ruhr, to see the results of their earlier visit.

***

The Gestapo caught up with the Auto Union in their Mercedes with no real problem. Their SS driver was an expert, well practiced in the skill of pursuit and capture of escaping suspects.

As the Mercedes passed them and continued onward, Ewan gradually breathed out. He realised he had been holding his breath ever since the speeding car had appeared in the rear-view mirror. Whoever the Gestapo were after today it was someone else. Marian stirred beside him opening her eyes awake immediately. "What's up?"

Ewan grinned tightly. "We were just overtaken by the Gestapo. They passed us without stopping."

"Do you think the first of the charges may have been found?" Marian looked worried for a moment.

"Look at your watch, woman. The first bomb went off an hour ago. You have been making up for all your lost sleep."

"You were supposed to waken me to take over the driving." Marian punched him on the arm.

"I was not tired, and you looked exhausted when we set out. I just guessed that your need was greater than mine, that was all." He pulled the car over to the shoulder of the road and stopped. Stepping out of the car, he stretched and stamped the kinks out from sitting in one position for the past three hours. "You can take over, if you will? We'll need to fuel, but nearer Essen, I suggest. I would rather we had a fairly full tank in case we need to get out fast."

"We have another 250 kilometers to go, so we need to get going. It will take at least four hours and it will be dark by the time we arrive."

Ewan grinned. "With luck, two more bombs will have made things interesting by then as well." He walked around the car to the passenger side and climbed in. As Marian pulled away from their parking spot she noticed he was asleep already. She was thinking that it was a talent he enjoyed, when she realised that she also was able to drop off to sleep almost on the instant in the same way. *It must be a spy thing,* she thought, and avoided a dog which ran out barking from the road side.

***

The service station was new and well lit. It was late and, apart from the attendant, there was no one about. The rest rooms were clean and the water hot. Marian used the facilities and stepped out to see the two men approaching Ewan, who had just been watching the attendant fill the tank on the Auto Union.

The men took care to approach Ewan from behind beyond his eyeline.

Marian slid the gun from her waistband and held it hidden by her handbag.

The leading stranger approached Ewan and said something.

Ewan lifted his hands and stepped back from the side of the attendant, who, unaware of any problem, was replacing the fuel gun.

Ewan spotted Marian standing in the shadow of the building. He nodded at the second man, whom he could now see, having turned as he stepped back, to bring the entire forecourt into view.

He spoke to the nearest man, "Who the hell are you?"

The man produced his I/d, "Kriminalpolitzei, Gestapo. Who are you, and where are you going?"

Ewan immediately changed his attitude to almost groveling. "I...I did not know. I am travelling on business to Essen. I have done nothing wrong, have I?"

The Gestapo agent looked at him with contempt. "You can stop pissing your pants. If it was you I was after, you would be on the ground already. I am looking for a man and a woman heading for Berlin. Have you passed anyone on the road during the last hour?"

"There were two cars travelling fast I recall though I did not see who was in them. Strange, now you mention it, there was another car leaving the petrol station as we arrived, there were two people in it, I recall."

The agent turned to the attendant. "Do you remember this car? Was there a woman in it?"

The attendant was flustered. "There was a woman bought the fuel. There was someone in the car, but I did not take much notice. I was busy doing my job,"

The Gestapo man swung round, not noticing Marian in the shadows. He called to his partner, who spun round and ran to their car which sat, with engine still running, on the road side outside the petrol station.

The Gestapo man followed his colleague to the car. The doors slammed and the car did a U turn in the road and shot off in the direction of Berlin.

The tension on the forecourt eased. Ewan followed the attendant to the office to pay the bill. Only then did

Marian, gun still in hand, walk over to the car and get into the passenger side of the car.

As Ewan walked out of the office, the Gestapo car roared back onto the forecourt. The agent in the passenger seat jumped out into the path of the bullet from Marian's gun. He dropped to the ground, his gun slipping from his dead hand,

The other man thrust the door open on the driver's side and reached for his gun at the same time. Either action may have worked. Trying both he was far too slow. He fell through the open door to join his dead companion on the forecourt.

To the surprise of Ewan, the attendant rushed out and kicked the dead man. "Bastards." He shouted, "Die, you swine." He turned to Ewan. "They murdered my brother. He was a student at University. Called him a Jew lover and shot him dead in front of my mother. She never recovered. So she has gone now, too. Go. Good luck to you, whoever you are. I'll clear up here and get rid of their car. There is no one about to bother me at this time of night.

Ewan went over to the car and joined Marian. They drove off once more, in the direction of Essen.

As they drove he kept his eye open at the many turnoffs to other destinations. Turned first to Frankfurt and then to destinations further south, until they were heading for Munich.

Marian looked at him enquiringly.

Ewan said, "I think we should get together with our colleagues. Then we can confer and identify targets without the problems of overlap which we are close to encountering at present.

Marian shrugged. Ewan spoke again his voice tense. "We have company."

Chapter Thirteen

Team Building

He put his foot down hard and the car accelerated the needle on the dial rising to 100 kph. It was still not fast enough to lose the vehicle behind them.

Ewan eased up on the accelerator and let the speed drop to 80kph. The following car slowed also. Puzzled, Ewan turned to Marian, "Why would they do that? Any ideas?"

Marian shook her head, then said, "Pull over at the next roadside cafe." In the early hours of the morning there were few restaurants or cafes still open. But eventually they saw the lights of an open place ahead and pulled over and parked.

They entered and ordered coffee and scrambled eggs.

The two men who entered shortly after them, ignored them. They sat at the counter and ordered coffee. They began talking to each other loud enough to be heard, and quite excitedly. Ewan and Marian looked at each other. Ewan nodded and drew his automatic under the table. Marian drew hers, slipping off the safety catch ready to shoot.

Ewan called to the men at the counter. "Eric, Klaus come over here, slowly and carefully."

The two men took their coffee and carefully brought their cups over to the table. They sat with hands in view on the opposite side, facing the Marian and Ewan.

"Perhaps you should pass your weapons over. No need to upset our hosts."

The men did not hesitate. The two guns were discreetly passed over. When the scrambled eggs were served there were no disturbing influences to upset the waiter.

"Right, now. I would like to know why you two are following us?"

Eric looked at Klaus, then shrugged. "The boss had your car bugged, privately. He heard that the Gestapo were showing an interest in you and your friends. We were sent as insurance."

Ewan looked at Klaus, "Insurance?"

Klaus took up the story. "The boss does not trust the Gestapo. They are too friendly. His own words were, 'That we look after you, because you are the only man he knows who can take out senior Gestapo officers, without suspicion falling on the wrong people'. We did not intend following you, we just happened to be in the area you passed through and picked up your signal. We decided to follow when we noticed that a Gestapo team was already on your tail."

"A Gestapo team?"

"They had an accident. Crashed into a petrol truck. Sad business. All four men died. Only the tanker driver survived."

Marian said, "The bug. It will have to be removed. It is obviously a risk we can do without."

Eric pointed to his pocket, at a nod from Ewan he carefully brought out a battered looking object of metal and Bakelite. "I removed it from your car as we came in. I thought it may be needed again, so I switched it off.

He placed it on the table, where it sat, the focus of all eyes. Marian removed it and placed it in her handbag.

Ewan said, "What is the boss up to? What is in it for him?"

It was Eric who answered. "You may not believe this, but in his own way, the boss is a patriot. He is willing to use the system to make money, but he is not happy with the Nazi's way of doing business. Many of his friends are Jewish, and he has already managed to rescue several of their families and get them to Switzerland. He has not gone soft. He has always looked after his friends. He has a code of honour. It does not suit everyone, but people who work for him are looked after. He guessed that you two were British agents. We will be at war soon. But, on the basis that your enemies are his enemies, he will help defeat them using any method he has at his disposal. We were sent to protect you. When we lost your trail we were ordered south to friends in Marseilles. It seems we were on the suspect list of the Gestapo, right beside you two." He smiled and nodded unconsciously. "Finding you again was pure luck."

Ewan listened and watched the two while Eric finished his speech. He shrugged, and returned Eric's, gun indicating for Marian to do the same with Klaus's.

"We are going to Munich first. If you decide to go to Marseilles, we won't stop you." Ewan looked at the pair, "There will be work to do if you come with us."

"We are your escort, remember? Munich it is. I'll let the boss know from a street telephone."

The escort checked in to a small hotel in Joseph's Platz. The others were staying with Sarah and Michael in the apartment they rented just around the corner in Zentner Strasse.

***

Gruppenfuhrer Karl Schumann was unhappy. There were three reasons for his condition and they were all standing in front of his desk looking decidedly uncomfortable.

"One of you tell me why, with all the resources of the Gestapo behind you, you have been unable to keep observation on two high profile people?"

The Major looked at his superior gloomily. "They must have found the bug," he said quietly.

"How could they find the bug if it was placed properly, in the correct place. After all, the whole idea of the secret location device is secrecy."

The conversation was one-sided, and it continued in that way for some time before the men were released to consider their shortcomings at length.

Schumann called his secretary. "Lock the door, Hanna. I need to relax."

He watched as the blond woman locked the door and then came over to the desk. She removed her knickers and sat on the desk waiting while Schumann prepared himself. When he was ready she lay back and spread her legs and received her master's offering, performing her part in relaxing him. It was an act that gave her little satisfaction. Schumann was only interested in his own part of the proceedings. When he was finished, she stood and went quickly to the small bathroom off the office to clean herself up before returning to work.

Her boss took his time dressing. Then feeling relaxed once more, he unlocked the office door and called for his car. His day would improve if he managed to spoil someone else's.

***

For Heinrich Stolle the day had gone well. The night before, he had escorted Edith home and she had invited him in. They had kissed and petted before he had left her. There was no question that their relationship would blossom, provided he continued to maintain his gentlemanly approach.

The Admiral poked his head around the door. "Heinrich, that little turd Schumann is calling round to complain that we are not keeping him updated with all our latest intelligence.

"Let us lay on a display for the unpleasant little fart. Dig out some tasty bits of interrogation statements for him to peruse. I presume he can read."

"Very good, sir. I have a recent batch he can read, including a knee-trembler from Norway, just to give him a thrill. It's a pity the prisoners are all gone. There is no one here to take his spite out on. I suggest the ladies disappear to the top floor in the meantime."

"Of course. Please arrange it." The Admiral disappeared, leaving Commander Stolle to his preparations.

***

Gruppenfuhrer Schumann stalked into the Abwehr office as if he owned it. "I am here to speak with the Admiral," he said, without acknowledging the fact that Stolle had risen at his entrance.

Stolle opened the diary on his desk. "Do you have an appointment?"

"I do not need an appointment. I am a General Officer of the SS."

"Admiral Canaris is an Admiral of the German Navy." Stolle stressed the word Admiral. I will enquire if he will see you. Please take a chair, sir." He turned and went to the door of the Admirals office, and knocked. He entered after hearing the reply from within.

Admiral Canaris smiled when Stolle revealed the identity of the caller. "I will make time to see the Gruppenfuhrer in five minutes. I need to finish these orders. Offer the visitor coffee, and make it yourself."

"Yes, Admiral." Stolle left the office, closing the door carefully. Facing the SS visitor once more, he said,

"The Admiral can see you in five minutes. Can I offer you coffee?" Stolle spoke calmly and politely, and inside enjoyed the fact that the SS officer was furious at being kept waiting.

Schumann controlled himself with some difficulty. He was unused to being balked. "No, thank you," came out through gritted teeth.

He sat down and tapped the sole of his highly polished boot with the swagger stick he was carrying.

***

Exactly five minutes passed and, as the impatient visitor was preparing to cause a scene, the Admiral appeared, in uniform, though without his hat.

The Gruppenfuhrer leapt to his feet and saluted with the Nazi forward upraised arm. Canaris flapped his right hand upwards in acknowledgement. "You wished to see me?"

"Yes, sir." The prompt reply brought the suspicion of a smile to the Admiral's lips.

"Come on through." He said, standing aside from the door to the office. Turning to Stolle, he said, "Do not disturb us for anyone other than the Fuhrer himself."

The suspicion of a wink could have been his imagination.

Stolle seated himself at the desk and pressed the button beneath his desk to start the recorder going in the admiral's office.

***

When the visitor had departed the female members of the staff returned to their places in the office complex. None were recorded as office staff. All were treated as agents and paid accordingly. All had been trained with weapons and hand to hand combat. All could—and sometimes did—go out into the field on assignments, even Edith. Her strength as an agent was her reticence, a natural shyness apparent in her body language and in her conversation. Whilst this was her normal demeanor, she was quite capable of adopting a domineering persona if required. A natural actress, her friends would not recognise her when dressed as an SS Sergeant on a 'stop and search mission'.

***

In the admiral's office, Canaris pointed out that the SS were mounting surveillance on the Abwehr offices. "All female staff must use the alternative exits. I do not wish them to become victims of some vindictive SS swine's venom." The alternative exits were secret passages that allowed the escapees to mingle with the other office workers from the many departments of the administration operating in the immediate vicinity.

"While you are here, Heinrich, any progress on the Helga Berger front?" The Admiral asked innocently.

Stolle grinned. He knew, and the admiral knew, that his romantic interest was in Edith Korder, here in the office. The actress Helga was a possible channel for contact with the overseas agents of the Abwehr.

"In fact, yes, sir. I have maintained contact with the lady, who has expressed a willingness to help as a courier. She is intending to visit the United States in just over a week. I have documents for the representatives of the German Bund in USA. Not ultra secret, but a possible test of the security of the service, for the future."

"Excellent. Her contribution could be extremely useful, as long as the USA remains neutral."

***

As Heinrich Stolle left the office that evening he looked for and spotted one of the watchers who the Admiral had rightly guessed would be there. He had arranged to meet Edith later that evening. She would be attending her class to learn English this evening. Not that she needed the instruction, her English was polished and comprehensive already, but it was part of her cover when in Berlin. He decided that he should lose the tail, if only to demonstrate that he could. Losing his shadow and making it look accidental that would be best. Making up his mind, he stopped and swung round, pantomiming frustration, and returned to the building. Inside he stopped and watched the tail to see whether he had noticed. The man had been looking at a newspaper. As he watched the man glanced up expecting to see his target walking past toward the corner as usual. A taxi came and deposited its passenger outside the building. Stolle stepped into the vacated vehicle and ordered the driver to take him to the Tiergarten. As he passed the watcher, he saw he was looking frantically all around seeking his quarry.

Stolle presumed his re-entry of the building had been missed by the man. Perhaps he had actually been reading the newspaper. He shrugged his shoulders. No doubt the man would invent some reason for failing to follow his assigned target.

At the Tiergarten Stolle left the taxi and strolled down to his apartment building. He was reaching for his door-key as the elevator door opened and he found Edith standing, waiting, beside his apartment door. Since they had only parted at the office half an hour earlier, he was surprised and troubled to find her here.

He did not query her presence, merely opened the door and ushered her into his bachelor apartment.

He took her coat as she stood and looked around the rather Spartan lounge. Then she turned to him and spoke for the first time. "How nice of you to invite me in like this." She held her hand up, finger to her lips.

He caught on fast. There was obviously some form of listening device in here. "I have been meaning to show you my humble abode for some time. Until now there was no opportunity." As he spoke she was waving a small box with an aerial projecting from it. A small light was flashing. As it moved, the speed of the flash increased until it became a continuous glow. Edith approached the lamp standing on a side table. "Oops. Sorry." She said, and knocked the lamp from the table. It hit the floor breaking the electric bulb. Her stout walking shoe crushed the fitting, demolishing the electric light ruining it beyond repair. The light on the small box went out.

"I believe that is the only one. I will check the other rooms just to make sure." She went through the rest of the apartment with her little box and finally returned to the lounge.

"That was the only device I can find. We should be able to speak freely now."

Heinrich looked at her. The shy quiet woman was alert and alive with energy. He said "Gestapo?"

She nodded, she was standing close to him he could smell her perfume. He turned and without thinking put his arms around her and they were kissing urgently both unconsciously drawn to each other. What followed was inevitable and wonderful.

Afterwards, they lay in his single bed, her head on his chest, aware that this was a beginning for them both.

Chapter Fourteen

Internal strife-Escape

"The Admiral knew," Edith said. "When I was recruited he told me. I was a widow. I loved my husband and I was willing to be alone for the rest of my life. He said. 'Give it time, things will change'. Then he said that I would be working for a man who had been through injury and had come out of it well, but would need support in his office work. That I could do.

When I met you, I realised that things were changing. I was going to lose my comfortable expectation of a quiet retiring life. You disturbed me. When you asked me out to that first concert, I realised that either I stopped things there at that time, or I was lost. And here I am."

She turned her face up to his. He kissed her, "I have decided that I will not let you go, ever." He said it quietly and firmly. "You need to know this because it makes us both vulnerable. I will speak with the admiral tomorrow. The Gestapo could threaten us through each other. If they suspect our relationship, we may find ourselves black-mailed into betraying the admiral. That must not happen."

"I agree. They will know I am here. What they must not know is that this is more than a social visit, or at best a quickie one-off. Though it pains me to say it, I suggest perhaps an assignation with Fraulein Berger?"

"If you ring her now, it is still early in the evening. They may well have a tap on your phone. It would divert attention. If not, the assignation would. As you are aware the Gestapo tends to regard women as objects to be used and cast aside. Let us help them continue to believe that."

Stolle reluctantly rose from the bed and reached for the telephone on the night stand. He looked at the small directory beside the phone and dialed a number.

Helga Berger answered immediately. "Fraulein Berger, this is Commander Stolle. May I call you Helga?"

"Of course. Heinrich, is it not?"

"Indeed it is. I am calling to invite you out to dinner."

"Why, thank you, Heinrich. That would be very nice. Where would you suggest? Somewhere discreet or would you rather a more public place?"

"Like the idea of being able to talk without shouting above the noise. Discreet, I think."

"My hotel has an excellent restaurant, and room service."

"Helga, that would be ideal. Are you free tomorrow evening perhaps? Say seven thirty."

"That sounds ideal. The concierge will direct you, to avoid fuss."

"Until tomorrow. Auf Wiedersehen." He replaced the telephone.

Edith reached out for him. "I think we need to reaffirm our partnership before that other woman comes between us."

***

Gruppenfuhrer Karl Schumann was not pleased. Whenever he encountered Admiral Canaris, the Abwehr chief, he came away feeling belittled, without any apparent reason. Sadly, this situation had not improved, and Schumann could not help thinking that the party would be better off without the Abwehr sticking its nose into things the Gestapo did better. He was almost certain that Canaris had conspired to get Jews out of Germany, to save them being eliminated like so many of their compatriots.

Schumann actually did not care about the collection into camps of Jews, Gypsies, and other dissident peoples. To him it was neither here nor there, provided they did not hinder the progress of the rebuilding of the Reich. They were just cattle like the rest of the people outside the Gestapo. It did not occur to him that the arrogant assumption of superiority adopted by the Gestapo was an expression of weakness. Then he didn't really care about anything that did not directly affect him.

Ascher Jung appeared to report on the progress of the inquiry into the death of Otto Gruber. There was nothing to report, so Schumann put his inquiry on the back burner and set him on the new task of finding things out, to use against the Abwehr. He then dismissed everything else from mind while he concentrated in reinstating the lucrative scam which had been halted by Otto Gruber.

***

The four sat around the coffee table in the lounge of the apartment in Joseph's Platz. They were silent considering the task they were faced with.

Michael had received word that the war would be with them within weeks, the build up on the Polish border making it apparent to any sensible person that there would be an attack in the very near future. It was already early August 1939 and the clock was ticking.

Michael had no option. The task facing them was going to be tricky at best and suicidal at worst. Professor Waldo was a one-off. The briefing stated that he was one of the greatest innovative scientific minds in the western world. His current research was in nuclear science, an area about which there was still little currently known. Falling into German hands was not a prospect to be allowed.

Unfortunately, it was likely to happen unless they could do something about it.

Sarah spoke, "We will need to go in and collect him, of course, but his family is the real problem. We know they are under the protection of one of the bureaus of the *Referat* (Polish Intelligence) in Danzig. Their protection is unlikely to stop a Gestapo snatch team and, with Ribbentrop about to sign a German-Russian accord treaty, the Russians may well come in on any attack on Poland. So we must talk of immediate action. Once Russia is off the table Germany is unlikely to hold off any longer. Time is not on our side."

Michael nodded. "That sums up our situation in a nutshell. I've drawn up a schedule." He passed a copy to each of them. "Take a look and see if you can knock holes in it." He sat back and rubbed his brow. He had spent some time working out the plan. He hoped he had got it right.

After a while Ewan said, "Transport?

"Aircraft to Warsaw," Michael said tersely. "Boat from Danzig."

"Can we depend on the boat?" Mark asked.

"Our friends from Peenemunde," Michael reassured them.

"Alright, then. I presume you have all read the brief. Sarah takes Ewan for the professor. Marian, Mark and I will collect the family. We will bring all of them to the boat. Sarah, getting the professor may not be easy. He may favour the Germans. If he cannot be persuaded to come, kill him."

Sarah nodded. "I understand." She looked at Mark, eyebrow raised.

Mark nodded. I get the message. If necessary snatch, but if it is not possible." He drew a finger expressively across his throat.

Michael continued, "Take Alek with you as back-up, we will take Klaus. We can use the private aircraft, the Beechcraft from the club airfield. The pilot had filed a cross country flight plan for six businessmen and their secretaries. All arranged by the Gestapo.

"We will drop off at Danzig. You will be in Warsaw by tonight. If you are able to collect him during the night the plane will not leave until morning.

"It also means we have to time the snatch of the family. With the professor gone, the family will be the next target. So though for us in Danzig it's 150 miles away from Warsaw, the telephone has made distance a poor safety margin. We must aim to be finished by the time the Warsaw party arrives. A swift snatch and go is what we really need."

They all looked at each other. Experience made it clear that forward planning seldom survived the first moves of the action.

***

The two cars swept through the entrance of the private airfield, the small insignia on both radiators ensuring smooth transit of the guarded gates.

Both cars came to a halt beside the parked Beechcraft standing with the engines ticking over and the air-stair in place.

The people from the cars boarded the waiting aircraft. The cars were taken into the hanger, to be parked until the party returned.

The air-stair door closed and was locked in place. And the Beechcraft started to roll forward towards the take off area.

The quiet of the airfield was shattered by the revved up engines of the Beech as it took off climbing above the end of the airfield into the morning sky.

***

In Warsaw, the lab where the professor worked was in turmoil, as the various scientists all tried to get their work prioritized.

In his assigned corner, the work of Professor Waldo remained uncollected, and unboxed. But then there was little to show, and little to go. The equipment was basic lab stuff, nothing special, and most of the work seemed to go on under his beard. The muttering of the voice beneath the beard was almost part of the background of serious noise.

He looked at the others contemptuously. Running around like rabbits, you would think the Germans were already here. For the real scientist there was no problem with whoever governed. People always needed scientists. The one small niggle of doubt was the stories they had been hearing of the scientists at Peenemunde. Their families had been held against their good behaviour. But apparently they had been eliminated and the supposed contact maintained with forged letters and messages.

He had been approached by the German Government last year to take part in a research program they were running. He had refused but from the sound of things he could well finish up working for them at a greatly reduced fee. As a scientist, Philip Waldo was not particularly interested in politics. He had a vague idea that the current German leadership were being aggressive, throwing their weight about in Europe. He had not really bothered about it until he heard the news through the grapevine about the people working at Peenemunde.

The telephone on his workbench rang. He looked at it in astonishment. It had not ever rung before to his knowledge. He had certainly never used it. Tentatively, he reached out and lifted it to his ear. The voice at the other end sounded a long way away. "Yes," he said. "I am Professor Waldo."

The voice at the other end started giving instructions.

Philip Waldo, listened for a few moments, then replaced the telephone on its stand. The telephone rang again. He shrugged and lifted it once more."Who is this?" He asked.

"My name is Michael Wallace. I am with the British Navy. I have been told that an attempt to abduct your wife and family will be made as soon as the invasion of Poland occurs. Sometime in the next week or so, I estimate."

Waldo stopped him there. "One moment. Did you call me before this, just a few minutes ago?"

"No. I have just reached a telephone and this is the first call I have made."

"Someone rang and threatened to kidnap my family, if I did not co-operate with them." Waldo sounded upset. "They did not give their name."

"That would be the Gestapo, the German secret police," Michael concluded. "What did you tell them?"

"Nothing. I put the telephone down."

"Good. There will be a team of my people with you very soon. Sarah, the leader, will identify herself to you with the words 'fission not fusion'. Do you understand?"

Waldo said, "Of course I understand. 'Fission not fusion,' is that correct?"

"Correct. I will gather your family and you will be brought to join them. We will send you to a safe place where you will not be in danger and your family will be safe." The phone rang off.

Waldo started to collect his personal things together. He managed to get them all into his old leather briefcase. He noticed the attractive woman who pushed her way into the laboratory.

She spoke to the senior lab attendant. He pointed to Professor Waldo, and bustled off about his work. The woman came up to the professor. He noticed that she was indeed very attractive. Her voice in English sounded cultured. The professor's English was fractured but passable.

"Fission not fusion," the woman said.

The Professor nodded and collected his bag.

The woman said, "No notes?"

The professor smiled and tapped his head, then his bag. "All I need," he said.

They left through the side door as a car drew up at the front door. Ewan and Alek were waiting. The car moved off immediately. The professor said, "First to the Hotel Central – my daughter will be waiting there for me." He looked around at the others. "She is visiting. We arranged to go out to eat later so I said I would collect her at the hotel."

Sarah asked, "Is she staying there?"

The Professor grinned, "No, of course not. It is far too expensive. We just meet there. That is all."

"Straight to the hotel please, Alek," Sarah said. "Then we will go to the airport."

"Right, boss. The hotel first, and then the airfield." The car drove off without being followed, while the snatch party was busy trying to find Professor Waldo at the lab.

***

The Central hotel was once the most exclusive hotel in Eastern Europe. Though it was showing signs of age, the doorman was as smart as his compatriots in Paris and London. He opened the door for the professor and his party, and reopened it as they left, now accompanied by the rather severe-looking woman dressed in a suit.

He had noticed the woman on other occasions. She was normally met by the professor, a known personality in Warsaw. He guessed the woman was a relative; the words lover and mistress did not seem to fit, in the doorman's mind.

The pretty woman in the group thrust a banknote into his hand. She breathed into his ear as she passed, "Perhaps you did not notice us passing through." He grinned and nodded, then watched as they all piled into the car and drove off. He opened his hand discreetly and folded the $100 bill carefully, slipping it into his inside pocket.

***

At the airfield they hit a small snag. At least that was Ewan's description of the event. A group of Polish Officers were awaiting their transport to some forward base on the frontier. They had been drinking. At the sight of the two women they made exaggerated bows and polite invitations to join them for a parting drink before they went to war.

"There is no war," Greta Waldo said. "Is there?"

This led to a discussion that the officers all joined into. And while the good-humoured chatter was going on, the Gestapo snatch group arrived.

"Time to go." Ewan said grabbing the professor. Sarah caught Greta's arm and they all began to move.

The Germans made the mistake of shouting for them to stop, that they were under arrest. They were drawing their guns as they burst into the departure area shouting. Unfortunately for them, they were speaking German. They realised their mistake when the first chair caught the leader across the chest, felling him to the ground and sending his Walther pistol slithering across the shiny stone floor. A gun went off and one of the Polish officers fell cursing to the ground. The remainder of the group, including the shooter, was tackled and brought down by the now angry group of officers. They were not actually killed, but there were broken bones among the prisoners when order was restored.

The police arrested the German party, confiscating their weapons. The wounded officer declared the flesh wound he had received to be nothing to worry about, and departed with his compatriots in the military aircraft which by then had arrived to take them to their airbase on the Polish/German border.

The German prisoners were jailed, awaiting process. They were eventually to be released when the German army marched into Warsaw, just a few days later.

Sarah, Ewan, Alek and their two companions were airborne en route to Danzig before the fight was over.

***

The big seaport was in a frenzy of activity, troops and naval sailors were everywhere. The two groups met by arrangement at a cafe near the docks.

"We have problems," Michael whispered. "There are Germans everywhere, and I have been told there are German ships in the vicinity, waiting to take part in the initial attack when it starts."

"In that case, we need to get out fast." Sarah said quietly. She looked at the Waldo family. The daughter, Greta, was still stone-faced as the Professor and his wife, with their son, discussed their imminent escape from Poland. Greta did not think they should leave. Her German friends had told her that the Germans were keen to have the professor working with their own people. He was highly regarded over the border. And, after all, the Polish and German people were closely related. There would be no real conflict. Just a quiet take-over, and an armistice between two neighbours.

She spoke to her family forcibly. "What are we leaving for? The Germans will make us rich. They have promised this. I would like to be rich for a change. Here, despite the prestige, I cannot afford nice clothes or go to the theatre when I wish. None of us do. What do these people offer?"

The professor looked at his daughter sadly. "Freedom," he said. "There will be money but most of all there will be freedom." He looked at his family. "Here we had freedom. That is about to disappear. Even if the British come to our aid, this country will fall initially." Turning to Greta, he said "Your German friends offer money. They offered the scientists at Peenemunde their family's lives? They then murdered them all! That is what the German promises mean. I will take a chance on the British and American promises. So far they have not broken any to me. You are my family. I must make the decisions, right or wrong. I will take the responsibility. If I am wrong, god help me. If I am right, we live for a while at least, in freedom." His wife squeezed his hand. His son took Greta by the hand and whispered, "It will be alright, Greta. I will look after you."

Greta smiled for the first time that morning. Her twelve-year-old brother would look after her. She squeezed his hand and said, "Of course you will. I should have known."

Their contact came into the cafe. He was in naval uniform. He walked over to Michael, managed not to salute, and passed him a slip of paper.

Michael read the note and then nodded to the bearer. "Two hours, pier six, Andorra." The naval man left. Michael turned to Ewan, showed him the note, "Check it out, please."

Ewan nodded, rose to his feet, jerked a thumb at Alek and the pair left the cafe.

Michael rose to his feet, took Greta's arm and slipped it through his., "Time to move to the second rendezvous," he called to the boy, "Paul, could you join your sister. I would feel better with another man with us." Paul came over happily to be the other man with his sister. Greta did not know whether to smile or struggle. She decided that smiling was the best bet for just now. The broken-up group left the cafe at separate times. All knew the new rendezvous point, so they took various ways, ensuring there was not a big party to attract attention.

***

As Michael, Greta and Paul entered the main harbour road, a man across on the other side noticed them. He turned to the girl with him and pointed them out. Greta noticed them. "Look, it is Carla and Matti," She waved and called out. Michael took one look and dragged her round the corner. The bullets chipped the bricks on the house beside them and Paul cried out as one of the chips drew blood on his face.

"Why are they shooting at us?" Greta cried. "They are my friends."

Michael had his own gun in his hand, "They were your friends. They are agents of the Gestapo, enemies of Poland. Here to kidnap you, to force your father to work for them.

"They were shooting at your brother and me. Killing Paul would convince your father that they mean business. He peered around the corner. Both German agents were half-way across the busy street. He looked round. Down the alleyway. He pointed to the others. Greta took Paul's arm and ran to the alleyway. Michael followed and waited by the corner of the alley, making sure that the followers knew which way they were going. The man, Matti, appeared at the corner. He was puffing, gun in hand. He stood getting his breath back. Michael took careful aim and shot him in the leg. He did not mean to shoot him in the leg. He had aimed for the body, but at least he had not missed, and Matti was on the ground writhing and bleeding.

Michael turned and followed the others along the alley putting his gun hand, complete with gun, in his jacket pocket, his finger on the trigger.

He was not surprised to see Carla appear at the other end of the alley, gun in hand. As they approached she raised the gun. Michael lifted his hand, still in his pocket and shot at Carla, who was still raising her gun. She stumbled and her gun went off, the bullet ricocheting off the brickwork and clattering into the rubbish bins outside the back door of a shop. She tried to lift the gun, still on her feet but swaying. "Polish schwein," she muttered and collapsed to the ground still muttering.

Gerda ran to her, only to hear Carla repeat the same words, "Polish Schwei....."

Michael lifted her up and took Greda in his arms as she sobbed. "She was my best friend, and she called me a Polish schwein. Why would she do that?"

Michael stroked her head. "She is a soldier, fighting a war. It's what soldiers sometimes do. Come on. We must meet the others. Warn them that the snatch squad are here."

They left the alleyway. No one had appeared, the shots unnoticed with the noise of the dockyard and traffic on the road.

***

The body lay sprawled on the dirty ground. A figure appeared looking from side to side to see if it was observed. Seeing no one, the man approached the figure on the ground. The scavenger, ignoring the wound in her chest, removed her clothing, right down to her white skin. He found her purse and collected the gun. The scavenger melted away, leaving the naked body lying in the middle of the alley.

Two years later, her gun was used by a patriot to shoot a German officer.

***

Michael, Gerda, and Paul made it to the rendezvous with time to spare. The others came in and joined them for the next stage of their extraction.

Having delivered the family members to Danzig, Ewan, Sarah, Marion and Mark took Klaus and Alek with them back to the airfield. The pilot was ready and they took off for a planned flight to Bremen. En route, they diverted to Copenhagen, and thence to Paris. By the time they crossed the border into Germany, Britain and France had declared war.

***

The big powerboat, now painted grey, motored into the busy harbour. The small ensign proclaimed it to be Polish, but the crew were all British. Below decks a unit of Marines waited, ready in case of problems. The big boat nestled alongside a ship already tied up at the dock. The first officer went ashore crossing the deck of the coaster alongside. He stepped down onto the quay and walked along to the big crane. The party was waiting for contact from the boat. "Stronghold?"

Michael stepped forward, "Bulwark." He said in answer. The first lieutenant saluted and spoke "Please follow me to the boat. Take care crossing the coaster. There are some sharp edges if you miss your step."

The party boarded the boat and, once all were settled below, Michael got together with the skipper as they left the harbour at slow speed. As they cleared the port the speed increased but not dramatically. The skipper, Lieutenant John Matheson, mentioned that there were enemy ships scattered around most of the approaches to Danzig.

"I'm hoping that the war does not break out for a day of two yet."

Michael looked at the calendar where the dates were crossed off. It was the 1st September, 1939. "Well, war has not broken out so far. Let's make some distance, and see how we go. There is nothing much we can do about it anyway, just put our heads down and run, I suppose."

The skipper smiled and said, "There should be a dram somewhere. Try the cabinet in the corner of my cabin. Help yourself."

Michael joined the team in the main cabin. "This could be a tricky voyage," he said quietly. "However, we are in the hands of an experienced crew who have been in these waters for several months and are accustomed to making their way about without detection. Please remember at all times not to show lights nor to make noises when we in quiet mode. Sound carries across water and there are people looking out for us, and boats like ours. They will shoot on sight, and worry later about taking prisoners from the shattered wreckage of the boat.

"After a barrage of bullets, that could be a pointless exercise. Also it would make our efforts over the past weeks a waste of time and lives.

"Finally, once we pass through the Kattegat, we should be clear of enemy influence. But, if war is declared by that time, all bets are off. The Nazi party have not demonstrated much respect for boundaries or frontiers, so the hazards of our journey could extend beyond the current sphere of influence claimed by Germany.

Chapter Fifteen

THE RAID

In Frankfurt, Ewan Fitzgerald was feeling odd. His normal élan seemed to have deserted him. He looked across at Marian Smith. She was sitting cleaning the pieces of her stripped-down Browning automatic laid out on a cloth on what was used as the dining table in their current apartment.

He had worked with her before and they had played husband and wife before. Up to now it had all been a game, but the unaccustomed restlessness that Ewan was suffering was not his normal sexual arousal. That was part of it, but there was more involved than that. In the past he had taken what was offered, enjoyed it and promptly moved on. This was not the same. They shared a bedroom for appearance sake, but they did not share a bed, or each other. Even on the train when they had carried out the operation on Gruber. They had cuddled for warmth, but no more than that. Now he found himself in the situation that so many others experienced. Should he or shouldn't he?

He sat, winding himself up to the point where he would have to speak or burst.

The doorbell rang.

Almost relieved, he took his own weapon out and went to the front door. "Who is it?" He said loudly through the door.

"The Angel and the Devil." The voice the other side of the door declared.

Ewan grinned and opened the door to Mark and Sarah.

They filed into the lounge.

Ewan was not surprised to see that the disassembled automatic had been locked and loaded in the interval between the bell ringing and the entry of the others. Marian was without doubt very skilled with weapons.

"What news?" Sarah smiled at them both. "How is married life?"

"Uneventful, so far," Marian said quietly. "But we are getting there.

Ewan wondered what that meant. "No news from Michael?"

Sarah shook her head. "It has been reported that the boat made it to Copenhagen, and an aircraft took the party on to England, but Michael stayed in Denmark. Presumably he was planning to return to Germany."

Mark took out a map of Frankfurt from his briefcase. "I have been taking a look at the setup of the Gestapo in town. I think, with a little ingenuity, we can make a difference here. One of the main drawbacks for the security forces is the habit of keeping secrets to themselves. It extends to the records they keep at local level. They are not shared with the next district even. It means that often the records are duplicated. But equally often they do not cover organisations crossing the boundaries from one area to another. Because of this fault, the destruction of records in this area removes many details of people which are kept nowhere else. I propose we destroy the local record office, and then do the same for the other areas around us. It helps us in two ways. Before we destroy them, we can take a look at what they've got. Perhaps we can blackmail some of our favoured people.

Sarah said, "I see what you mean and approve on the face of it. But I do think we should carry on doing positive things before easing back to the negatives."

Ewan said, "What have you got in mind?"

"I wondered about sabotaging the airfield. Since the war began, the aircraft from here seem to be flying every day and night. I thought if we used some of our explosives and trick gadgets we could cause problems for the Luftwaffe security. You realise that they hate the Gestapo. If we create enough trouble, we can ensure that the Gestapo take over the enquiries. That will upset the Luftwaffe even more.

"It will all lead to breakdowns in the Luftwaffe and, hopefully the Gestapo presence on the airfield would cause more disruption.

"Given the factors so far, each aircraft we can sabotage means one less in the air over Poland, and on any other front they may choose to attack."

"I like the idea." Ewan added, "Especially since as a boy I used to put sugar in the police fuel tanks. Sometimes I would crack the distributor caps. I think it worthwhile establishing a way into the airfield which we can use on a regular basis. Let us check up on the ways in and out controlled by the authorities. I have an idea we can add one of our own which nobody will question. Alternatively, use one that exists already but is not used. We might be able to take it over for our own use."

The others all looked at him speculatively. He could almost hear them thinking.

"How do we go about installing our own gate?" Mark said, musingly.

Ewan looked at him pityingly, the vivid memories of doing just what he suggested still fresh in his head. "The airfield is surrounded by a chain-link fence. Gates in such a fence are installed using galvanized poles welded together to form an oblong portal. A chain-link covered gate is fitted to size. For a fence of some age the easy answer is to locate a similar fence elsewhere. The best would be on a disused site. Cut out the gate and frame complete. Choose a dark night and time the patrols. We erect the whole frame and gate in place. Then, in between the patrols, we lace it up. Finally we cut out the door size piece of chain-link. Job done."

"Surely, someone will notice a new door in the fence?" Marian commented.

"It will not be a new door. That is the point of locating a disused fence and removing a gate from it. It will tone in with the used look of the existing fence." Ewan said, patiently.

"Won't the patrols notice an extra gate?" Mark asked finally.

"It's possible, but not really likely. Remember there is several miles of fence with poles and wire all round. The gates have padlocks. If they stop to look, what do they find? A locked gate a bit rusty, part of the structure of the fence padlocked, with no signs of being opened from one year end to the next."

Sarah looked around the group. Each member nodded. "Right, first things first." She turned to Ewan. "I presume you have seen a suitable gate already?"

Ewan shrugged and nodded. "What do we need?" I'll collect Alek and Klaus, We'll manage the gate. You all scout the airfield. We need a suitable site for it to be erected, preferably somewhere that the gate can swing either in or out over a dropping slope. It will save leaving signs of it opening and closing scraping the ground under it."

***

The darkness was split by the shafts of light from the headlights of the patrol vehicle. Despite the hooded cowls over them, it was still possible to see the stretch of fencing as the perimeter track curved to follow the line of the boundary of the airfield.

The three squatted down waiting for the patrol to pass. The others, already inside the airfield and on the wide expanse of grass, were well beyond the lights of the security patrol. Once the small truck had passed, they moved up to the gate. The lock had been left open for them. As soon as they were through, they made their way across the perimeter track onto the grass stretching away to the runway at least one hundred yards away.

They began running alongside the runway towards the lights of the apron in front of the hangars. There was a row of fighter planes standing beside the apron to one side. On the other were several twin engine bombers. The fighters were being worked upon. The bombers were quiet and partly in shadow. They were the target for tonight.

As Ewan, Klaus and Alek approached the aircraft, Sarah came to meet them. "I think the fighters at the far end have been attended to already, so I thought it would be a good idea to booby trap them. What do you think?"

Ewan grinned, his teeth shining in the reflected lights. "Sounds good to me. Bring the bags. Alek, Klaus lead the way."

The four passed across the front of the line of aircraft being serviced. The other planes at the far end, six in all stood, silent and evil looking; the shark's jaws painted on the engine cowlings looking menacing in the reflected light.

Ewan pointed to the first two. *Me 109's,* Ewan decided. "Those are yours," he said to Klaus and Sarah. "We'll take the next two, and split the last two."

They all set to work, attaching the made-up charges into the wheel roots and under the pilot's seat. Timers were set for one hour ahead.

As they completed their tasks, the mechanics working on the aircraft started to collect the tools and return to the hangars.

Ewan could not resist it. He placed charges in the three Messerschmitts, but missed the fact that one of the mechanics was still working. His shout brought other workers and guards from the nearby hangar. Ewan broke and ran. He stopped suddenly, swung round and opened fire with the MP3 machine pistol he was carrying. The man who had given the game away died on the spot. The others dropped and two of the sentries opened fire at random, unaware of Ewan's exact location.

Klaus and Alek spread out on each side of Ewan and started to fire well-aimed shots at the growing bunch of armed men facing them. There was the sudden roar of an engine. A half track with a pedestal-mounted 20mm gun came round the corner of the far hangar. The driver hit the accelerator and the vehicle speeded up. The gun started to fire. Ewan suddenly realised it was firing at the soldiers and mechanics. He guessed that Mark and Marian were in charge. Calling to Sarah, he told her, "Use the truck as cover and come and join us. We will all leave together, using the half track."

As the vehicle approached them, they followed Sarah, leaping on board one by one and immediately dropping below the steel sides, their fire adding to the barrage of the 20mm gun. Marian, who was driving, steered to catch the propellers of the fighters standing in the row.

The steel window frame, having lost its glass already, hit the blades in turn, causing damage to each one. Then she turned up the field and increased speed once more, putting distance between the saboteurs and the guards.

When they reached the far fence she drove through without stopping, finally crashing the truck into the ditch running beside the main road.

As they gathered to return to the cars they heard the first explosion, followed in turn by another six. Sarah said, "Let us not wait for the rest to blow. We should really be long gone before they come looking for the people who spoiled their pretty planes."

Without further discussion the group left the airfield, returning to the city via the back-roads. The main routes were closed off to make way for the passage of the fire and safety trucks howling their way to the disaster scene.

Back in the apartment there was a signal from London.

***

Michael Wallace crouched down in the bottom of the dinghy, waiting for the current to take it into the eddy beneath the timber pier. As the water swirled and speeded up, driven by the incoming tide, the aimless drift of the boat took on direction. The shadows of the pier swept over the small craft. Michael raised himself from the bottom boards, his reaching hand found a strut forming part of the framework. This halted the boat's gyrations. Now stopped, he was able to pull the boat to a point where he could climb out onto the pier deck and stroll ashore.

The small port of Wismar was not his first choice of an infiltration point, but that was the only port he could get into, now that the war had officially commenced.

The stick he was using to legitimize the limp in his left leg was one his father had brought back from Germany after the first world war. It had accompanied him through the Schwartzwald and had beaten off the attack of several would-be Brownshirts who were anxious to strip his companion, to better enjoy the well-toned body barely covered by her shirt and shorts.

All three attackers had felt the power of the stick and had been disappointed in their purpose. His father had mentioned that then Hannah had laughed, and stripped off her clothing. She had left Michael's father with memories which still brought a smile to his face. Now walking with the stick, Michael adjusted the set of his uniform hat and, remembering to limp, stepped through the dockyard gate into the street beyond. He turned left and made his way to the rail station, where he boarded the Berlin train.

The first class compartment was empty when the journey began, though the guard appeared with a lady passenger who was feeling unwell.

He apologised for disturbing Michael, and left the lady to herself in the corner. When he was gone the lady turned to Michael. She looked him in the eye and said, "Hello, Michael Wallace. How nice to see you again after all this time. How is your father?"

Michael looked at her carefully, something about the blond woman, past middle age but still pretty fit he thought. "Hello, Hannah. It must be 20 years since you left England."

"You are right. It is actually 19 years 9 months. It was not possible for me to stay in the circumstances. I was not cut out to be the wife or mistress of an English gentleman. Life was just too formalised. How is your father? I miss him you know?"

"He misses you, of that I am certain. My mother died shortly after you left. He took it badly. Now he has settled for the quiet life, I believe."

"Your mother asked me to stay and look after you both. I don't know if you knew that. I did not stay. There were too many other matters pulling me. I have two children of my own. One is your half brother. I was already pregnant when I left. It was one of my reasons for leaving. Your father does not know."

Michael nodded slowly. "Now what do we do?"

"I came into this carriage because the other carriage was noisy and crowded. The guard comes from my home village. He never allows me to travel second class. You need not worry about me. I can tell you that there are two Gestapo on the train and neither will be missed if they fall off. They are not popular in my area and there has been growing resistance to the actions of that maniac Hitler, who is, even now, frightening his close associates. The so-called Blitzkrieg, is not working as well as he expected, and he is blaming his inner circle of senior officers. General Walther von Brauchitsch, who commands the invasion, has the sense to absent himself from Berlin."

"You are well informed?"

"I am in the loop, if that is what you mean. I am a major figure in the 'Women's League.' I hear all sorts of things." She leaned forward. "The Gestapo are in the next carriage trying to get the guard to leave a microphone in here. They do not like me and wish to blackmail me into sleeping with their boss, some sewer rat from the Berlin gangs."

"Are they likely to pay us a visit?"

She nodded. "I have to think so."

"Let us prepare for them shall we? Come sit beside me, I will see for myself if you are as cuddlesome as my father said you were."

Hannah laughed and joined him on the seat at his side. Michael put his arm round her and hugged her. She nuzzled his neck, and he felt her breath on his ear."

The door of the carriage was wrenched open. Both ignored it. Michael kissed Hanna on the lips in front of the two black leather-coated men standing in the doorway.

The leading man, red faced, shouted at them, "Stop this performance immediately."

Michael looked up at the angry man. "How dare you speak to an officer in the Kriegsmarine in that tone of voice. Get out of this compartment, before I have you thrown out."

The red-faced man was taken aback to put it mildly. He was unaccustomed to being spoken-to in this way.

Michael released Hannah and stood up to his full height. His rank was now clearly to be seen on his cuff. At his throat was a Pour le Merit cross, and an Iron cross with a cluster, was on his chest. The other medals were for sea service in the Spanish War.

He leaned forward and looked into the face of the angry Gestapo man. "My part in this war is important. Your part is to be a weasel sneaking around back doors, fucking prostitutes and women who cannot fight back. Now get out of this compartment before I personally throw you both out, and off this train."

The Gestapo man turned to his companion drawing his pistol from beneath his overcoat as he did so. Michael did not hesitate. He thrust the man into his companion, who crumpled as the bullet meant for Michael was inadvertently shot into his partner. Michael grabbed the stick and smashed it against the Gestapo man with the gun still in his hand. It hit the back of his head with a soggy thud and the man collapsed to the floor. The bullet-wounded man was dead, and, when Michael checked, so was his partner. The stick had once more been wielded effectively.

In the corridor the guard looked appalled, Michael said to him, "Would you like to explain what happened here?" The guard shook his head looking very scared. There was no one else watching, he knew he would suffer and probably his family too.

"Open the door." Michael indicated the outer door on the other side of the corridor.

The guard nodded and opened the door despite the wind, and held it. The dark countryside was empty of lights. Michael took the wallet and gun from the dead man and slipped them into his pocket. Then he hauled the man to the door and tipped him out into the night. He searched the second man, took his gun and wallet, and then hauled him over to follow his partner into the darkness. The door closed. They all three examined the floor for bloodstains, and other signs of the incident. Hannah found a badge under the seat, obviously from one of the men. Otherwise there was nothing to show for the lives of the two Gestapo men. Michael checked the wallets of the pair. The money they contained, he gave to the guard. The documents and ID he decided to keep. They were all placed in his briefcase. The guard left Hannah and Michael to themselves and returned to his duties elsewhere in the train.

Michael looked at Hannah. "Are you going to kill me?" She asked quietly.

"Good lord, no. Father would never forgive me." He grinned. I was actually going to kiss you. I got a brief breath of what attracted my father to you." He leaned forward and kissed her seriously, a contact reciprocated with enthusiasm.

They separated in Berlin, she to her children—her husband was dead—and Michael to Frankfurt to link up with his team.

***

It was evening. The team sat around the apartment while Michael explained how the boat had survived the escape from Peenemunde.

"The voyage was tricky. When we made it out into the Baltic, we found we had a hostile navy almost wherever we looked. We made a run for it to start with. Luckily, none of our pursuers was fast enough to catch us once we really got going. As we passed Fehmarn we were blocked off by a destroyer. I believed that we were sunk at the point. But that little beauty had a few tricks up her sleeve. The skipper, John Matheson, just pressed a few buttons on the control panel and the boat slowed just a little. Then there was a whoosh. We turned to one side. The torpedo we launched took the destroyer in the engine room. It blew up. The Marines came on deck from then on. When we encountered the E Boats, we had the edge on speed. But it was the bazooka the Marines had with them which made the difference. It was designed for killing tanks, but it worked fine on the armoured side of an E boat.

"We made it to Copenhagen and I decided to do the last bit by air. When I put the family on board I realised that, if I went with them, there would be a good chance they would keep me in London. So I thumbed a lift on the boat back into the Baltic and landed at Wismar.

"On the train back, I met an old friend of my father's, and two Gestapo men, but they left."

Ewan produced the two guns Michael had added to the armoury. I've filed the numbers off. I presume these were from the two agents"

Michael shrugged. "There was nothing else I could do. Now it's your turn. What have you been up to since I left you?"

Between them they told Michael about the raid on the airfield, It seemed that all twelve of the Me 109's had been destroyed. The bombers they had targeted were also gone The explosions they had set on the bombers had inflicted collateral damage on the un-sabotaged ones, so the base had been seriously hampered for over one week, until new aircraft had been flown in. The security at the airfield had been tightened up, but the new gate had not been discovered, leaving their way in and out still secure.

Chapter Sixteen

Bonding

Ewan and Marian were once more on their own. Michael and Sarah had moved to the city of Munich to create a base in Bavaria; Alek and Klaus were still in their apartment around the corner.

Ewan found his feelings for Marian more and more difficult to suppress.

Eventually, Marian let him off the hook. She had been aware of Ewan's increasing feelings for her and, despite her own for him, she had tried to convince herself that there was no real genuine affection between them.

They were sitting alone in the lounge. Alek had left. He had been visiting them, as Klaus had found an old girlfriend to call on and was out for the evening.

Ewan looked at Marian when he thought she would not notice.

Marian had noticed and she said, "Ewan, have you got something to say to me?"

Ewan jumped as if he had been stung. "Me? What do you mean?"

"You have been sitting there as if you were trying to get up the courage to come over here, and kiss me until I agreed to go to bed with you. I'm right, am I not."

"More or less," he said resignedly, realising he had been found out.

"Well, for Pete's sake get over here and get started. I can't hang on much longer."

Ewan sat still for a moment not believing what he was hearing. Then, without further hesitation, he sprang off his chair, joined Marian on the settee and kissed the first woman he had fallen in love with in his entire life.

For Marian he was the first man she wanted to make love to for no material reason. Falling in love had never occurred to either of them so far. Now it had happened and they would just have to learn to live with it.

***

Heinrich Stolle was in Munich visiting Edith's family. He had been in the area for the Admiral and realised that while he was here he could do a little research on the new love who had come so dramatically into his life. He loved the city of Munich. There was a light-hearted atmosphere which always affected him. He wished that Edith was here to share it with him. He conducted his business and then strode off to seek the address which had been the home of Edith's parents, the Krauss family, for the past thirty years. He checked the number on the slip of paper where he had noted the address.

Then he stepped up to the front door, and rang the bell.

Footsteps approached the door and it opened slowly. "Frau Krauss?" He asked the small, slim woman who stood there.

The woman shook her head. "Not here," she said. "Not at this address>"

Stolle looked at the paper where he had written the address. He was certain that it was copied correctly.

"Do you know the Krauss family?" He asked.

She thought for a few moments, then shook her head. "I have lived here all my life. That is not a name I recognise."

"How about the name, Korder?"

Stolle noticed a flicker of recognition in her eye at that name. He went ahead to say, "There is no trouble associated with these people. I am a friend of some people in Berlin who gave me the names to call upon."

The lady went to close the door, but Stolle was too quick He stopped the door from closing and stepped inside. "I think we should sit down and have a little chat. I am Commander Stolle of the Abwehr."

The lady looked frightened now. Heinrich nudged her into the lounge and suggested she sit down. "Is there anyone else here?" He asked.

The woman shook her head.

"So tell me about the Korder family?"

In a faint voice the lady began to speak. "The Korder family lived in the upper part of the house. Herr Korder was in the silver trade and he was in business with several other silver traders, many of whom were Jewish. In the early 1930's the anti-Jewish movement was at its height. Herr Korder did all he could to protect his friends, but his address was discovered. One night the Nazi's had broken in, raped Frau Korder and hanged Herr Korder, claiming he was an undercover Jewish man. The local leader of the Brownshirts threatened everyone. If they talked, he would pay a visit and accidently burn their house down, with them in it. Nobody has dared to talk since that time."

"Is the man still in the area?"

"Yes. He is the head of the local Youth movement. Wilhelm Dehn."

"Thank you, madam. I will not reveal your name. But there will be things happening, and justice will be done."

Heinrich Stolle decided then and there that the Admiral might well be interested in the story of Edith's family.

Meanwhile there was another matter he was scheduled to deal with while he was in the area. He stepped into the Post Office building and took a telephone booth. Using his pocket book directory, he rang a number that was a cut out for one the contacts he had acquired whilst in the proper navy, the part which sailed ships and actually fired their guns.

The call-back came within seconds of his replacing the receiver. An address was given and a time, one hour ahead.

***

He was greeted with real enthusiasm by former Petty Officer Martin Horst. He had survived the attempt to have his rank stripped with discharge from the Navy, rightly attributing it to the efforts of his Officer, Lieutenant Heinrich Stolle. His eventual discharge had been honourable with the pension earned and paid to him for his 20 years service.

There was of course justification for the case brought against him, but it was for offences tolerated everywhere. The case had been brought vindictively by an officer who had attempted to muscle in on the trade which Martin Horst had developed.

Stolle was ushered into a comfortable office, and seated by Martin, who was looking decidedly prosperous. The pretty woman, who was in the office at the time, went to bring coffee and cake for their honoured guest.

"So, Commander, what brings you to Munich?" Martin asked.

Heinrich settled into his chair and looked keenly at Martin. "I was in Munich for other reasons. Something came up while I was here." He told of his discovery about the treatment Edith had received from Wilhelm Dehn. "I would really like to see that man punished. But I don't quite know how to do it without causing problems elsewhere."

Martin leaned back in his chair. The pretty woman came in and set down the coffee and cake for the two men. Martin introduced Heinrich to his daughter, Marlene. "This is my old friend, Heinrich Stolle."

"It was you who saved my father from a prison sentence." She smiled and shook his hand. "Thank you, sir. My mother would be happy to join us in thanks, if you have time to stay to dinner."

"Sadly, I will not be able to stay on this occasion, but I will try to arrange things next time I come to Munich."

Martin broke in at that point, "Heinrich had a problem with your friend, Wilhelm Dehn."

Marlene immediately tensed. "I think it is time to do something about him."

Heinrich looked at Martin who said, "That shit groped all the girls in her class at school."

"I can still feel his hands on my body," Marline said with a shiver. "We really have to do something about him."

Martin thought for a few moments. Then, slowly, he spoke, "You will be happy to hear that Wilhelm Dehn's days are numbered. Arrangements will be made for his removal from office for embezzlement of party funds."

"He had been found out, has he?" Heinrich said with a grim smile.

"He will be." Martin said, enigmatically.

"Where did he put the stolen money?" Marlene asked.

"I haven't decided yet," Martin said with a small smile. "I think Switzerland. Don't you?"

***

In the train back to Berlin, Heinrich went over his visit to Munich in his mind. On the whole it had been a success. He would tell the Admiral what he had discovered about Edith's husband, and report on the reason he had visited the southern city in the first place. He was aware that the Admiral took a personal interest in his staff. He would like to know the real background to Edith's story.

Heinrich would not mention his visit to Martin Horst. Some things were better left unsaid. He settled down to read his book for the remainder of the journey.

***

Elsewhere on the train Ewan Fitzgerald sat contemplating the note he had received from his 'crime lord' boss, Sigmund, real name, Dieter Braun. There was not a great deal in the note. Just that there was a move afoot to replace, Rudolf Hess, once one of Hitler's favorites. His place would be taken by Martin Bormann, once Hess's deputy.

Dieter was under pressure to assist in the removal of Hess by arranging an accident. Dieter liked Hess, so the accident was to be re-scheduled for the would-be assassins.

Ewan was well pleased at the request. Dieter Braun had been helpful to the agents and this was a way to return a favour and carry out the agent's brief at the same time.

Alek was sitting in the next compartment. The team set up of always operating in pairs prevailed. Since Alek knew the two killers and could therefore identify them, he was the ideal choice for the partner.

Ewan's targets were one-time members of the mob in Berlin, though neither were Berliners. Both came from the Dortmund area and had arrived in Berlin having shared a cell in the local jail. They had formed a team to survive the Berlin underworld and gained a reputation for carrying out whatever task they undertook.

***

Upon arrival in Berlin, they were met by a runner who passed Alek a set of keys for an apartment nearby. When the two men found the apartment they found the keys of a car, and a note. The car was in the underground garage beneath the apartment building. The weapons were hidden in the usual place.

Alek had retrieved the dripping package from the bathroom cistern and both weapons were on the blanket covered table. Both men cleaned and oiled their guns before they did anything else.

A messenger delivered a packet of documents that evening. When opened, the documents turned out to be the details on the two killers for hire, who had been tasked with the killing of Rudolf Hess.

The weather was not good. The city centre was alight with Christmas decorations despite the war. In Berlin it appeared there was no need for a blackout. None of the British bombers could reach the city and return, and the French seemed to think that the war was some sort of joke. After all they had the Maginot Line, a well defended string of forts along the border between Germany and France. Why should they worry?

Ewan looked at the maps in the newspapers sadly. The forts stopped at the border with Belgium. "Do they ever learn?" he said to Alek.

Alek grinned. "Why should they? A war gives politicians an excuse to spend money without proper accounting. That means two things. Lots of jobs for the boys, plus plenty of women to play with. What more could any red-blooded politician want?"

"These two men we are after. What do you think would be the best way to deal with them?" Ewan was interested in any suggestion, especially since Alek knew them both.

Alek did not have to think about it for long. "Women! They are both fond of the girls and not too fussy either, from what I've seen."

"It's Christmas time. Parties and fun; there should be a way to get the boys off with a couple nice girls."

"We would be better to import them. Use girls who do not know who they are dealing with. Here in Berlin everyone knows everyone else. I think we would be better off to speak with the concierge at the Adlon, Karl Curnow. He will find two new girls for us, preferably non-German speaking, who could be returned to another place without trouble."

"That sounds good. Then we need a venue with a balcony at the right level."

Alek thought for a few minutes. "I think I know a place. I better ask the boss though., he might be using it."

***

Horst Weller and Walter Schultz were both from the Dortmund area. They had been together as a team for three years now and had found it a profitable partnership. Their specialty was in arranged removals, and over the years they had removed a number of people for a variety of reasons. Mainly money! Although lately, it was more and more for position, though money still ranked high on the list. Their current contract was from a person whom they realised was a cut-out for someone high in Government. But then the target was probably the most senior person they had ever been asked to deal with, short of the Fuehrer himself. No wonder an accident had been ordered.

***

Ewan's problem was fairly complex. He had to arrange an accident for two men who specialized in accidents. While it was possible that they may not even consider that they might be victims, there were no guarantees in the removal business.

Alek came back with permission to use the apartment with the balcony. The concierge of the Adlon, Karl Curnow had found two Romanian women, Alexis and Greta, both suitably endowed.

***

The willing women found little difficulty in picking up the two removal men. Ewan had considered the problem of making sure the two were brought to the apartment. He need not have worried. Both men travelled light, keeping their possessions in easy-to-transport bags, purchasing clothes wherever they were, rather than carrying suitcases full of clothing from place to place.

They arrived at the apartment with their two hand carry bags, fully prepared for the time their lives with the two pretty women. Horst was very taken with the dark-haired girl. Though Walter had professed to be quite happy with the blond, Horst had the feeling that Walter was trying to get him drunk so that he could have the dark-haired girl.

The seemingly light-hearted chatter when they arrived at the apartment covered a darker atmosphere between the two men. Though friends, there was a rivalry which arose, often when they were planning an operation. Horst sometimes felt he was number two in the partnership, and this did not always sit well with him.

Walter was the bigger of the two and used his greater bulk to bully his way through. Whilst not browbeating as such, it came close, on occasion.

Over the years they had been together the pattern had built up, and Horst was becoming less tolerant of his partner's assumption of the lead on all new operations.

Now, as he sat stroking the thigh of his dark haired companion, he was well content with the way things had worked out.

Walter on the other hand, accustomed to getting his own way, was not quite so happy. As the drink flowed, it seemed the girls were well provided for. He sat and became more and more frustrated, watching his partner's hand disappearing up the skirt of the woman he had decided should be his. He grew more and more morose. The blond, Alexis, tried to distract him, but as the evening passed Walter drank more and more. Eventually, he got up went over to the dark girl, Greta, who was in a close embrace with Horst and dragged her off him and made for the bedroom. Horst, who was only half dressed, tripped over his pants in his haste to get up and stop his partner. Walter was halfway into the bedroom when Horst got free and lunged at Walter.

Greta stumbled away from Walter, her steps restrained by her panties pulled down to her knees. She yanked them up as she joined her friend, watching as the two men clashed.

Both men were pretty drunk and finding difficulty in keeping upright, so the fight was mainly pawing at each other. They progressed back into the lounge area. The French doors to the balcony were closed but not locked, as the pair stumbled around, each trying to hit the other, they reeled toward them,

Ewan, who was waiting for them to become completely drunk, saw an opportunity. As they stumbled off balance toward the balcony, he came out from behind the curtain and slipped the catch.

The two men hit the doors which then burst open. The cold air outside was like a wet douche starting to sober the men up, but not before they hit the ice on the small balcony.

As both suddenly realised their precarious position they swung their arms to get their balance. For the first time Horst hit Walter solidly.

Walter reacted, hitting the rail, still off balance. With a yelp he went over, his cry trailing his falling body, past all four stories to the ground.

Horst poked his befuddled head over to see where Walter had gone, as he leaned, his foot slipped, and with a wail he followed Walter to the ground, impacting solidly on the body of his dead partner.

In the apartment Ewan closed the French doors and the curtains, Alek picked up the two bags the removal men had left behind and Ewan collected their coats.

The two women were both packed and ready to go by the time the men were at the door. Both knew better than to hang around when the police were likely to appear.

With a last look around Ewan closed the door with his gloved hand. They used the stairway to descend to the basement garage, where their car was parked.

The two Romanian ladies were on their way to Cologne by train within the hour and Ewan and Alek were in the safe house discussing the evening's entertainment.

Ewan's report to Dieter was succinct. "There was a fight between the removal men over women. They accidently fell over the balcony, slipped on the ice while they tussled. It was an accident!"

Dieter commented, "The package will be in the locker when you leave Berlin."

***

As Ewan told the others when they rejoined the group in Munich, "I think he thought the accident was engineered. It was, in fact, an accident."

***

Commander Heinrich Stolle lay in bed contemplating the sleeping face of the woman beside him. He admitted to himself that this woman had completely captivated him. With a wry grin, he moved his short leg out of the bed, swinging himself into a sitting position. Rising upright he hopped over to the bathroom door. He showered and dried himself off. He was unsurprised to find Edith still asleep when he seated himself, still naked, to fit his prosthetic lower leg. It was not a difficult process. The doctor had been careful with his amputation. The end of his limb was well padded, and the fitted artificial limb had been well made and adjusted to be as comfortable as it could be. He rose to his feet and started dressing, taking care not to disturb her.

Fully dressed and about to leave, he heard her stir."I trust you were not considering leaving without kissing me goodbye."

"I thought you were still asleep." Heinrich said as he bent to kiss her. He could smell the faint scent of her perfume, or perhaps soap, the warm nearness of her was intoxicating to him. He kissed her, feeling the lazy arm go round his neck, "Do you have to go right now?" She whispered in his ear.

"Sadly, yes. I must. The Admiral, as you know, does like to be surprised in the morning on occasion. This is one of them. I will see you in the office later, I trust?"

He kissed her again and she released her arm.

Outside, he walked to the office in the cold morning air. There was snow on the rooftops and, though the streets had been swept, there was fresh snow on the ground, forcing him to take care with his artificial foot.

***

As he suspected the Admiral followed him into the office. He had only time to make sure the heating was turned up and the coffee was on, before he heard the sound of the Admiral's footsteps.

"How did the Munich visit go?" As they sat drinking that first coffee of the day, the Admiral opened the conversation. "Did you find out the story of our enigmatic Edith?"

Heinrich looked up in surprise. He was unaware that the Admiral knew anything of his quest to seek the story of Edith.

He found himself telling the Admiral of all he had discovered regarding Edith and her husband. When he finished, Canaris said, "Perhaps we can do something about this man?" Heinrich started to say that he already had done something, when he was interrupted by Canaris. "Of course, there is nothing to be done. He is after all, a good party member."

Heinrich nodded gravely. "Of course, though such a man can be difficult to trust in a critical situation, don't you think?"

The Admiral sat and thought about that for a moment. "Such power, misused once, could be misused again, perhaps."

The subject closed there between them, though there was a reminder, almost one week after the New Year. A bulletin from Munich under a confidential seal reported that Wilhelm Dehn had been investigated. It had been proved that he had been embezzling funds from the party and placing them in a numbered account in Switzerland. Unfortunately, Dehn denied the entire affair and drew his pistol on the arresting officers. He died of his wounds without divulging the number or in fact the name of the bank concerned.

Commander Stolle smiled when he heard the news, "As I once heard an American friend comment, 'What goes around, comes around'."

"I believe that is a satisfactory conclusion to the case we discussed earlier." The Admiral said enigmatically.

Chapter Seventeen

Spy games

Helga Burger returned to Tempelhof Airport, tired and feeling in need of a shower. The journey from New York to Lisbon by the PAA Yankee clipper seaplane was comfortable enough – the onward flight by the Lufthansa. Focke Wulf Condor was not quite so luxurious.

She returned to her apartment and found messages from her agent, Heinrich Stolle, and Carl Gerber. Ignoring them all, she had a long hot bath, and went to bed.

The following morning she made contact by telephone with both of her 'admirers'. She was then collected for her appointment at the Babelsberg movie studios in Potsdam, on the outskirts of Berlin. The chauffeur delivered her at the door to the executive offices.

The office of the current occupant was reminiscent of a movie set itself, complete luxury, plus a casting couch of mammoth proportions.

The executive director was flanked by two visitors: on his left sat Gruppenfuhrer Karl Schumann, in full SS uniform complete with military honours from the Spanish campaign; on the director's right sat a rather insignificant looking man in a black suit wearing round glasses, his black hair glued firmly to his scalp with hair oil. His eyes studied her coldly and sent shivers up her spine. Her feeling was that this man was evil.

Herman Edleberg was fairly harmless, his interests focused on boys and business. He was married but it was a convenience rather than serious. "These gentlemen are here to discuss a movie we are planning with a serious part for you if you wish to take it. May I introduce Gruppenfuhrer Schumann, SS." He waved at Schumann who rose and took her extended hand. He gave a short bow. "Charmed."

The other man was introduced as Herr Martin Bormann of the Fuhrer's staff. Bormann did not rise to greet her. He merely nodded. His mouth made a grimace that could have been a smile.

Helga was seated by an aide who was then dispatched for the coffee and cake which seemed an inevitable part of any meeting with vaguely social pretentions.

The current production, 'Jew Suss', was near completion and Helga was wondering why she had been called. As far as she was aware there were no other projects in view.

It was Bormann who spoke. "We were interested in your view of the Americans. You were there recently. Since you are known to be rather more than many of the brainless beauties who live in the movie world, it is of interest to us to have some idea of how the other side of the Atlantic sees us."

Helga was surprised, shocked even to be consulted in this way. What she did not know was that Martin Bormann was a stalwart follower of the arcane. He lived in a world where astrology carried more weight than astronomy. In a recent session with a favoured fortune teller he had been informed that Helga was an important focus point in the immediate future of the Third Reich.

Since the publicised return of the actress from England and the USA was in the news, he recruited Schumann to accompany him on the visit to the studios.

The fact that Helga was going to visit the studio to discuss a possible new role was included in the article. A phone call was all it took.

Helga recovered her composure swiftly. "I presume you want the truth?"

Bormann nodded "Please."

"In general, Germany is regarded as a bully. There are areas where every action by the German government is regarded as criminal. Following the Anschluss, there was muttering and antipathy toward the Germans. Many of more recent immigrants were incensed at the annexation of their homeland in such an arbitrary manner. The invasion of Poland was a hammer blow for the pacifists. There was uproar in many parts of the USA. It led to many people returning home, in case a more general war broke out barring them from returning.

"In Britain, when the assault on Poland came, though they were prepared, it still had an impact. The army received a rush of applications, the Air Force and Navy too. Though the country is unready, the spirit of the people is high.

"There is no sign of the US joining with Britain at the moment. The politicians are calling for isolation from this European disturbance. They do not want another world war. To sum up, for what it's worth, USA will go to war, but not yet. Britain will grow through war years, with USA or not. They will, as always, be the force to be reckoned with."

Helga sat back and waited.

Bormann rose to his feet. "Miss Berger, you were not asked to observe the situation in either country. Your natural skill at being aware of what goes on around you has been clearly illustrated here. My thanks, for your clear and patently honest report of your observations. It makes a refreshing change from many of the reports I receive from people who say what they think I wish to hear. Auf Wiedersehen."

Followed by the Gruppenfuhrer, Martin Bormann left the office.

Helga looked at Herman Edleberg. "What was that all about?"

Edleberg wiped the sheen of sweat from his brow. "They scared the hell out of me," he said. "They turned up here this morning. I was all prepared for the handcuffs, until they asked if you would be here today. I'll be honest, darling. The relief was almost orgasmic."

"What happened to the telephone, Herman? I had no idea that they were here. How could you just let me walk in on them like that?"

Herman spread his hands out expressively. "What could I do? The door opened and they were there. That dishy Gruppenfuhrer and the odious little man, Bormann. I hear he is very close to the Fuhrer. But would you upset him? I know I wouldn't dare."

Helga was on her feet. "Whatever you had in mind for this morning, I am not in the mood. Call me some time next week and I may answer you. Until then, I will not be interested." She swept out of the office.

Herman sat down in his chair, looked the calendar in the form of two mermaids supporting his list of appointments. The entire morning had been dedicated to Helga Berger, and she had gone by 9.30. He shrugged, pressing the intercom switch he called his secretary. "Ingrid! Send Charles in, will you. I'm wasted. Entertaining the Gestapo is not good for me. Oh, and hold my calls till lunchtime. There's a dear."

***

On her way home, Helga stopped off at the Post Office and made two calls on the public telephone, the first to Carl Gerber, the second to the private number of Heinrich Stolle. She then went home.

Heinrich Stolle called at her apartment within an hour of the call. He accepted the package of notes she passed him without comment. As he drank the coffee she placed before him, she detailed the content of her meeting that morning with Martin Bormann. She also registered her feelings, referring to the aura of menace that the man exuded. A mention of the presence of Gruppenfuhrer Schumann caused Stolle to feel a little worry. questioning to himself, 'what was he doing there with Bormann, Hitler's new deputy?'

At the office Stolle made for the Admiral's office immediately, only to be told that Canaris was attending a meeting with the Fuhrer himself, in the planning suit at the Reich's Chancellery.

***

Michael in his Carl Gerber role received his call through the cut-out number in Berlin. He called Helga and promised to be with her within two hours. This required the use of a plane, which luckily was available. He was able to be at Helga's apartment by the deadline he had set. Like Stolle he was disturbed to hear of the meeting at the studio with Bormann, immediately questioning in his own mind why Bormann would bother. Up to this time the allies had no real idea of the secret nature of the man, who became far more than the secretary everyone believed him to be. His quiet transition into one of the most powerful men in the nation took most people by surprise. The reflection of his savage implacable attitude to those he regarded as opposed to him began to be felt more and more, as the influence of Rudolf Hess declined.

***

Carl Gerber received the small package of documents passed over to him by Helga and was considering leaving when he realised that she was shivering despite the warmth of the apartment.

He walked over to her and slipped his arms around her. "If you don't mind I will stay here tonight." He felt her body relax at his words. "It is getting late and the weather is not good for flying."

"You flew here?" Helga asked.

"Yes. I was elsewhere when you called, so I flew here as soon as it was possible. I had the impression that you were really upset, and you needed me." He looked at her almost apologetically.

To his relief, she smiled, "I'll get the spare bed ready." She bustled off with something to occupy herself, to deflect her thoughts from that terrible man.

They ate together quietly talking, discussing the impressions she had brought back from her recent visits. They also talked of everyday matters. The subject of the invasion of Poland was ignored, though the matter was now close to conclusion. The armies of Germany and Russia had done most of the carving up of the country, which they would maintain until the inevitable split occurred.

For the actress the comfort of having a companion to share the evening with, was enough. Later, after they had retired to their individual beds, her cry in the night brought Carl to her side to reassure her and join her in the warmth of her bed.

When he left in the morning Helga was her old confident self once more. When the Admiral had a private chat with her at Stolle's request, she was able to put the entire incident behind her.

***

For Michael and the teams there was a more significant role to play. In discussion it seemed that whatever calming influence Hess had on the Fuhrer, it was now a thing of the past. While Hess was still too popular to be removed openly, there would probably be another Bormann-inspired accident arranged.

Ewan said, "Let's kill Bormann."

The others looked concerned. Michael said, "Getting close enough will be difficult. If we only damage him, the repercussions could be bloody and a lot of innocent people could be involved."

Sarah commented, "I think Gruppenfuhrer Schumann might be a lesser target, but as Bormann's hatchet man, it could dissuade the next in line. Apart from all else, he is a much more available person. Someone who's arrogance could do half of our work for us."

Mark said, "I'm inclined to agree. Much though I would be happy to see Bormann part this mortal coil, I am willing to settle at this time for Schumann."

Marion had listened to the talk among the others. She was not really pulled one way or the other. "Let us take a look at both people, Bormann and Schumann. Both deserve whatever we decide to do to them, so let's set up a plan for both. We can take them in either order."

The conversation became general though, in the end, little was accomplished at the time. It was Alek who resolved the question that they had all been trying to answer. "If we could have Schumann eliminated, either by his colleagues or by enemy action, it would not highlight the group. Since the concealment of our presence is still important, we should concentrate on that, rather than grandiose plans which would give the game away, and have every counter espionage organisation hot on our trail."

Alek's comment made sense, and the group realised that they were wasting time. They got down to the more sensible options offered by the more overt movements of the SS Colonel.

For the interim, at the suggestion of Ewan, it was agreed that they would take another look at the airfield. The gate was still in place and, as long as the security force ignored it, they could gain access whenever they liked. They all agreed—and even London approved, only too aware of the disparity in numbers between the Luftwaffe and the RAF.

At Ewan's suggestion, they decided to acquire more of the gates with frames, and install them in some of the airfields in France, to give the local resistance the opportunity to sabotage the aircraft on the ground.

Marian commented, "Judging by the number of collaborators we have news of in France, we may have difficulty in passing on any gates over the border. Though I suppose it is important to try.

Ewan laughed, "You may well be right. But there is nothing stopping us from doing the job for them if we are there anyway." He looked around the room all seemed quite happy about the idea. Truth to tell, all were fed up with sitting around waiting for things to happen. Any operation was better than doing nothing.

Most of the airfields depended on chain-link fencing, with roving patrols for security. With that in mind, Klaus and Alek disappeared to vet the airfields up to the French border. Marion and Ewan went searching for gates. Michael and Sarah went to France, leaving Mark to look after their base.

All kept contact with Mark, who was supplied with a cut-out number in case the security forces got too curious.

***

During the absence of the others an opportunity came to stir things up in Munich itself. At an assembly in the square opposite the cathedral there was scheduled to be a parade of the local regiments. The salute was to be taken by General Von Rundstedt, from a saluting base beside the steps of the cathedral itself.

There was little to do that one man could not handle, and Mark decided to take the job on himself. The sniper rifle they had was ready for use. The gun had been tested and the telescopic sight aligned properly for a range of up to a mile. The shot would be much closer than that. He thought from Augustine-strasse, in one of the buildings with line of sight to the saluting base.

Mark was in the Cathedral as the square was being set up in advance of the parade. From the front door of the cathedral he was able to assess the line of sight to a point beyond Augustine Strasse, actually in Kaufinger Strasse which would give him a better chance of escaping.

***

For the third time Sarah redirected Michael along a different road. The two previous choices had been abandoned when they discovered road blocks in the way. This time they were able to parallel the airfield on a minor road obviously dating from the original construction period. The airfield dated from the First World War. It had been built by the German army, and had been taken over by the French Air Force subsequently.

A permanent set of hangers and revetments with subterranean fuel tanks and barracks for the maintenance staff, an officer's mess and a control tower. The security fence was what else? Chain-link.

Michael grinned. I believe that some of the locked gates in the fence have never been opened, and likely never been checked. They drove along the road, which passed through a farmyard, and continued, to join the main road about one mile beyond. In that time they saw one patrol vehicle which followed the perimeter road around the airfield at approximately thirty miles per hour. The vehicle had four men in it including the driver. Two facing the rear were smoking, the other, a corporal was seated next to the driver and talking to him. None appeared interested in the small car driving along outside the fence.

Sarah said, "Bored guards, poor security. I think this would make an interesting target."

"We'll take another look before we leave. Meanwhile, I suggest we do a little local snooping."

They spent the night at the village auberge. There they discovered, regardless of the claims that Alsace was traditionally German, the actual people were not. In fact they were inclined to be more French than the French, and bitterly resented the presence of the occupation troops.

From information received through London, Michael was aware of the local agent's identity. He contacted the woman, who was able to give further background about the airfield, which operated as a bomber base for raids on Holland, Denmark, and the south of England.

Using directions given by the agent, they located a quarry, no longer in use, that had a chain link fence, complete with a gate and frame which was salvageable. With the assistance of three local partisans, they managed to retrieve the gate and install it as part of the fence around the airfield. The most difficult part was locating a suitable padlock. The dirtying of the gate was mostly done already by the weather. Only in the places where it had rubbed off was treatment required.

Chapter Eighteen

The Lady Officer

The couple went on into France as far as Metz, where they located another airfield, which was quite busy when they arrived. They checked the area thoroughly before making any moves. Sarah noticed several German women in officer's uniforms working with the staff in the town. They had Luftwaffe rank and emblems on their uniforms and seemed accepted by the men they worked with. They were billeted in long hutments, erected for the purpose it seemed.

Sarah gained admission by merely walking in. The building was used by transients in addition to the permanent staff from the airbase.

For Sarah it was surreal. As she entered, head high, she noticed that despite her lack of uniform, the others present deferred to her.

When approached, she found it was with respect and the offer of assistance. She had the wit to mention that she expected to be posted here in the near future and was just looking the place over. She made the observation with tongue in cheek, and to her surprise she was given a tour of the premises without further question.

Outside once more, she mentioned her experience and her excuse for being there.

Michael said, "Wait in the car. I'll be back in a moment." She saw him run across the street to the building she had just left. She watched, appalled, as he entered.

He emerged within a few minutes and strolled over to the car.

"What was that all about?" She said angrily. "I thought I lost you there for a few moments. What were you doing?"

"Whoa, stop. Give me a moment." He took a breath started the car and moved off. Then in measured tones he said, "I went in enquiring if Grafin Herzog was still there. They were mystified at first. Then, when I mentioned you had called in within the last half hour, the penny dropped. You were the lady that had been given the tour! And you had left not five minutes ago. I said thank you, and got their promise not to mention that the Grafin had been there. Then I left."

She said, "And they believed you?"

He laughed. "It's your posh upbringing. When you are in the presence of serfs, they react like serfs. Had you been in the presence of your own class, they would have treated you as an equal."

Sarah looked at him in astonishment. "Why would they do that? I am nobody special."

"Dear Sarah, nobility will out wherever you are. You take with you an air of superiority that is entirely natural. There is no international barrier which can alter such a situation. You are what you are, and it is easier to work with it than against it. Here, in a country where arrogance is virtually a way of life. We must flaunt it!"

"They will not keep the visit to themselves."

"I certainly hope not. When you go back in uniform I expect them to all know who you are and what you are. You will be senior in rank to most of them, and they will accept that of course. You can then be kind to the nice ones and arrogant to the nasty ones. It should be fun."

Sarah looked at him in surprise, "I am going back then?"

"Of course, this opportunity is too good to waste. You may well be able to copy, or at least memorize, information that London can use. First, we must find you a suitable uniform."

***

Dressed in the uniform of a Luftnachrichten-Flugmelde-Stabsführerin (Major-Plane–Spotters branch, Luftwaffe) Sarah entered the town base of the Luftwaffe in Metz. The busy office was involved with the dispersal of a new squadron of aircraft at the airfield on the outskirts of the town. She carried orders to examine the set-up for the reception and the identification of the variety of aircraft operated from the airfield. The name on her orders was Emma von Traube, but she was immediately recognized by the staff as Grafin Herzog.

The vehicle they provided was a staff car and an Oberhelferin (senior female auxiliary.) to drive her to the airfield. She was escorted by Hauptführerin (Captain.) Hansie Goebel, a rather serious twenty-eight year old native of Brunswick. The uniform she wore was well tailored and showed off a figure that a model would not be ashamed of. Seeing the two women together, one of the male officers remarked to a colleague. "Wow!"

"In your dreams, sonny." His superior decided was the appropriate response at that particular moment.

The open tourer sped down the main road to the main gate of the airfield, where the driver brought the car to a halt while the passenger's papers were examined. The barrier-pole was raised and the car proceeded to the administration block, where they were received by the Station adjutant, Oberleutnant Freyer.

They were entertained to coffee while they awaited the appearance of Oberst (Colonel) Karl Leuter who commanded the base. Leuter was an ace from the Spanish civil war, having shot down seven fighters, two Russian Yaks and five Curtis Hawks. He suffered from a wound he received. It was obvious to Sarah that her companion, Hansie, was either already sleeping with the man, or earnestly desired to do so. Studying him, she found herself admiring her taste.

"Stabsführerin von Traube," he bent over her hand and brushed it with his lips "A pleasure to meet you. And Hauptführerin Goebel good to see you again." He carried his left arm stiffly, obviously no longer having full use of the limb.

He seated himself and looked at the two women. "You have come to look over our aircraft, I hear. I have arranged to take you for a short circuit around the field to give you an over-view of our establishment. I have a Fieseler Storch on standby for the purpose."

"That would be most helpful. I have arranged to be here over two days at least if that is convenient?"

"We would be delighted, and you will of course dine-in with us at the mess this evening."

"I'm afraid I do not have my mess dress with me here, though it is in Metz with my gear."

"Your driver can fetch your bags and you will be our guest here on the base." He turned to Hansie, "You will of course also stay and keep the major, company I trust."

"Of course, sir. I will brief the driver and she can bring my gear also." Hansie rose to her feet, and left to make the arrangements accompanied by the adjutant.

Karl Leuter looked at the officer seated in front of him, "What will you do with the information you collect here on my airfield?"

Sarah looked at him and, with a small smile, said, "I think, maybe, I'll pass it over to that man Churchill, Winston Churchill, is it? I will put it in an envelope addressed to 10 Downing street London." She laughed, "Actually, I have no idea whatsoever, where the information will go. They tell me nothing. If I am captured, I will have nothing to tell."

"I think my boys will enjoy having your company tonight." The Colonel smiled, though I have no fears of you finding matters beyond control."

The mess night was noisy, but no worse than dining-in in a British Officer's mess. The young men were, in many ways, no different to their opposite numbers on the other side of the Channel.

At the end of the evening Sarah was escorted by most of the young men, to her quarters. Her companion, Captain Hansie Goebel, disappeared shortly after the Colonel left the party. As Sarah had already observed the Captain had her own priorities as far as relationships were concerned. There were other female officers at the dinner, but it was evident that they were all spoken for, long since.

Sarah slept undisturbed for the remainder of the night and was ready, as soon as breakfast was over, to get on with her duties.

The airfield was split up into sections, with a bomber halb-geschwader (half-wing), three fighter staffeln (squadrons), and one special service staffel.

The bombers consisted of three squadrons of Heinkel 111, and three squadrons of Junkers JU88 dive bombers. The bombers were grouped in dispersal areas, close together for ease of maintenance. The special service squadron had variants of several different types of aircraft, and included the Storch which had carried them on their flight around the airfield. It was based in its own dedicated hanger. The other two hangers were in use for the fighter staffeln.

Over the next two days Sarah catalogued the aircraft on the general service list, and on the final day of her stay she listed and classified the Special Service squadron.

Her guide was a dapper young man with the rank of Oberleutnant. His name was Ludwig Hirsch. He gave Sarah the creeps.

Among the aircraft there were two updated variants of the FW 190. Both armed with different weapon sets. There were also two ME 109, test aircraft, as yet unclassified. They were being developed by a specific team of experts, one of whom was escorted the entire time by armed guards. Sarah was told in confidence that he was an Armenian Jew whose family were being kept as insurance to compel his cooperation. Sarah raised an eyebrow. "Are you saying that we cannot produce such an expert from among the German people?"

Hirsch shrugged, "Given time perhaps, but at the present moment, no."

"And this man's family is held to ensure his good behavour?"

The face gave the game away. Sarah realised it was the same situation employed at Peenemunde. The man's family was dead, gone. He had been kept ignorant with forged notes, and prerecorded messages.

She pressed him, tapped her nose and said, "So he believes?"

Almost in a whisper her guide said, "They were all sent to the new camp at Auschwitz, to test the system." With a small movement of his hand, he drew his finger across his throat.

Sarah nodded slowly, desperately keeping her rising fury under control. Realising if she strangled the disgusting little shit, she would compromise the entire operation.

The odd aircraft out was the FW Condor, a passenger airliner which had undergone considerable alteration. It was basically in the configuration used by the Kriegsmarine, the bomb-bay doors fitted to drop depth charges, and/or a torpedo. Only the doors had been extended for a bigger bomb load, and special racks had been added to take a single oversized bomb.

"I realise that this is an experimental aircraft modification, but what sort of bomb would such a sized bomb bay merit? It would be huge!"

The guide said proudly I believe we are developing the bomb to end the war. One dropped on London. No more London."

"What does that mean, you silly man. One bomb could not wipe out London!" Sarah said, impatiently.

The small man drew himself up to his full height. "I am not a silly man. I know for a fact that, as we speak, there is a bomb being created which will wipe London from the face of the earth. It is known as an atom bomb. My brother is one of the scientists working on the project"

"And when did you last speak with him, may I ask?" Sarah was relentless and quite ready to cause an accident for her guide.

"Just three months ago. He said they were making good progress and that it would be ready by Christmas; a fine present for Mr Churchill."

Sarah sighed with relief. They anticipated that they would have at least another year before they needed to slow things down again. If the man's news was that old, then he was not aware of the spanner they had shoved into the works at Peenemunde."

"Your brother is at the site in Peenemunde, is he?"

Her guide looked at her sharply. "What do you know about Peenemunde?" He said angrily.

"What I wish to know, is what do you know about the experimental station there? I am an inspecting officer and it is my duty to know of such things. How is it that you know? As far as I am aware, you are a junior Luftwaffe officer, without such clearance. Do I assume that your brother has spoken to you about this?"

The man was now getting worried. It showed in his demeanor. "I happen to be the pilot of this aircraft. It is my duty to know what load I will be carrying."

"Very well. I shall say no more on the subject, nor I trust, will you. It is not a subject for general discussion. There are too many flapping ears about these days. Let us get on with the tour." It had occurred to Sarah that she could have pumped the man for more information which would have been of use to the group, but she also realised she would have to kill him then, because, loose mouthed as he was, he could well finish up repeating his discussions with her to others. It already seemed that he had said too much, and for the rest of the tour she was concerned and pre-occupied with the question, whether she should report him or not.

The matter came to a head in the office of the Colonel late the same afternoon. As she reported that her survey was complete, Karl Leuter said, "I have received no confirming paperwork from command, regarding your purpose here. In normal circumstances, I would have had an advisory memo at least?"

A chill went up her spine at these words, "Do you always get your memos so promptly?" She spoke casually, showing no signs of the turmoil within.

"In this case yes. I would expect the memo to be here before you arrived." The Colonel's voce was calm and untroubled.

"You saw my orders, Herr Oberst. I am not aware of the internal systems of every air base I visit, and I must say that this is the first time I have been questioned in the matter."

"You mentioned that you had carried out a similar task in Augsburg?"

Sarah shrugged, "I did?"

Leuter said, "I spoke to my old friend, Otto Fremel, who is in command at Augsburg, he tells me that he has never heard of you, or your survey."

Sarah relaxed in her chair. "Oops. I mentioned the possibility to my boss and he laughed at me. Now you have found me out. If I told you this was just an excuse for me to contact my boyfriend who is a pilot here, you would not believe me?"

Oberst Leuter shook his head, and reached for the intercom on his desk.

Sarah shook her head. "No, Colonel." She put her hand on his and proffered her ID card with the other.

Karl Leuter looked at the card. The photograph was quite good and was undoubtedly that of the lady who proffered the card. It stated that Fraulin Emma von Graben, was a Kriminalinspector of the Kriminalpolitzei. The warrant card was signed Himmler.

Karl Leuter sat back in his seat. "What does the Gestapo want here?"

"You have a FW Condor here undergoing conversion to carry a different load."

"True. This is something that is known only to myself and the riggers and fitters, and even they have no idea what the conversion is for."

"I know." Sarah said quietly.

Leuter looked up swiftly, then relaxed. "I suppose you were told before you came here?"

Sarah shook her head, "Oh, no. That is not the way we work. I learned of the purpose of the aircraft here. I knew nothing before, though obviously my superior did."

Leuter had the feeling he should not even think of asking the question, but he asked anyway. "Who is your superior?"

"Herr Himmler does not like to be spoken of, so I expect you to keep that information to yourself." Sarah looked at the Oberst with steady eyes. "Would you like his number?"

Leuter shook his head and said, "What did you find? How, and who, told you about the Condor?"

"Would you believe me, if I told you, the young man who is scheduled to fly the aircraft when it performs its mission."

Karl Leuter sat back in his chair, shaking his head sadly. "Hirsch thinks he is going to fly the Condor. He brought it here and was allowed to oversee the alterations. He will not be permitted to fly the mission, and now he will be visiting his loud-mouthed brother in Peenemunde, which is a short distance from the sea, He is well connected, so he will not be stripped of his rank and shot; he and his brother will go sailing."

Sarah said, "Sailing?"

"Neither has any talent for it, but typically both know all about it, as they know all about everything. It will be no real loss to the Reich, and perhaps better than the firing squad."

"I presume, in that case, that a verbal comment on that subject is all I need to make?"

"If you please. The family would not like to discover that they have such a man in their midst."

"I am expected at Peenemunde next. There has been some sort of trouble there. Perhaps I could offer the Oberleutnant a lift?"

"I think this is one occasion when the Luftwaffe will take care of its own problems. But thank you for the offer." He rose to his feet, "Now, if all is in order between us, I presume this visit never happened."

Sarah rose in turn, "Colonel, in another time this could have been a happy occasion. As it is, farewell and thank you for your cooperation." She donned her hat and saluted, then left the office to join Hansie and her driver for the trip back to Metz.

At her request they dropped her at the Railway station, where she was collected by Michael. No longer in her uniform, she was now just another relative arriving on the Paris express.

***

The entire team collected for the Metz operation. The selected spot for the new gate was in the shadow of a copse of trees, there were no perimeter lights. The patrols depended on the vehicle lights which included a spotlight mounted above the windscreen. The section chosen was on a long straight to allow plenty of warning for any intruder, entering or leaving.

They timed the patrols, which like every other airbase they surveyed, ran to a timetable. The routine for fitting the gates was down to a simple system. The uprights were sunk into holes and quick drying cement poured in. The gate and frame was placed in situ, against the wire, and laced all round. Then the following night, after the cement had dried, between patrols, they opened the gate outward, carefully cut the wire section of the fence around the frame and removed it, rolled it up and placed it in the van. The gate was then closed and the lock attached.

Three days later the team arrived, and drove onto the perimeter track. They each had a target. Their vehicles were Luftwaffe trucks.

Alek with Mark drove one truck, and Klaus drove the other truck inside the fence.

Chapter Nineteen

Sabotage

Karl Leuter generally enjoyed the post of Officer-in-Charge at an operational airfield. He would rather have been in Germany, where the local populace was less hostile. Metz was not the worst place to be. Most of the local people spoke German anyway, and, with Hansie available at weekends and odd other occasions, life was not too bad. He was aware that his wife who stayed in Berlin had her own agenda in his absence, but he was not complaining. When he was there she was available exclusively to him, and having the full attention of a beautiful actress was, as the other members of his staff put it, beyond luck.

He flew the Storch back from a visit to the satellite airfield situated at Verdun. The regular visits to the other field were a relief from the routine on the main field, and a chance to get away from the demands of the telephone and the Ministry, in form of Feldmarschal Goering, who had the irritating habit of snap visits to keep them on their toes.

The runway lights were lit for him as he arrived back at the base. He taxied over to the apron of the Special Service hanger as the lights were switched off behind him. His kugelwagen, used on the airfield, was there with driver to take him to his quarters beside the officer's mess. The air force grey vehicle was open at this time and easy to climb into, something he appreciated as he grew older.

He was in his bath when the noise started. First, it was a series of explosions, then the warning sirens. He got out of the bath and wrapped a towel round himself, reaching for pants and uniform shirt. The door banged open and his servant appeared to repot that the airfield was under attack.

"Who by? I hear no aircraft?"

"Saboteurs, partisans! No aircraft." The man reported.

"Get my gun," Leuter shouted. "And arm yourself. Is the car outside?"

"The Kugelwagen is there still, sir."

"Move!" The Colonel shouted.

Outside there was pandemonium. There were vehicles heading for the aircraft hangers. Pilots with guns in their hands piled into cars and got in the way of the security forces.

Over beside the three hangers, fires were burning. The station fire engines were jangling bells as they tried to avoid the confusion and get to a place where they could operate.

As he watched, the Special Services hanger went up in flames, the aircraft inside exploding and showering the other aircraft with burning fuel.

Three of the parked FW190 fighters, engines roaring, broke away from the line of parked aircraft. They lined up to take off without the benefit of the runway lights. The first roared down the runway veered off the hard runway onto the grass, ground-looped, and exploded.

The other two made it off the ground and exploded before they reached fifty feet. Leuter groaned, three of his pilots wasted in seconds. The Special Services hanger doors were jammed. *Perhaps the heat of the fire,* he thought, and drove there to try to get them open.

They had been locked and a truck had been driven across the two doors to help prevent them opening. Leuter swerved the car round to the side door and found that locked too. But there was a fire axe in the glass case beside the door. He smashed the glass and then took a swing with all his strength at the hinges of the door. It burst open with a bang and flames shot out, singeing his hair and face. He gasped, inhaling the fiery air, and assured his death within minutes. But through the door four men made it out to live,

The colonel fell back on the ground, his front blackened, clothes burned to cinders and his skin seared and peeling off his bones. Mercifully, he took a breath and died.

His servant held him and sobbed, not immediately accepting that his boss, and his idol, was dead, just like that. Not killed leading a flight of fighters, or a cavalry charge, but killed by a saboteur's fire bomb.

He was forcibly removed as the fire fighters cleared the area. There were munitions inside the hanger.

Taking up his rifle, the orderly/servant set his helmet straight and went looking for the people who had killed his Colonel.

There were men running around everywhere he looked. He spied some men in black overalls, creeping around the broken tail of one of the bombers, wrecked in the first string of explosions. He assumed that they were some of the saboteurs, so, lifting his rifle, he shot two of them before they could escape. He did not realise at the time that he had shot two of the mechanics chasing the saboteurs.

Mark and Alek had been attending to the bombers. Because of their close parking, the planes were easy targets. Two refueling trucks, parked among the aircraft, were an obvious target, and in both cases Mark opened the valves to allow the fuel to flood the ground beneath the aircraft.

Mark met up with Alek. They lit a small charge and threw it into the nearest Junkers 88. There was a satisfying bang, and the plane burst into flame. The fire raced across the puddled fuel on the ground, leaping from aircraft to aircraft. The two tankers blew up with spectacular results, scattering flame and bits of metal throughout the area.

***

Michael and Sarah were finishing off by mining the fuel dump. They had decided to mine the dump, rather than to blow it like the rest. This was a way they could upset matters for a second time later in the night, without risk to themselves.

While Michael continued stringing the trip wires, Sarah took a tour around the central hanger that housing the aircraft being worked on, both fighters and bombers. She was certain there was a bomb store somewhere close. It had not been evident when she was on the base doing a survey. A low doorway caught her eye. She realised that she might have found it. She spun the wheeled handle on the door, which opened with a hiss. Cool air was sucked out by the heat of the fires outside. She entered the room and looked at the neat stacks of bombs. Then from her bag she produced a small pre-formed charge and inserted a detonator taken from the side pocket of the bag.

She crouched and placed charges between the first stack of bombs, and up against the noses of the second stack. Then she cracked the fuses and crawled out.

Looking around, she located Michael. "Drop it and run!" She said, grabbing his hand. He did not hesitate. She raced with him, off out onto the open airfield. They were running into the dark. There was little of them to see against the background of night.

The Colonel's man glimpsed their running figures and raised his rifle. He took careful aim. As he went to squeeze the trigger, he felt himself grabbed and sucked into the air by a tremendous explosion. Then nothing!

Sarah and Michael hit the ground as the bomb store went up. The explosion lit up the sky, and was followed by a series of other explosions, as the other rooms within the bomb shelter blew up in turn. The ground shook and the underground air raid shelters collapsed, creating a huge hole in the ground where they had been.

Sarah looked at the scene behind her. The entire Special Service hanger was gone, nothing left but a heap of burning rubble. The next hanger was wrecked, though there was one wall still standing. The other hanger was leaning drunkenly away from the seat of the explosion, The fire, which had been blown out by the blast, had re-ignited and was blazing well, lighting the scene, highlighting the extent of the disaster. The rows of aircraft were either burnt out or in process of doing so. Survivors were stirring and beginning to appear in the light of the fires.

Michael grabbed her hand. "Run for your life!" He yanked her to her feet and ran up the field to the waiting truck. As they arrived Ewan appeared carrying Marian, who was bleeding from a wound in her shoulder.

Klaus had the engine running. Alek, and then Mark appeared, his overalls torn and a bruise on his face. Klaus put the truck into gear and drove sedately down to their gate.

Alek produced a big wide rake and did his best to clear the marks in the grass where the truck had come through the fence. He then closed and locked the gate,

Klaus dropped his passengers off and took his truck round to the main gates. There was pandemonium, as people were trying to get in and out of the airfield. The sky was lit up with the fires, though now there was only the odd explosion, to punctuate proceedings.

It was when the fuel dump exploded that Klaus decided to leave the truck where it was, engine still running. He strolled away down the road toward Metz. As he walked he decided that he was pleased that he had chosen to be anti-Nazi. It was sad to see so many people killed, but they had made their choice. He had made his.

This was a battle he had won. He had no illusions. There would be other battles. Some he would win, others not. When the time came he would deal with it, he and Alek between them.

***

The group re-assembled in their safe house. Marian's wound had been dressed by the mob's surgeon. "The wound would heal nicely." He assured her. There would be little sign of scar by the time it healed completely. He was, after all, a specialist in cosmetic surgery.

There was no public announcement about the events at the Metz airfield. The deaths of the Colonel, with a list of his pilots and ground crew, were recorded as killed in action, their location at the time of death not announced for reasons of security.

Michael and Sarah, with Ewan and Marian, travelled to Frankfurt as soon as Marian was well enough.

Mark had been following up a lead on the scientist who had been employed on the base. Conrad Reuter, whose wife and son were being held hostage, was a specialist in atomic physics. He had been well aware that the job he was doing on the air-base was a waste of time. He was pretty certain that he would be shifted to a more meaningful job, now the air base was closed for repairs.

Mark had managed to make contact with Reuter. He had sent him a message, informing him of the true situation regarding his wife and child, asking him to continue as if he knew nothing. The message promised that he would be contacted soon and that an opportunity would be made for him to avenge his family's murder. If he doubted the truth of the message, ask for an answer from your wife that only you and she would know.

Conrad Reuter would have worked for the Nazi's if they had simply asked him. He was Russian and he knew he would be rich if he cooperated with these people. The problem was that the Gestapo had jumped the gun. His wife and son had been snatched before he had been approached. He had not been given the opportunity to make a deal with them. He asked his wife about her favorite soft toy, lost after the family moved. He could not believe she would have forgotten her pet name for it. He realised his informant was correct, it was not his wife sending him messages. He felt the fury at the betrayal. Since they had killed his family, he would get his revenge, one way or another. Kill as many of them as he could, ideally with a fission bomb. He thought that in the Ruhr an atomic bomb would be effective, wiping out millions of people and destroying the machinery of the industrial heart of the country.

Realistically, he was aware that it was unlikely that research would reach that stage in time for him to do anything about it, but he could dream. Meanwhile, he had to see what this contact had to say. At least he had managed to get in touch. It was the first time anyone outside the immediate circle of permitted personnel had been able to do that.

Mark stayed in Metz where Conrad Reuter was held. The destruction of the air field had meant re-assignment of quarters elsewhere. Metz was the nearest place, and the Gestapo safe house was used as a temporary measure, while the inquiry was conducted. Reuter was a suspect, of course. Though, considering the supervision he was under, there seemed no real chance that he could have organized the event. The descent of a group of Gestapo agents from elsewhere allowed Mark the opportunity to join in and speak to Reuter.

The Gestapo agents were now considering whether there would be a point in keeping Reuter within the system or taking him out straight away. It really depended on the outcome of the present inquiry.

Meanwhile, Mark had arranged for a method of contacting Conrad, and for Conrad to contact him.

***

Heinrich Stolle had become seriously involved with Edith Korder. There was no doubt in his mind that she was the one. She, in her turn, had been shaken to her roots by the impact that this man has made on her life. There were no more doubts in her mind. Heinrich had proved himself through every test she could think of. Were he to ask her to marry him, she would accept in an instant.

He entered the office looking serious and went straight through to the Admiral. Canaris looked at his number two, surprised at the interruption so early in the day.

Stolle wasted no time. "Sir, the airfield at Metz, all the aircraft, plus 67 men and women on the base has been wiped out, probably by saboteurs. The Commandant, Oberst Karl Leuter was killed in the incident."

"Sit!" Canaris said, "Edith, coffee please. Include yourself and join us."

Edith came in with a tray with coffee pot, cream, sugar, and three mugs. She set the tray on the desk and sat down with the two men."

She poured the coffee, and handed the mugs round.

"This news is not good, mainly because we had no inkling of actions on this scale occurring. Later in the war, I would have expected the local partisans to be in action. This seems to me to be a commando raid, not partisan activity. In other words, I suggest this activity was imported, not local. You both realise that the Gestapo will probably decide it is local, and round up and kill a hundred or so local people in retaliation."

"They may be right, of course, but it is unlikely. The saboteurs used explosives and detonators of a level not found in the area," Stolle added. "Maybe a night drop of munitions, paving the way for future partisan activity."

Edith spoke, "Given that you are right, there has to be a embedded group within the country, German speaking and trained in sabotage and weapons in general."

Canaris noticed Stolle's surprise. The inclusion of Edith in the discussion, and her subsequent input, had been something he had not taken into account. "You were not aware that Edith is an agent?" He said, quietly. Everyone who works for me is an agent. Edith, at the moment is recovering from a spell in the Middle-East where she was captured by bandits. Here in the office she still performs her duties. Incidentally, your relationship, which has not gone unobserved, is not part of her duties, and is inspired by the lady herself. So, if you are considering asking her to marry you, please feel free. It is nothing to do with work."

Stunned, Heinrich Stolle looked at Edith. She, in her turn, looked at him.

"Is this true?" He asked her.

"Absolutely," she answered, waiting, holding her breath to see what he would say.

"If I asked you to marry me, you would give me a personally honest answer?"

She nodded, unable to speak in the tense atmosphere of the office at that moment.

"So will you?" Stolle said, caught up in the same tension.

"Will I what?" She said breathlessly.

"Will you marry me?" He asked.

"Of course, I will." She said calmly, now it had been said clearly and openly.

Canaris broke the spell. "Congratulations. We can arrange the ceremony later this week. Meanwhile, to get back to the situation on the table, how have we missed these saboteurs?"

The other two turned to the Admiral and set their minds back to the present situation.

Stolle remembered the two bogus Gestapo agents from the Berlin train. "Remember the killing of that Gestapo asset, the member of the mob, Gruber. He was getting rid of all the so-called deviants. Remember he was blown up in his compartment. Someone dropped two grenades down the stove chimney."

Canaris nodded, "What about him?"

"The Gestapo questioned others in the train and found two so-called Gestapo agents elsewhere in the train. Correct I/D, everything. Except they were not on Gestapo records. They were obviously agents. They have not been captured or seen since.

"Also, the Metz Luftwaffe office has a record of a female officer, Stabsführerin von Traube, who came to do a census of all the aircraft assets on the air base, just a few days before the raid."

"So what? These things happen."

"She is not recorded as an officer in the Luftwaffe, either under her own name or that of Grafin Herzog, another name apparently, that she did not use while in uniform.

"She was originally identified as Grafin Herzog by a man who dashed into the office when she first made contact and asked for her by name. He then immediately asked them not to mention the title when she reported for duty, thus ensuring that they would accept her, whatever name she used. Don't you see? They were a team, a man and a woman. Then, three days after her inspection of the base, it is blown to hell and gone."

"It does make sense," Edith said. "Targets of opportunity, they call them. There will be a reason they are here, but there is obviously a time lapse until they can perform the function they were placed here to carry out. My guess would be they were here before war was declared, so they are possibly British. As you are aware they are a devious bunch. Certainly not the idiots the cartoonists make them out to be. And some speak German!"

"What project would they be bothered about to the extent of placing agents in place, before war is declared?"

All three contemplated this puzzle for the next few minutes.

The Admiral said, "The atomic energy project."

As he spoke, Stolle said, "The Peenemunde scheme."

"Surely, they are one and the same, are they not?" Edith added.

Canaris answered her, "Yes and no. The place hosts several projects, one of which involves work on atomic energy. But it also hosts experimental rocket research. It features one of the biggest concentrations of scientists in Germany, including many Jews, whose families were held hostage against their good behaviour."

Stolle said, "You said were?"

"There was a break-out. Most of the Jews escaped to the west to Britain and USA."

"But their families? What happened to them?" Edith asked.

Canaris turned his eyes away and in a flat voice said. "Our Gestapo friends decided keeping the actual families under control was a waste of resources. They maintained contact by letter only."

"You mean they…..?" Edith put her hand to her mouth.

Stolle said, "They murdered them? All of them, women, and children?"

Canaris nodded, "Sent them all to Auswitz. Used them to test the equipment." He continued, "How did the scientists find out? Somebody opened the files up and distributed them to the huts where the scientists were kept. The fence was cut and most escaped. Those who stayed were eliminated of course, they could not be permitted to pass on what had happened to any new people who were brought in.

"Do you believe that it was this cell of agents who arranged the break-out?" Edith asked.

"It has all the earmarks of a smooth, professional operation. The planning: a boat came alongside the quay at Peenemunde, the German scientists, and wives where applicable, were invited to a party by a titled lady, a Grafin. So the German specialist team was abducted. The Jewish scientists were released, and all escaped. The lid came down immediately. Security covered the entire operation. They actually stole the radar from the offshore islands so there was no trace of the boat when she sailed. The result is that the research program into the splitting of the atom has been set back possibly for years, and a large percentage of the expertise has gone over to the other side." The Admiral sat back and looked at his two companions. "We need to find these people, before the Gestapo gets their hands on them. Our so-called colleagues have a habit of shooting first. If they actually take them alive, what they would do to them does not bear thinking about. I think you will agree.

"In our hands they can be a source of information and a conduit to the intelligence service in Britain, in fact, of incalculable value, to our own intelligence efforts."

Chapter Twenty

Keeping up the pressure

Ewan smiled at the assembled members of the team. "I think that went rather well."

The others around the room all nodded in agreement.

Marian said, as she felt a twinge from her wounded shoulder, "At the risk of being personal, I think the return of one shoulder wound, against countless casualties, an unknown number of aircraft and a lot of buildings, was a pretty good deal. Only next time it will be someone else's turn to take the bullet, please!"

The group laughed and the drinks went round once more.

Michael rose to his feet and, taking up a place against the mantelpiece, he called for attention. "We have been successful at every job so far. The reason is mainly because we have kept our presence secret." He paused, thought for a moment, and then continued. "The Gestapo are searching for the two rogue agents from the Berlin train. The Abwehr have been preoccupied elsewhere." He paused again and took a drink, looked at each member of the group, seeking and getting their full attention. Only then did he continue once more.

"That situation will change. Make no mistake, the Gestapo have a very wide base of agents throughout this country, and France will swiftly join the network. We will need to retain our low profile, and if the Abwehr get in on the act, watch our step even more.

"Our next operation is already planned, but we will go though the nuts and bolts of the set-up over the next few days. Our immediate concern is to get Marian back on her feet and ready to go out into the field. The next job will need all the skill and ingenuity we can muster between us. Alek and Klaus will be our outside contacts for the next two weeks at least, meanwhile, contain yourselves, and keep your weapons handy. I will be travelling to Berlin to our contact there. She has a contact with the Abwehr. Hopefully, I will get some feedback through her, but there are no guarantees. In my absence, as you are all aware, Sarah is in charge. Please stay indoors and let Alek and Klaus do the legwork. The briefing pack for the next target is with Sarah. Use the next week for planning what we will do about it."

He left them together in the lounge of the apartment and went to his room. Sarah joined him a few minutes later. He passed over the briefing package, and when she turned to him, he kissed her. "I'll be back by Friday, all things being equal. Look after yourself. Keep a tight rein in Ewan. He is inclined to be a little impetuous at times."

Sarah looked at him seriously.

Michael threw his hands up. "Ok, I know. You know him as well, if not better, than I do. I'll say no more." He turned, picked up his small bag, and made for the door. She was there before him, stopped him and kissed him again. "No more sleeping with the enemy, understand?"

He nodded. "I understand!" Then he was gone.

***

Gruppenfuhrer Schumann slapped his boot with the leather-covered crop he habitually carried when in uniform. He called through the door to the outer office, "Jung!"

His man entered the office promptly, and stood waiting for whatever his lord and master wanted.

"Do you have any news yet on the two bogus agents who killed Gruber?"

Ascher Jung hung his head. "Sadly, no, sir. I believe they are spies and probably British, but I have no proof."

Schumann scratched his chin. Despite the close shave he had that morning there was a small area that the keen blade had missed. It was irritating and it had happened before. "I believe we have been missing something. Take a look and see if there are any other cases where false credentials have been used. Look everywhere in the occupied area of Europe."

Ascher Junk straightened up, grateful for the excuse to get out of the range of that damned stick, which on more than one occasion had been used against his back and head.

In the back of his mind he had an idea that there had been a recent case of a female Luftwaffe officer who had been an imposter. perhaps she….Then he remembered that the impersonator had been believed to be a Grafin. He had heard about a Grafin before, somewhere.

He was back in the Gruppenfurher's office within minutes. "Sir, the Metz airfield disaster."

"Well, what about it.?"

"The woman was believed to be Grafin Herzogsterm, in the Peenemunde affair, it was a Grafin Helene von Klause that abducted so many of the scientific staff in that boat. In both cases the woman concerned was autocratic, and beautiful, what are the chances?"

"The bogus Gestapo agents!" Schumann said.

"If you are correct and the agents are British, where else would we find an aristocratic woman who speaks German like a native. That means either the saboteurs are German or the abductors are, or maybe both."

Jung stopped and waited to see is his gamble had paid off.

Gruppenfuhrer Schumann was mulling over the information that Jung had brought. It all seemed to fit in an odd sort of way.

He spun his chair around and spoke to Jung, "The rail stations, Metz, Munchen, and try the airfields see if they have anything for us, flights to the area of either of these events. Find the girl and we find the others involved. There have to be more than two people. Judging by the reports from the airfield, there could have been as many as ten, or more even."

Jung left the office in a hurry, leaving his General deep in thought.

***

The package of information on the subject of the next target was bulky. The background information on Schumann, the target was a sad litany of brutal bullying and abuse. He had risen through the ranks of the party through his ruthless use of the people around him and his compete lack of sympathy for the people he trod upon to get to his position. He was still not in the place he really aspired to. Richard Heydrich had just taken that place.. Schumann had been suspected of trying to arrange for Heydrich to meet with an accident, but there was insufficient evidence to proceed with.

What the Team really needed, was a venue inside Germany so that they could link Schumann to whatever incident they could arrange. The fact that Heydrich was homosexual had not impeded his career in any way, another factor that upset Schumann, a committed homophobic.

So, thought Ewan, *we have one very nasty man, Heydrich, and Schumann, even nastier if that was possible.* The idea of getting near Heydrich was, to Ewan, a joke. He was guarded by a troop of SS twenty-four hours per day. He seldom ventured beyond the confines of the headquarters building where his office had accommodation included.

Ewan spoke with the others and they discussed possibilities. They decided that Heydrich's security would not allow them access without exposing the team. "In the circumstances, can I suggest we eliminate Schumann rather than Heydrich? It is going to be difficult enough to achieve that aim. Ploughing through the paperwork will involve enough problems, certainly more than the tasks which we've undertaken so far." Ewan's suggestion made sense to the group and they agreed accordingly.

Ewan composed a message for London informing them of their suggestion.

***

In the offices of the Abwehr, Stolle had reached a similar conclusion to the Gestapo's, regarding the events of the past months. The identity of the woman and or, man involved in the train killing, was the key to the apprehension of the team of saboteurs operating in the country. The only clues to their identity were the facts that the woman had an upper class air, and was regardless of her hair colour, brunette. This information came from the Gestapo on the train who observed her briefly naked.

Edith suggested that they would probably have a base somewhere in the centre of the country, where they would have access to transport in all directions. Because of the transport hubs, she suggested Frankfurt. "Not exactly the middle," she commented, "Though roughly halfway, between north and south, with good communications in all directions.

The Gestapo settled for Berlin. Stolle heard that piece of information through channels not normally used by the Gestapo, Which made him extremely suspicious. In fact, he need not have been because, having made their deductions, they had got no further with their enquiries.

The Abwehr operated in a completely different way to the Gestapo, despite the obvious connections to the Navy, Admiral Canaris, and Commander Stolle et al. Their agents were all undercover, and operated without fanfare, mostly abroad. But, like all spymasters, Canaris had a network of agents in his own country also. A wise move in a nation so preoccupied with competitive organisations that duplication of effort was an everyday occurrence. This often resulted in them cancelling each other out.

The Abwehr man in Frankfurt was Walter Kroll, a retired businessman. This allowed him to roam at will and sit around talking with the old men, without them feeling they were being grilled. Because they were always there, they saw things others did not.

When he received the request to advise the office of new people moving into the area, he was able to recall the arrival of Alek and Klaus. On checking up on them, he discovered they were mob gunmen, so he lost interest.

***

Mark was told to bring Conrad Reuter away. A night landing of a Lysander would be laid on to collect Reuter. He would be going to Britain from choice. He turned to Sarah for advice on getting him away from the Gestapo in the first place.

"Distraction," she said. "If they can be distracted in some way, you would have the opportunity to move him. Once you are out of the building we can make him disappear. Then we can talk about the uplifting of him to Britain."

"A bomb in the basement. Would that do, do you think?"

"Sounds good! Can you arrange it?" I was just thinking of ideas, remembering that there is a garage below the offices in the basement of the building. That makes it conceivable, I believe."

Sarah smiled. "Provided your man can get away from the people guarding him. You know as well as I, most plans do not survive the first ten minutes."

Mark listened to her, fascinated by her clear enunciation, correct grammar and impeccable delivery.

Sarah looked at his preoccupation. "What is it?" She said. Is there something you don't understand."

Mark shrugged. "I just like listening to the sound of your voice."

Sarah laughed. "Cheeky boy." She said through her laughter. Then she stopped suddenly, realising what he had said.

"Do you think I have a distinctive voice, Mark? Would you recognise my voice, perhaps on the telephone?"

"Without fail. I can hear your voice in my sleep sometimes, when I'm having a night-mare."

He grinned, "Seriously though, I have no doubts about your voice. It is distinctive, so that, even speaking a foreign language the tone and the timbre comes through.

Sarah realised that it could be a problem. The one thing to avoid in this particular game was identifying features, in her case her manner, and now apparently her voice. It was important for her to take heed of these things in her movements around the country.

***

They moved a team to Metz. For obvious reasons, Sarah did not take part. Mark used Klaus to keep the close eye on the garage beneath the Gestapo safe house. The building itself was a modern block with three stories, located on a corner allowing two points of egress, one on each of the street walls. The garage entrance was next to the window on the high street. There was a steep slope down to the underground car parking area, which was spotted here and there with the pillars supporting the upper floors of the building. Originally, the parking was for people occupying the other users of the building, but, since the Gestapo had moved in, nobody had challenged their assumption of the entire area for their own use.

The other apartments were on the other side of the building, which meant the other occupants had no need to contact their neighbours, short of a power cut, or some other disaster.

Mark made his plan, and advised Conrad by note to be ready during the morning of Friday, in two days time. The note continued, 'there will be a diversion. It will be noisy. Come out with the rest of the people. I will be waiting with a car. M.'

Conrad appeared at the second window on first floor of the building. He stood looking for at least three minutes. Then he nodded twice and turned away.

Mark had received the reply he hoped for and went off to prepare the diversion. The others had several suggestions to make, but the best suggestion had come from Mark himself. A bomb placed under the body of the vehicle, and a back-up of three people.

"Why, only three others. We have plenty of people who could do your, job."

"I trained as a Marine in the States. We have a similar set up to British Marines. On special jobs we work in a team of four. Any other questions?"

Chapter Twenty-one

Snatch & Shoot

The Mercedes stood waiting at the kerb, the engine burbling healthily. The driver sat, looking bored in his high necked SS uniform, not a happy man. His thoughts were far away from Metz. They were back in Wurttemberg, where his wife was struggling to make ends meet on a soldier's pay. She had been used to the money he made at the selling during the day and on the tables in the evening. Even when he had first been conscripted it had not been too bad. He had made a pretty good living out of the other recruits and, later out of the Jews he had rounded up. Here there was little extra to be made. The sergeants had all the loose gear sorted out and the various fiddles that would have been available were out of reach, what with the greedy bastards he had to drive about hogging all the perks. Women, money, drink, there was never the offer of a piece of the action from the Gestapo. As he sat in his own world railing against fate, he did not notice that someone had crept up alongside the car and left a bundle tucked into the spare wheel standing on the running board of the big car.

Alek smiled to himself, as he wandered tipsily back to his place of concealment in the alley just 20 feet from the idling Mercedes. The sight of the Gestapo vehicle had virtually cleared the street when it arrived.

From his place, Alek saw the Gestapo men rejoin the driver and watched the car drive off. He lifted his arm and punched the air once,

A car at the other end of the alley drove off to chase the Mercedes on the parallel street, which joined the street used by the Mercedes approximately two hundred yards ahead.

The chase vehicle, driven by Klaus, then watched as the Gestapo car drove down into the underground car park, beneath the Gestapo building. Klaus then pulled up beside the figure of Mark leaning against the wall of the building opposite.

The SS driver appeared from the garage entrance smoking a cigarette.

Mark pressed a button on a small bakelite box. There was a pause, then the building opposite shuddered to the shock of the explosion., Flames burst forth from the open garage entrance. People began pouring out of the building as the fire alarms rang with that piercing intensity, urging people to seek safety. Conrad came out of the building with a bunch of girls. They all rushed across the road. The rear door of the car was already open when a girl, and Conrad, leapt in. Klaus did not hesitate. He let out the clutch and let the car ghost away, leaving the incident behind.

In the car Mark asked, "Who are you?"

The pretty woman, who had entered the car with Conrad, looked at him anxiously. "I'm with him," she said. "You must be Mark!"

Mark looked at Conrad, who shrugged his shoulders resignedly. "What could I do? I needed help, and Wilma offered it."

Mark shrugged in turn. To Wilma he said, "You realise the Gestapo will be looking for him. – and you?"

"Yes, of course. but we have done nothing wrong."

Mark nodded his head in agreement. "They will still kill both of you if you are caught now."

Wilma did not look too happy about that idea but it was too late now to go back. "You have something in mind, I presume?"

"Probably a short trip to England. or a long walk to Spain. It is likely one of the two."

"I think I would prefer the quick trip to England. I like it there." Wilma sounded almost cheerful at the prospect of going to England.

Conrad said nothing. He just sat gloomily waiting for whatever happened.

***

The streets of Metz behind them echoed with the sound of sirens, and lights flashed on the roads through town. But they missed all that by being out of town before the place was organized.

Klaus did not go to the agent's safe house. He went to a house kept by his boss instead. The caretaker recognised him immediately and the car went into the garage while the people went into the house.

Mark rang Sarah and informed her. "We have an extra fish that we cannot throw back. It looks as if we will have to put her in the bag with the others."

"I'll let them know what is happening and they can possibly take whoever we have." The phone went down as Sarah rang off. Turning to Ewan, she said, "Contact base and tell them we have two for collection, one of each, not just the one."

Ewan nodded and went through to the back room where the signal gear was located.

He would code the message. When it went, it would go in four seconds. They would decode it at the other end, and, hopefully, the reply would have a solution.

***

In Berlin, the office of the Abwehr was informed of the loss of the scientist from Metz. Stolle suggested that the agents they were seeking were responsible.

"I have no doubt they are," Canaris said quietly. "Another example of the incompetence of our Gestapo colleagues."

Edith said, "Perhaps we should go to the area and see if we can spot anything that they may have missed."

"I'm afraid that they will be far from the scene of the crime by now, Edith. My guess is they will take out a highly placed person next. It will keep the security services hopping about, wondering what they will do next. I think we know what they are here for, so I suggest we prepare a trap. We will bait it with a lie. They will have to follow it up because they cannot afford not to."

"Trap? We really will be gambling with this one." Heinrich Stolle sounded doubtful.

Edith smiled, "We cannot really lose. Although we are guessing, it's a pretty solid guess, and, if we are wrong, who is to know? Certainly not the Gestapo. If it tips off the agents that we are on to them, it could cause them to either withdraw, or make a mistake that will allow us to capture them. As I said, we are in a win – win situation."

Both men looked at her calculatingly. Stolle spoke first."You could be right, though we will have to keep the Gestapo out of things. They would give the game away, tramping about with their big boots."

Canaris smiled. "Don't get carried away. Whatever trap we set may not work. The information must go out in a discrete manner, a slip of the tongue at a party, that sort of thing. Perhaps a publication that reveals a little too much.

"First, we have to speak to an expert in the field. We have to predict something that is possible, perhaps tried and passed over, and on re-examination. Do you get the picture?"

Stolle picked up the story. "Then we will need the place where the breakthrough has been made." He paused, thinking. "Perhaps a research establishment. One that we can cover with our own agents. We cannot afford to use outside forces. Too much can go wrong, too many different agendas."

The admiral considered the matter, looking at his two closest colleagues, but looking through them, working things out in his own head. Finally, he clicked his fingers. "I think I know just who to consult about this. Leave it with me. I will get back to you after I have spoken with my contact."

***

Later that morning. Edith arranged a flight for the Admiral to Munich. The local agent in Munich met him and drove him to Erding, a small village north east of the city. They stopped at a chalet house, and Canaris got out of the car. "Call for me this evening. You may have to wait for a while."

The agent, Peter Weiss, smiled. "I'll be here, sir."

Canaris watched the car drive off. Then he turned and walked off around the corner into the next street. It was not really far, but it was another world. The small cottage was an original Bavarian thatched cottage with small lattice windows and roses growing in the garden, and creeper across the face of the building.

Canaris walked up to the front door. It opened and he walked straight in. The girl who opened the door was young, and hauntingly beautiful. Her lustrous, black hair fell to her shoulders. Her dark eyes were warm as she recognized her grandfather's old friend. She led him to a room at the back of the house where his old friend was seated.

Jacob Akermann was undoubtedly Jewish. He had all the attributes associated with the race, and when he opened his mouth to speak it was confirmed. "Shalom, Wilhelm. What can I do for you that brings you all this way?"

Golda spoke, "I'll bring tea."

***

When the car appeared that evening Canaris was seated on the wall in front of the chalet house. He had no idea who lived there, but the wall was comfortable to sit on. Peter Weiss, the agent, collected him and returned him to the airfield where the Junkers Ju 52 passenger aircraft waited to return him to Berlin.

Four hours later, the Admiral stepped out of the car at his office. He decided to sleep on the bed he used there on occasion. His wife would be, by now, asleep. He would not disturb her.

***

Ewan Fitzgerald was singing softly as he drove into the parking place at the office building used by his boss. He left the small disk on the dashboard to indicate that it was a mob car. It would therefore be left alone.

Ewan took a taxi to the gardens at the location of the SS headquarters. He seated himself there watching the passing parade of people. He watched the two plain-clothed men who appeared as the Mercedes drew up outside the building. Schumann came out with another man whom Ewan identified as Ascher Jung. They got into the car and it drove off.

Ewan was intrigued. Ascher Jung was known, though not as a member of the SS. So why was he with Schumann and travelling in the official car?

At The Adlon, Ewan took a room for his stay in Berlin. A quiet word with the concierge cleared up the matter of Ascher Jung's presence at the SS HQ. Karl Curnow was able to verify that Jung had been undercover for the SS for some time, though he had done jobs for independent operators from time to time. In Curnow's opinion, it was with the permission of his masters, to establish his credentials as a freelance. He was now openly an overt operative of the SS and on occasion wore uniform.

Ewan realised that there would be no real problem assassinating Schumann, but it would be advisable to dispose of Ascher Jung at the same time.

Having seen the level of security that the Gruppenfuhrer surrounded himself with, Ewan realised the whole affair could be handled by one man with a silenced rifle. Looking at the buildings in the immediate area he worked out that, shooting in this area would demand dedication accuracy and a death wish. Unless.....A silenced rifle perhaps, a different entrance, or even waiting in the basement for the car to come in. He would check and see. He had been informed that the Gruppenfuhrer had a habit of returning direct into the garage and using the elevator to reach his office on the third floor.

Ewan decided to make preparations for both scenarios, just in case.

***

The job was completed on the fourth day. A car was brought to the door of the office. An explosion the other side of the visitors' area, drew everyone's attention,

The Gruppenfuhrer had just come through the door when the explosion occurred. As he stopped, a spray of blood jetted from the side of his head and splattered Ascher Jung, who was standing next to him. Self-preservation would have normally dictated he drop to the ground and seek shelter. But, with his boss bleeding blood and brains, he was stunned for the fatal few moments he would have needed to survive.

The second bullet hit the base of his skull where the cranium and the vertebrae met. The bodyguards had no idea where or what had happened, just that their charge and his assistant were dead on the ground. They had heard nothing and seen nothing. The bullets had come out of nowhere.

***

Ewan lowered the rifle. He closed the car window, laying the rifle on the floor in the back of the car. He turned, climbed into the front seat and started the car. Before he drove away a soldier called on him to stop and raised his rifle to cover Ewan. With seconds to react, Ewan rammed the accelerator down. The car leapt forward and the soldier fired. The bullet smashed the windscreen and drew a red welt along Ewan's cheek. The soldier was thrown aside by the bumper of the car and lost his rifle.

Ewan was away, before the soldier had time to recover. The car rounded a corner and was gone. All the soldier could tell the investigators was that the shooter had dark eyes and wore a trilby hat. The car was a black Opel.

As Ewan escaped he noticed the confusion at the SS building and the growing crowd of uniformed personnel scattering across the square.

The car was left down the back alley behind the old abattoir. It was deserted there. Ewan stripped the rifle and packed it in the fitted briefcase. His cheek bore a red line where the bullet had passed, and burned the skin without actually touching him. In the mirror he could see the mark, but there was no break in the skin. It would need attention, but there was nothing he could do, a doctor would need to look at it.

***

Back at the Adlon, the rifle was now stripped down and cased in an innocuous looking brief case. Ewan went up to his room. Seated at the desk in the room he wrote out a signal and coded it for transmission. He rang the doctor whom the mob used and arranged to see him. Then he spoke with Sarah who was in Frankfurt. "Target achieved."

Chapter Twenty-two

The Raid

Sarah passed information back, which caused Ewan to study a big map of the continent in his room.

Sarah was also studying a map. Mark and Marian had reported in. The imminent arrival of Albert Kessler, who as Eric Rohm had been in the initial group to come to Europe, was expected.

The latest information on the atomic energy research was that it seemed that there had been a breakthrough in the research program. Since it was found in an area already exhaustedly covered, or so they thought, much of the initial work had already been done. There was now a chance that by the following year they could have the basic program for a bomb.

The worrying thought for the allies research team was that their own people were now following the same line of inquiry and had made a breakthrough. The news from their sources in Germany implied that the Germans had made the same deductions and had broken through also, making it a race against time. Something needed to be done to halt the progress of the German effort.

The team was there in place for just that reason. Kessler was there to support and, if possible, find out exactly how far ahead—or behind—the German team was.

Ewan was there first, the mark on his face liable to be there forever, though at present it was concealed to a great extent by the medicament used by the doctor to reduce the burn and ease the swelling which had accompanied it. His position was currently to the south of the establishment. The abbey had been the home of a nuns' order. The occupants were still there, though they had suffered being moved to what was once the animal quarters. Their cells were now in use by the German research team, but they still had the use of the chapel. Otherwise, they were expected to feed and serve the intruders, in return for their continued accommodation and rations.

Thus far, only two of the younger nuns had been raped. The current commander of the establishment had given strict orders that any interference with the nuns would result in extreme punishment. The examples set to cost the two guilty men were sufficient to maintain the commandant's embargo. Both had been beaten by the Sergeants, eight of them. One of the culprits would be unable to use his tackle for anything, except voiding his bladder from now on. The other was discovered to have a weaker heart than expected. His death was recorded as accidental. After drinking unwisely, he had been hit by a truck. That was the story his parents were given.

***

Of all this Ewan was ignorant, but his observations did highlight a certain amount of unexpected fraternization between the younger nuns and the SS men who were the security for the research labs.

Another important discovery was that this was a crack company of SS troops. They had seen action in Poland, after their baptism of fire in Spain. This was no bunch of old men and kids, like many of the other soldiers assigned to protection duties.

He was awaiting the arrival of the others. Each was coming from different directions, and since the reason for the journeys might be questioned, in the case of the two women, inquiry was made into attendance at the Church Music School in Regensburg.

Two were travelling salesmen in the form of Eric Rohm and Hans Richter. Alek and Klaus were with friends and required no reason for travelling there.

Michael came and joined Ewan at the observation point. He had been back in the car sending and receiving messages.

"My hunch is that this could be a trap to draw us out," Michael said to Ewan.

Ewan turned to him. "Do you really think so.?"

Michael thought for a moment. "I had words with Albert… Eric, I mean. He is the expert. He said it is most unlikely that the Germans have reached a solution just like that.

"The work they did prior to this 'breakthrough' was exhaustive. To go back to it, when there is so much else to do, so many paths to follow, does not really add-up. The more I think about it, the more I'm convinced it's a trap.

"Accordingly we—you and me—are going to investigate the carvings in the chapel. which are reputed to have occult ramifications. You may be aware, or maybe not, that Adolf Hitler is very conscious of the occult. He is a believer and seeks reassurance anywhere it can be found. The so-called worlds of astrology and witchcraft are very real to him. Thus, all suggested locations of centres of the occult are of particular interest. The result is that all the con men and quacks are coming into their own, hoping they will be able to get a piece of the current action: power, money whatever."

Ewan looked at Michael. "You're pulling my leg. Nobody is that daft, to believe all that rubbish. Even if Hitler does, nobody would be stupid enough to try and con Hitler?"

Michael looked at Ewan. "What are we doing?" He said with a grin. "A year isn't it, no... over a year, neared two." He corrected himself. "You can be my assistant."

"Thanks, boss. Just what I need."

"Our job is to get Eric into the labs to take a look at what they are up to. Personally, I will be searching for the trap. Perhaps we can spring it to our advantage."

Ewan was not overcome with the idea of penetrating a place with three platoons of troops on guard. But life was an adventure, wasn't it?

***

Eric carried his bag into the tea rooms in the town centre. Mark Randall was sitting at a table with another man. When he saw Eric he called him over. "Eric, it's been a long time." He turned and said to his companion. "Eric Rohm has been a friend since we were at school together. We are officially rivals, but we both work for companies who serve the third Reich, so competition at this level is pointless."

His companion smiled, held his hand out to Eric and introduced himself, "Karl Weber. I work at the Abbey."

"Interesting," Eric said. "I thought it was a nunnery?"

"Oh, it is still a nunnery. It has just been taken over as a research lab."

"Are you then a researcher?" Eric asked. He called to the waitress for coffee.

"Good lord, no!" Karl Weber said. "I am just one of the admin staff. I keep the books."

"Just as important as anyone else in the labs. We all have our place in things. One without the other is only half of the business."

"Eric was in the Polish campaign and prior to that he was in Spain. He holds the Iron Cross, you know, presented by the Fuhrer himself."

Eric looked uncomfortable. "You need not have said that. Karl will think I have been boasting."

Mark laughed. "Boasting! It was all over our local papers. Why it made the Munchener Zeitung. You were famous at the time."

"Enough of me. I am interested to hear about these nuns." Eric said.

"Well, there are some things which surprise me." Karl tapped his nose knowingly. Both the others leaned forward to hear better. Karl laughed. "I think maybe I will keep that to myself."

"Oh, come on, Karl. Eric has suffered in this war. He could do with a little lift."

Karl shrugged. "Oh, well. Alright." He leaned forward once more and began to speak. "I am not a nosey man but, like you, I was curious about nuns. You know what they all say: no men. What do they get up to? Well, when I went there first, only one month ago, I was all eyes. Now, some of those nuns are real lookers, and, though their habits cover things up, they also reveal." He used his hands to demonstrate a bosom, and patted his bottom suggestively. "I thought it would be amusing to nose around a bit. I discovered that the Commandant of the security here was strict. He would not allow any interference with the nuns, but his men did not get the message. Two have been caught and one castrated, or near enough. The other died. He got his message across, I believe. So you can imagine my surprise when I spotted the Abbess entering a room in the cloisters." He held his hand up to stop the questions from both the others. "I did not mention that the nuns had all been placed in the animal accommodation, the barns at the end of the Abbey. Their rooms had all been taken by the research staff, and the Oberst. There was the abbess entering the room of the Oberst.

"As I passed the room I heard the activity within. That creaking bed was seriously bad news. Well, having heard the story of the two punished soldiers, I was amazed. But then I realised that some of the other rooms also had an active performance going on. Just between you and me, I got the impression that the so-called nuns were window dressing. I am living in a room in town here, so I asked my landlady about the Abbey. Were there many young nuns from the local area. She laughed at me, She said the old cow who ran the place had been struck off the list, or whatever they do to disqualify nuns."

"Unfrock," said Mark.

"Wow, that is a good description for the old cow. She had been renting out the nuns to the local businessmen, telling the novices and young nuns that they were undergoing training to be able to understand the situation of the poor whores and rape victims whom they were expecting to deal with on a daily basis in future."

"But that is like running a brothel."

Karl nodded. "That is why the abbess was, as you say, 'unfrocked'. All the nuns disappeared along with the abbess. Then, one year later, six weeks ago, an abbess appears with a new set of nuns. We are told that they are moved to the cattle sheds, as the research labs are being set up." He giggled. "I have not bought a test tube since I arrived. Bedding, rations, ammunition and furnishings I have purchased, food and drink. But nothing technical whatsoever, and …" He sniggered. "I am sleeping with a nun, young enough to be my daughter."

The door of the tea room opened. He looked and his face paled. "So, gentlemen, I am afraid I cannot help you. We have business hours at the Abbey and office supplies are purchased there." He looked up at the officer standing there. "Oh, Oberleutnant. I did not notice you there. I was just telling these two salesmen that we only make purchases in working hours at the abbey." He rose to his feet. "I must be getting back to the office, Thank you for the tea, madam," he said to the owner.

The officer watched him leave. "Papers, please," looking at the two seated men.

Both produced their papers. He examined them studying each to check the likeness and make sure they were the persons described. "You are here on business, gentlemen?"

"As always these days, Oberleutnant. You are stationed in this area are you? It is unusual to see members of a crack regiment in such a backwater."

"That is none of your business, Herr Richter. How long will you stay here?"

"Off tomorrow, I'm afraid. We do not get much chance to laze around in this business."

"And you, Herr Rohm. Do you also leave tomorrow?" He looked at Eric as he spoke.

Eric shrugged. "I only arrived this afternoon. I will be here for tomorrow and leave the following day."

"You do not like this place?"

"Oh, the place is fine. it is just that there is nothing happening here. No night life, if you know what I mean. It can be boring, especially in the winter."

"I would not take much notice of the man who was with you. He believes he is important, and tends to boast about his place. In fact he is a minor clerk with expensive habits. Good day, gentlemen."

Both sighed with relief when he left the premises.

***

They all gathered together later in the evening. The ladies had been in at the Church Music School, looking at the prospectus and chatting with the Principle. It seemed that the school had been run by the same administration for many years, and had no connections with the abbey whatsoever. The way the Principle talked of the abbey made Sarah ask the question, "What is the story of the abbey? Everyone I have spoken to has avoided the subject."

"The story is not a happy one." She told Sarah the same story that the men had heard.

She said, "It sounds like a badly set trap to me."

"Looks like it. But I would still like a look inside." Eric said.

"I'll see what can be arranged. I think I have an idea to make that possible." Ewan commented.

Sarah said, "But if it is a trap, why take the chance of springing it. Surely, we would be better off leaving it alone, and withdrawing quietly."

"That is an idea, but I have to be sure we are not facing a double bluff. The deliberate setting up of this pathetic trap worries me. While the trap is poor they have used a crack SS unit as security. So we have a mix of good and bad involved here. I am seriously worried that this whole set up was created to deceive us over where they are with their work on the bomb.

"But we do not even know if there is a lab here. Our friend from the tea room said there was no equipment brought for a lab." Mark made the point.

"That makes perfect sense if they are covering things up. That man told us things he should not have been aware of, if anyone was really trying to run a secret lab unit."

They agreed to see what Ewan could come up with.

***

He had a breakthrough with the sight of a well known scientist, who appeared when all of them had apparently left the area.

The man, who was photographed for Eric to look at, was immediately recognized. Eric said, "That man should not be here."

The confirming point came when Mark found a man in Munich, who had been involved in work in the area digging underground shelters beneath the Abbey. The point the man made was that there were already extensive crypts beneath the buildings, sufficient to the point where they were big enough to satisfy the needs of the abbess at the time. There were people waiting for the digging to finish to install water and power to the underground rooms. He was not able to confirm that the places were completed, since he finished his part and had been sent home, but he had no reason to believe that they did not finish.

Given this information it was essential that they either destroyed the place, or got in and discovered how far the Germans had gone with their research.

Chapter Twenty-three

The Raid part 2

The team reached the decision to examine the place further. Mark and Ewan worked out a pattern of surveillance. Based on the assumption that they would not keep the scientists underground all the time, the two men made a careful survey of the grounds area, and then settled down to watch in the most likely places for a concealed exit.

Sure enough, they only had to wait one day before finally, they saw the concealed exit open. A closed van emerged and drove off in the direction of Munich.

Sarah and Michael followed the van until they saw it discharge its passengers in the busy main street of the city. Sarah took photographs of the passengers as they emerged from the van. There were sixteen of them, men and women.

They left the place, parked the car and circulated on foot, finding two of the men and following them. They were making for a small hotel and when they went in they did not come out. Michael followed them in and watched them going upstairs together. He turned to the receptionist. He indicated the stairs. "Those two." He crossed two fingers, raised them and raised an eyebrow.

The receptionist shrugged. Michael reached across the counter and gripped the man's shirt front. He yanked him forward half across the wooden surface. "When I ask a question I expect a reply."

The man was quivering. Michael thought he was on drugs.

"They are regulars I have not watched. But I have been in there with room service. They share the bed."

Michael put him down. "How often do they come?"

"Twice a month,, sometimes three times."

"Do you know where they come from?"

The man sneered, "They think they are clever and don't fill in the form for the Police. I let them think that I have forgotten about it. They come from Regensburg."

"You know this?" Michael said casually.

"They were talking about it, when I went in last."

"They mentioned the place?"

"No they mentioned the choir school and the little boys of the choir."

Michael did not show the distaste he felt at that mention, and of the possibility that the men may be pedophiles, in addition to being homosexual.

He produced the Gestapo credentials. "I have never visited you. You know nothing of me. Oh, I dropped in to check your license."

He left and returned to Sarah. "Did you get the picture going in? She nodded, "Good, we'll wait and get one coming out."

***

They drove back to Regensburg and rejoined the others.

Eric, thought and then spoke, "I think the two men must be Werner Schuss and Nicholas Hertz. Both, talented and both march to a different drum – a polite way of putting it. It is a convenient euphemism when heterosexuals, who do not wish to say the dreaded word, for personal or business reasons talk about the subject.

"With sixteen in the van, I guess the wives are there, part of the underground world they have created for their own convenience."

Ewan said, "I located the base for the troops. They are at least fifteen minutes away. I guess they keep twelve men inside and eighteen outside. They should not need more inside. Outside, I would periodically train and set up surveillance. That was how I would keep the men on their toes. I would also run regular training sessions to teach them self reliance, just in case they lost their officers, of course. But they are not me, and I have seen little to recommend their officers for."

"Do I get the impression that you are not impressed?" Michael sounded amused. "It does mean that we maybe have a few more things in our favour."

"How do we go about it then?. I presume there will be an attack?"

"There certainly will, As soon as I get the weapons sorted, we can get on with it." Mark went off in their van and the others settled down for more surveillance. When he returned there was no sign of the others. He drove around to the entrance of the bunker. Finding the opener was no problem when the entrance could be approached openly. Mark had driven up without attempting to avoid any watchers.

He found the control and pressed it. The flap rose from the ground and a ramp lowered, enabling him to drive the van down into the area below where vehicles were parked.

Uniformed guards stepped out with guns in hand. "Step out with your hands up," the sergeant called.

Mark slid the door open and stepped out,, holding his hands up, with papers in his right hand. "These are my delivery documents." Mark called.

The Sergeant came forward cautiously. "There is no delivery scheduled," the Sergeant said.

Mark looked at him curiously. "Were a bunch of people brought here earlier today? Maybe an hour ago?"

The sergeant lowered his MP3. "Yes. How did you know?"

Mark grinned. "That's what the delivery is for, where are they? Do you know?"

Bewildered, the Sergeant said, "Yes. They are in the holding cell next door. Why?"

"That is why I'm here. If you'll just move them into the back of the van, I will get rid of them for you."

"But you said you had a delivery for us."

"That's correct. I brought the van."

The Sergeant shook his head in exasperation.

Mark said, "Tell me about it. One minute, I'm sitting at the house with a lady ready to tear my clothes off. Next thing, I'm driving a bloody van, to a place I've never seen, to collect people I don't know, to take them to another place I've never heard of. Frustration is another word for Special Service." He shook his head dropped his arms and took the MP3 from the astonished Sergeant.

"Move!"

The Sergeant turned and walked back toward the other two guards." Both had lowered their weapons. Mark called to them, "Just lay the guns down on the counter top. Do not try to use them. I'll blow a hole through the sergeant to get to you both."

He drove them into the office.

"Keys?"

The Sergeant indicated a keyboard.

"Cell?"

The sergeant followed by the two privates went through the door to the right. There was a grilled cell there.

"Unlock it."

The three went into the unlocked cell. The keys were still in the lock. Mark turned the key and withdrew the bunch. He tested the door to make sure it was locked and walked down to the next cell. The group all sat, looking a little down until they saw Mark. He unlocked the door. "The guns are in the back of the van just through the door there. Help yourselves, and come back here. Where is Ewan?"

"They took him through to talk to him," Sarah said.

The others assembled, armed and dangerous. Sarah passed a silenced automatic to Mark. "Do we know how many guards are here?"

"As we thought, only twelve. The Oberleutnant is here. So count thirteen. Three in the cell, ten to go," Mark said.

Sarah nodded, "Good. Lead off, Mark. Let's go and see what this place has to tell us."

He led off through the inner door, opening it cautiously, gun up and ready. There was a corridor ahead and no indication of what was behind each of the doors.

Holding the silenced automatic in front of him, he tried the first door. Turning the handle quietly, he opened it gently, inching it without making a sound. He heard heavy breathing in the room. Peering round the open door he saw a bed with someone asleep. There was a key on the inside of the lock. He quietly removed it and slipped it into the outside keyhole. Then, closing the door, he turned the key and locked it. On the opposite side of the corridor, Sarah shook her head and closed the door. Side by side, they made their way down the corridor opening the doors to a series of empty rooms. All apparently accommodation, as all were furnished and had made-up beds inside, though, apart from the first room, none was occupied. "Eight rooms?" Mark commented, "At least eight people."

The door at the end of the corridor was more substantial. It opened onto a landing with a stairway going down and another going up. Eric, Sarah, and Marian waited while Mark ran up the stairs. At the top was another heavy door, through which was a corridor similar to the one below. Mark opened the first room door. Like below, just accommodations. He looked around the empty room and noticed a cardboard box with framed certificates of qualifications in Physics and Chemistry stacked in it. They were all in the name of Corbin Hyack.

Back with the group, Martin mentioned what he had seen.

Eric knew the name. "He would not be wasted in a diversion, he is an important man in research."

Sarah indicated the down stairway. "Let's go find Ewan."

Mark took the lead once more, and went swiftly down the stairs. The door at the bottom led into a small guard room. The three guards were alert and all grabbed at their guns. Mark did not hesitate. He shot all three. then again, to make sure. The three men sprawled onto the floor, Sarah looked at the diagram on the desk. The rooms of the basement area were all titled.

Eric looked, noting the various labs. "This is the mother lode he said quietly."

Sarah said, "We need to move. The guard is scheduled to change in 35 minutes." She pointed at a roster also on the desk.

Mark looked at the list of rooms. "Management," he said succinctly, "That should be the place. Eric, you and Marian stir things up in the labs. Don't take risks. Sarah, we go direct for Ewan."

Sarah and Eric both nodded, neither disputing the fact that Mark had taken the lead.

Mark held his hand up with three fingers. He folded them one by one. At the third finger Eric pulled open the door. All four ran in making for their targets. Mark and Sarah left the other two and made directly for the Management office. Ewan was seated on a chair, with his hands and ankles bound with what looked like sisal string. He had a bruise on his cheek but apart from that seemed unhurt. The others in the office were startled and froze at Marian's command, "Hands up."

Sarah went around and lifted the weapons from the officer, the sergeant, and the two privates.

She then cut Ewan loose. He took the weapons from her and hung them over his shoulders.

Turning to the civilian in the room he said, "Please give me a reason to shoot you. Where are the other soldiers?"

The man took the warning seriously. He opened his mouth, and the officer said. "Don't you dare tell them."

Ewan smiled. "We'll take you with us."

The man sweated, but then made up his mind. "They are below in the lower bunker, preparing to ship treated material to Peenemunde."

The officer shouted at him. "You are a dead man. I will hunt you down and kill you."

Mark shot him. The silenced automatic made a sort plopping noise. The Oberleutnant dropped dead to the floor.

Ewan said, "Where do we access the lower bunker?"

The manager said, "There is a password. You need it to get in there. The door is over there." He indicated a door in the corner of the lab, visible through the glass of the window between the two rooms.

There were people working in the lab, ignoring what was going on in the office.

Noticing the puzzled look on Sarah's face, the manager said, "Its one way glass we can see them, they cannot see us."

Mark tied the other soldiers and the Sergeant up with string, first removing the tunic from the sergeant. He tried it on. It fitted more or less, as did the small forage cap the sergeant wore. Taking over one of the MP3s, he turned to the manager, and said, "Let us go and relieve the men in the lower bunker."

Together, the pair left the office. Ewan and Sarah watched them walk through the next door lab to the door in the corner. The lab staff ignored them.

The manager knocked at the door and said something into the small box mounted on the door jam. The door opened. The two people went in.

***

The watchers were getting nervous, waiting, until finally the door opened. The manager walked out, followed by five uniformed men, followed in turn by Mark in the sergeant's tunic. The soldiers were all carrying their MP3's, though none made any move toward using them. They entered the office. Ewan relieved the soldiers of their weapons. Eric appeared. "I have some recruits and two prisoners, five people in all. Marion is preparing them for the van."

"Anything else?

"Let us look into the safe," Eric said. "All the findings should be there, placed every night for security."

"Tsk, tsk," Ewan looked at the manager, who was sweating once more,

"You did not ask. I did not know. Please."

"Open the safe."

"Sarah! Go with Mark and remove the people Eric set aside. Marian with you—between you should manage."

The open safe was being emptied by Eric. He took all the papers, a stack of money, and a row of highly machined parts laying in a row on cotton cloth. He bundled all into a bag, slammed the door shut and spun the wheel. "Let's go," he said. The prisoners and the manager led off through the door into the corridor. Marion was waiting by an open cell door. The prisoners went in and Ewan locked the door.

Mark discarded the sergeant's tunic. The entire party boarded the van.

Chapter Twenty-four

Escape & Evasion

On the way back to their base, Ewan called Alek. "We need a place to keep six people out of sight and secure from search parties. They should not be too much trouble. Two are kosher, by the way. Will that be a problem?"

"No, we've handled that sort of merchandise for the bosses in the past. For the moment, take them to the warehouse north of Munich. I'll clear it with the boss, and meet you there.

In the van, Sarah asked Eric, "How many of your people are unwilling?"

Eric grinned. "It sounds odd, but three are willing, not all for the same reason. Two are Jewish. Usual story, families held hostage. They know that they were sent to a place called Ravensbrück, and that people do not leave, once they are taken in. One is sick of his carping wife and sees this as a way out of her clutches. The others all said they enjoyed the research, but knew nothing of the politics of the Nazi party or their methods."

As the van drew up outside the warehouse, Alek appeared in an Opel car. He opened the doors and the van drove in. There was ample room inside, as the Beechcraft took up only the rear part of the building. There was an upper gallery floor, with rooms along one side of the building. It was to that floor the group was headed. The manager from the site was nervous. Ewan said, "Do you have a wife, or anyone else I need to worry about?

The man looked quite shocked for a moment, then said, "I am not married, nor do I have a girlfriend, or boyfriend for that matter. I do have a dog at home, and I do not like to leave him alone."

"Is there anyone you can call?"

"No, but I don't live far from here."

"Let's go." Ewan said. To Sarah he called, "I'll be back in a short while."

He went over to the small car standing by the wall. Alek joined him.

"I heard the conversation. You are now known. I'm not. I'll take him to fetch the dog. Besides, I have the keys."

For a moment, he thought Ewan would argue, but he just shrugged. "Take care," he said and watched the small car leave through the partly-opened front doors.

He walked over to join the others. Sarah looked at him. "Thought you were going out?" "Alek has gone instead. Now, what do we do?"

"Sit tight for the moment. Though I think we should see if the Beechcraft is in working order.

The rear doors of the warehouse were opened to an unobstructed field, big enough for the aircraft to take off and land. They pushed the machine clear of the doors. Ewan climbed in and switched on. The battery was charged and the instrument panel lit up, the needles coming to life. Ewan studied the panel for a few minutes. He called out, "Without starting the engines, I cannot be certain, but it looks to me to be ready to go."

Sarah said, "Will it reach England from here?"

"No. Switzerland we can manage. England or Spain are just too far for this baby, without extra tanks."

"Extra tanks?" Sarah inquired.

"Yes, they are slung under the wings. Once their fuel is used up they can be dropped, discarded."

Sarah left it at that. But they kept the plane at the open doors nonetheless, just in case.

***

Michael had been stuck in Berlin, having gone there to meet Helga Berger. She had news and papers for him. Sarah rang the number he had given her. Karl Curnow, the concierge, at the Adlon answered the telephone. "Herr Gerber? Yes. I will find him for you."

Michael came on to the telephone, and, in carefully chosen words, Sarah managed to convey that the lab had been raided and several scientists had been recovered. All were safe, but transport would be needed.

Michael promised to call the number she gave him, when he had news for her.

***

Alek rang Ewan from the post office in town. He and the manager were clear of the manager's house, with a suitcase and a little dog.

Ewan asked Alek about it. Alek said, "We were just in time. The dog came out, peed on the garden and then we left. As we turned the corner, they were coming to see if there was anyone home."

"You're sure it was our friend they were after?"

"There was no doubt in my mind. There was no hesitation. They drove straight to his house."

Ewan nodded thoughtfully. "You got clear?"

"Absolutely."

"How is our dog lover?"

"Scared shitless."

"Should be happy to take a trip and have chat with us then. I dare say he will have a certain amount of information for our boffins."

Alek said, "Boffins, what is this boffins?"

Ewan laughed. I'll tell you when you get back here. Take it carefully and don't get caught."

Alek put the phone down and noticed there were more police about than normal. He collected the car and his passengers, and put some distance behind them, before turning off and making his way back to the airfield.

***

Klaus rang from the safe house. "I am on my way now. I have cleared the place up. Done my best anyway. I'll join you soon. Oopse! Visitors. Must run." The phone was dropped and the sound of gunfire could be heard. The phone was lifted. "On my way!" The voice was Klaus's. The phone went down, and the buzz of the disconnected line could be heard.

***

The session in the warehouse did not take long. The entire crew was there, apart from Michael and Klaus. The manager, Gunter, and the group from the lab were seated in the Beechcraft. They did not need rocket science to guess that the searchers were going to be calling soon. They had to split-up fast.

Eric, Mark, Marian and Alek left in Alek's Opal. Sarah and Ewan waited with the aircraft for the call from Michael. It was full dark by the time Michael called.

"On the chart near St Etienne, a place called Montbrison, there is a private airfield. It's in Vichy, so-called Free France. The contact name is 'Canard'. Squawk twice. He manages the place and should be able to fill your tanks. There is another just outside Biarritz. It is probably near enough to reach friends in Portugal. If in doubt get into Switzerland and dump the plane. There are friends there, but enemies also. Good luck. See you in London."

Nothing was said of the party in the Opal. They would disappear and make contact in the usual way with London.

***

Klaus did not make it out of the safe house alive. He killed four of the SS men and two Gestapo. The Gestapo made the mistake of approaching him as he lay, fatally wounded, on the floor of the lobby in the little house.

The booby traps, rigged for just such an emergency, had been activated when the front door was smashed. Klaus was lying on the pressure plate on his side, holding it down with the weight of his body. The two black-clad Gestapo men approached. The smaller of the two hooked his foot under the body. "Let's see if we know him." With a laugh he rolled Klaus over onto his back. Klaus smiled at them as the pressure pale was released. The bomb was not huge, but it set off the other charges in the house. Everyone in the lobby, including Klaus, was obliterated. The other charges brought the rest of the house down, taking the search teams with it. Thirteen dead, and four seriously injured. Klaus would have been proud.

***

The Beechcraft managed the refueling at St Etienne, in the early hours of the morning. They hid the aircraft in the hanger during the day and departed at midnight for Biarritz. Keeping at low altitude once they were through the mountains, they made it to the grass airfield outside Biarritz before true dawn.

Their final flight got them to Porto, on fumes.

***

For the other group, there was mixed fortunes. The journey north from Munich was split at Nurnberg: Eric and Marian heading for Frankfurt, and Mark and Alek for Berlin.

Alek found another car for Mark and himself, while Eric and Marian continued with the Opal to the Frankfurt safe house.

Mark and Alek made good time on their way to Berlin until the owner of the car they were driving reported it stolen. A police car took off after them in Bamberg. They managed to evade it.

Alek admitted he had stolen the car.

The next stolen car was taken from a closed garage beside a vacant house, and had been that way for a long time. It was owned by a senior official in the Nazi party. As Alek pointed out, he was being chauffeured everywhere he went. Since the driver he used was accustomed to providing all the services his employer may ever need, there was little likelihood of the car being missed for the foreseeable future.

Mark accepted this reasoning, but insisted on having the number plate changed, despite the protestations from Alek that the number was a privileged one which could smooth the way wherever they went.

They made contact with Michael in Berlin, and were told to lay low for the next few days.

***

In their new quarters, Alek served up coffee and said, "How would you like a little entertainment this evening. I have a friend who has several chums who enjoy a party. It would cheer you up."

"I really do not need cheering up," Mark replied. "But do not let me stop you. I can go out and give you the use of the house for the evening."

Alek thought about it."Good. I will take you up on that offer. How about, you don't come back until midnight."

Mark thought about it, then nodded. "Midnight or after, fine. Don't wait up." Mark rose to his feet and picked up his coat and left.

Alek grabbed the telephone and got to work.

***

For Mark there was no problem. He stopped a taxi and was taken to the Adlon. There, Karl Curnow, the concierge, was able to fix him up with a seat at the ballet. The payment was to escort a protégée of Karl's. He was assured that she was respectable and would expect to be taken to dinner after the performance.

Taken aback, but intrigued at the same time, Mark agreed. He was given a room key for a room held by Michael for emergencies. "You will find a case with evening wear suitable for the occasion. It belongs to someone of your size, I believe. I will send a valet up to press the clothes."

"But you do not even know me?" Mark said hesitantly.

Curnow smiled. "Friend of Herr Gerber. I believe. That is good enough for me."

The astonished Mark left, key in hand, for his room, where he was met by a valet who unpacked the suitcase there and took the evening dress and shirt away. Mark took one look at the bathroom, happily stripped off and stepped into the bath.

Dried, and in the dressing gown provided, he was sipping the glass of schnapps he had poured when the valet returned with his clothes for the evening.

"If I may suggest, sir, I can attend to your day clothes while you are out and have them ready for you when you depart?"

"That would be excellent," Mark replied, and emptied his pockets into the dresser drawer, before allowing the valet to take his crumpled suit and other clothes away.

He was expected to meet his partner for the evening in the lobby at six forty-five. So, shaved and dressed, he was there in place by six forty. Karl Curnow indicated a woman who had her back to them, standing just inside the front doors. "Her name is Margarethe Froelich, and she is Austrian."

"Herr Curnow, I know the lady, and she knows me as Hans Richter."

Kurt looked at him shrewdly. "Then I know who you are, and I am reassured that you will look after my niece. Enjoy your evening". He passed over the tickets for the ballet, and the table booking for later. Then he watched as Mark walked over and greeted Margarethe. He saw the way she greeted Mark and, satisfied, he turned to deal with another matter requiring his attention.

***

Kurt Albert Curnow had gained his position as concierge of the most exclusive hotel in Berlin despite the competition of a formidable number of other worthy contenders. His Austrian background was both a recommendation and a disadvantage at the same time. In the end, it was because of the in-fighting of the Berlin applicants that he managed to enter by the back door. Having been engaged on a temporary basis while a selection process was being undertaken, he had managed to impress the management by his commitment to the position and his undoubted talent for this most exacting of jobs.

An element of luck had come into things when an attempt had been made to abduct one of the guests, a personal friend of the general manager. His recognition of the driver of the limousine which came to collect the guest, or rather his non-recognition of the driver, who had been nominated to drive the lady, led to his alerting of the Hotel Security Manager, who, though wounded in the ensuing shoot-out, prevented the kidnap. It brought recognition to the security manager and to the concierge, both of whom were assured of their posts from that time onward. For Kurt, the Nazi party confirmed his opinion that, unfortunately, scum always seems to rise to the top. Whilst he was a confirmed patriot, his innate sense of right and wrong had rapidly placed the people he had to deal with in the category of like and dislike. The death of his pregnant wife ensured that for him. The Nazi party was scum, and deserved to be exterminated. Otherwise, those he liked were good. the people he disliked were bad. This simplistic code was followed by his friend the security manager also. In this capacity the Abwehr he accepted, the Gestapo he hated. Cooperation with people like Ewan, Michael and now Mark, went without saying.

Chapter Twenty-five

Interlude

For the fifth time Heinrich Stolle attempted to concentrate on the papers in front of him. It was never easy for him to immerse himself in paperwork in the way the Admiral did. He envied his boss's ability to just sit down and concentrate. The work just seemed to melt away for him. On Stolle's desk it multiplied.

Edith came through, and sat on the chair beside his desk. "It is time to go home, Heinrich."

Stolle looked up. Edith never referred to him by his first name in the office. He looked at the door to the outer office. Edith nodded and pantomimed 'Gestapo'.

Stolle got to his feet and silently walked to the door. He grasped the handle and slammed the door shut. He said loudly, "That damned door lets in the draught, Edith. We really should have something done about it. Hang on. We did get it fixed some fool has left the front door open. He wrenched open the office door and was faced with a man with a bloody nose, standing between the office and the open front door.

He thrust the man aside and walked to the front door and slammed it shut. The sound of the door slamming brought a stranger out of the Admiral's office. Papers in hand, he stood looking down the barrel of Stolle's pistol. "Come all the way out. Place the papers on the table. Then raise your hands in the air. The man at his own office door started to speak, then shut up as he felt a gun at his neck.

Edith said quietly, "Place your gun on the desk beside you, and take a pace forward." The man did so.

Stolle concentrated on the office of the Admiral. "Anyone else we should worry about?" He asked quietly. "The wrong answer will undoubtedly be fatal."

The man in front of him shook his head.

"Step back into the office."

The man turned and re-entered the Admiral's office.

"Edith, bring the other intruder here please." Stolle was icy calm.

Edith and the other man entered. Edith was now carrying the other man's gun.

"Your weapon. Out. With two fingers only. Place it on the desk on this side."

The man did so, saying, "You are making a big mistake. You will be sorry."

"I am deciding whether to shoot you out of hand as burglars. I strongly advise you to keep your mouth shut until I tell you to speak. Do you understand?"

The man said "I …Oh…." The shot was not as loud as Edith thought it would be, but it caused the man to grab his leg and drop to the floor.

"Do you hear what I am saying, now?" Stolle said clearly. "Nod, if you understand me!"

The man nodded still clutching his leg from which blood was leaking.

Edith pushed the other man over to his wounded partner. She took the first aid box down and, without a word, passed it to the man to attend to his friend.

"Why are you here?"

As the man opened his mouth, Stolle said. "Remember! Answer the question nothing else, why are you here?"

"I was ordered to examine the papers I would find in this office."

"Are you aware of whose office this is?"

"Admiral Canaris, I believe."

"Do you know who he is."

"Head of the Abwehr, I believe"

"Did you think you would get away with it?"

"Before I realised that I had been partnered with a complete idiot, I did. yes."

Stolle turned to the man with the bloody nose. "What's your excuse?"

"Orders," she said sullenly.

"You are contractors, I presume. Who employed you?"

"I do not really know. You know what it is like. A phone call, a drop, with an address and the job, and a drop-off for the result."

"And what happens if you are caught?"

"Dumped, I suppose. It has not happened before. Mind you, I had a sensible partner then."

The other man broke-in then. "I thought it would be easy. With just the woman there, she wouldn't be any trouble. We knew the boss was away."

His partner hit him round the face. "Working with trash. That's what I said. Trash."

"What were you told to look for? Same rules!" The gun was up again.

"Anything at all. Specifically, correspondence with other senior officers, Admirals, Generals, details of plots, anything to do with a plot to depose of the Furhrer."

"Edith, have you made the call?"

"Yes, sir. A few minutes only."

"Meet him!" Stolle sounded serious.

Edith left the room. The three men stood looking at each other.

In the outer office, there was the sound of voices. Then the door opened and an SS officer entered. He lifted his pistol to shoot Stolle. Edith shot him in the head. He dropped with his gun unfired.

Stolle turned his gun on the idiot and shot him between the eyes. "He shot the SS man. Did you see?"

The other man nodded. "He was mad, lost his head. I tried to stop him. He shot me in the leg."

"Come in, Edith. Give me your gun."

She passed over the weapon. "It's his gun," she said, "It's the gun he was carrying when he came in."

"Good," Stolle said, putting the gun in the hands of the dead man with the bloody nose.

The outer door opened and the Admiral came in. "Been busy while I was away? I do not altogether like having bodies all over the place." He sat down in his office chair. "Edith, Could you empty the pockets of these men, and then call the cleaners."

He turned to Stolle. "Anything you couldn't handle?" Stolle shook his head. "Good. Leave a gun and leave this man with me. You think he might be worth saving?"

Stolle thought for a moment, then nodded as he left the office.

Three men came with a big laundry basket. Both bodies fitted in quite well. The carpet was lifted and replaced with another. Then the men left.

With the injured man securely in the hands of the doctor, the Admiral, now seated at his desk said, "There have been attempts to unseat me ever since I gained this job. Gruppenfuhrer Schumann of the SS was being groomed for this job before someone removed him from the list. I have no doubt someone else will be already selected. It is a fact of life in this job. I am an old man. I have had my day, I suppose. What you must be sure of is that you have a back door to escape through. Of course, I expect you to take Edith with you. I know it is rumoured that she has been my mistress. Well, that is all it is, a rumour!" He looked at Stolle keenly. "I have watched your progress in this office since you first arrived. I do not want change, but, when I think the time is right, I will have you transferred out of here to a more secure position. If I misjudge things, then please take seriously my instruction about a back door.

"Now who killed the Gruppenfuhrer?" Once again all business, he opened a file on his desk and said, "Do you think it might have been our team of British agents?"

Stolle smiled thoughtfully, "It is an intriguing notion. I wonder if they realise that they were actually doing this department a favour?"

"That is what I like about you, Heinrich. You have the knack of seeing the entire picture rather than only what is immediately in front of your nose."

"It does presume that there is someone operating in Berlin once more."

"It crossed my mind, and why not? This is the centre of a great deal of activity."

Stolle interjected, "There must be several of them. That attack at Regensburg was not the work of amateurs, or partisans. Let's not deceive ourselves. Planning on that scale was not the work of a bunch of yokels. This team has been around, and evaded capture, for what…two, perhaps even three years now? All must speak German like natives, and all seem to have the acting ability to be whoever they need to be."

Canaris looked at his deputy with a rueful smile. "Do you know? I believe you admire these people."

Stolle said, "Probably as much as you do, sir. Further, I wish they were working for me!"

Canaris shrugged. "You are right on both counts. I also would be happy to have them working for me."

***

Mark Randall, as Hans Richter, was enjoying his evening out with Margarethe. Her training in England had prepared her for the task of entering the night life of Berlin.

As a member of the von Lutzlow family, she slipped into her role of titled aristocrat, diffidently, as the daughter of Captain von Lutzlow of Austrian nobility. The Captain had photographs and would proudly talk of his daughter in Berlin, to anyone who would listen. Thus Margarethe had a provenance acceptable to the Berlin glitterati.

The link with Curnow was explained to Mark as the evening progressed. He was a friend of the family as long as she could remember. His home was in the same village. A contact of value to both of them. His acceptance of her current role fitted his criteria.

The natural worry which Mark felt working with Margarethe over the next weeks was gradually lessened by her professionalism. Their feelings for each other had not abated, but both held back because of the work they were doing gathering intelligence. The entry of USA into the war came and the door closed on the US embassy. The Christmas festivities were, apparently, more important than minor things like making an enemy of the most powerful country in the world. The occasions, when the pair of them were most at hazard, were when they would undertake an excursion into the country to meet unknown contacts. The trip to Charlottenberg had been uneventful, but the need to carry on toward Stendal entailed risk, because they would have to by-pass roadblocks on the way. They made it to the rendezvous early, having managed to miss the checkpoints with a combination of luck and geography.

***

At the meeting place, the two agents carried out a careful survey of the immediate area. Luckily, there was little open ground to cover. The woods around there tended to be open woodland rather than the dense forest elsewhere. Satisfied, that they were not observed, they settled down to wait.

The contact turned up, late, but not too late. He was based in Stendal and had news of the movements of rail traffic to the Baltic. Mark went to the contact's car with him to collect maps and copies of delivery schedules. While they were there, Margarethe wandered into the woods to relieve herself. There she saw the ambush being set up. She quietly made her way to their car which was on the opposite side of the road to the meeting place.

She flashed the headlights once. The car was facing the car of the contact. The signal was seen and Mark grabbed the papers from the contact. "Run! Get out of here! Ambush!" That got through. The man dove into his car to get away. Mark ran across the road and jumped in to his own moving car, with Margarethe at the wheel.

Down the road and out of range, they stopped to change places. The contact was long gone, away ahead of them. They turned off and made their way round by side roads back to the Berlin road. A car appeared behind them. They stopped in at a local café, where they drank chocolate. The car which had been following them also stopped and waited a short distance down the road, out of sight of the cafe. There were two people in the car, a Mercedes, a car that could have overtaken them at any point on the road.

Mark said, "We have a problem. Those people are following us. They would not sit out there otherwise. I am afraid we will have to dispose of them."

Margarethe nodded, "If we must. I will go out of the front door and distract them. I presume you can go out the back and come up behind them."

Mark smiled, "You can read my mind."

"Of course I can. I thought you knew that from the very beginning."

Mark kissed her and grinned, then he left through the rear door of the café. Margarethe rose and strolled out of the café toward the road into view of the car. Then she changed direction and stopped to stretch. Her blouse strained as she raised her arms, outlining her breasts. The two men in the car, parked and sheltered by the woodland along the road, both leaned forward to enjoy the view. As she relaxed she saw Mark approaching the rear of the car, gun in hand. She also noticed a third man in the trees near the car, creeping over behind Mark. There was a gun in his hand. Margarethe left the men in the car to Mark and, out of sight of the road, took out her own gun. The man behind Mark was concentrating on remaining quiet as he stalked his quarry. She was behind his eye-line, so she took a chance and ran to close the range. Time seemed to stretch as she stopped. Taking a deep breath she leaned against a tree, raised her gun the way she had been trained, squeezing the trigger as the gun came level, she experienced the shock of the noise as the gun fired. The man creeping up on Mark flinched. She fired a second time. The man's body twitched. He folded over and hit the ground without a sound. The woodland noises all around stopped at the shocking sound of the shot.

In the stunned silence that ensued following the shots, Mark quickly leaned into the car and shot the startled driver and his companion. Then, putting his gun away, he looked around and saw the body of the third man for the first time. He walked over to Margarethe, who was standing, stunned at the fact that she had just killed a man. Mark took her hand and held her close, "You just saved my life," he whispered. "Thank you."

They stood for a few moments. The woods around them came back to life. There was no frenzy of activity from the café or elsewhere, so they strolled to their car and drove off. Either, the folk in the café did not notice the shooting, or they did not want to know what was happening outside.

The entire episode was over in minutes. Margarethe sat silent and Mark allowed her to process the event in her own mind. He drove rapidly without comment. Eventually, Margarethe stirred and said, "Is it always like this?"

Mark thought for a moment. "I think it is different for everyone. For me, I work out if it could have been avoided. What would have happened if I had not killed? In simple terms, the easy answer is: did I save my own life or the life of my colleague, or friend? Sometimes I decide that they deserve to die because of acts they have performed. Every time, for me, is different. In a case like today, it was them or us. Kill or be killed. We are not in a position to take prisoners, nor do we take chances and wound them. It may disable them today, but they will still be a threat in the future."

He drove on in silence. Finally, he felt her relax. She rested her head on his shoulder, and dropped off into a restless sleep. Darkness fell and Mark drove on.

Chapter Twenty-six

Kill The train

Michael had established a new safe house in Potsdam. It was nothing special to look at, and was in a position where people were coming and going all the time. Living in Germany was becoming more difficult for all the ordinary people. Rationing had been established and the black market was now very much a part of the local economy. Of course, for some there was little difference. In the Adlon hotel things could be obtained as they always had been. They cost more, but so what. It's only money. Power was the real currency. If you had power, people performed for you. A baroness would invite you to her bed, if the price was right. The Luftwaffe officers on leave found easy pickings among the womenfolk of the upper echelon of the government. The women involved excused themselves by claiming they were doing their duty for the brave boys who kept the skies clear over Europe.

Michael was entertaining Helga Berger. It meant staying in Berlin, so he had a room in the Adlon Hotel. This was to save travelling to Potsdam in the late evening, and provided a private meeting place for Helga, without divulging his safe house address. It also gave him a chance to contact Kurt Curnow, to debrief him and find out what was happening from his viewpoint.

Kurt's life was surprisingly easy, his wife having been one of the casualties of the early days of the party.

She had had the misfortune to be pretty and pregnant, on a night when the Brownshirts were prowling. Her end was neither pretty nor painless. Though she was not a Jew, it was convenient that it was dark. For the Brownshirts, a woman was a woman.

Though he was dealing with murderers on a daily basis because of his position, he was beneath their radar. By cooperating with the mob, and with people he suspected were enemy agents, he was working against his wife's murderers. In addition, on several occasions he had been in a position to dispatch drunken party members. The skinning knife he plied had become a well-used weapon. It gave him some satisfaction to actually contribute to the war effort in such a direct manner. Entertaining Michael in his apartment, he told the story of his wife. "So you see, Carl. My attitude is never going to be politically correct. I hate the bastards and use every opportunity to get revenge in whichever way I can. I realise you are not who you say you are. I have known it since we first met."

Michael went to get up, but Curnow waved him back to his seat. "My position entitled me to this apartment, within the hotel. There has been an attempt early on to create a garden. The building on the flat roof area of the hotel is surrounded by the peaks of the roofs around it, thus the project failed. The service elevator had been installed at the time, with the garden in mind, to serve this rooftop building. The building was turned into an apartment for the General Manager's mistress. His wife had soon put a stop to that. When I took over the job as concierge, it was reinstated and tidied up. It was decided I should remain on the premises. I have my own housemaid to clean the place and look after my clothes. She is not a live-in servant, though, if truth be told, I believe she would like to be."

Michael smiled, "You do have a very pleasant life style, I must say. I have the impression it is not difficult to find the occasional bed-mate in this pied a terre of yours?"

"In fact, my apartment is visited whenever I feel the need. Women come and look after me and provide information that I occasionally feed to the Abwehr, and, sometimes, to people like you. The object is to hurt the Party in any way possible.

"When I sleep with some senior party member's bit on the side, sometimes his wife, it is deliberate. It gives me a certain amount of control over them, if you know what I mean."

Michael looked at the man standing in front him, maybe an inch shorter than himself, sandy hair, well controlled. Well dressed and groomed. Neither handsome nor ugly; a normal face with a friendly smile, with a hard slender body. He spoke, "As you are aware, I share your hatred of the Nazi party. The control which everyone once welcomed has now become a burden for the people who allowed it. In my own way, I do all I can to destabilize the entire setup. Any information you are able to give me go's to a good cause."

As Michael descended in the service elevator, he was careful to check in the corridor that there were no people loitering there before he pushed through the swing doors and walked along to his own room door.

***

Back in his own room he undid the package he had been given as he left the apartment on the roof. The contents were a mix of information, the most important being a schedule of movements by rail of materials required for the production of rockets. The significant element being references to a V2 rocket, a weapon of unknown designation so far.

Though still under development the V1 Flying bomb was already known about, though it's capabilities were still being assessed.

"What was a V2?" Michael asked himself the question. He put the schedules to one side and examined the other papers. The second report he uncovered answered the question. The V2 project was for a rocket that was capable of leaving the atmosphere and entering space giving it a range of over 500 miles, perhaps further. That could mean an intercontinental weapon a rocket that could maybe carry a warhead to Washington?

Michael realised that this was news that could not wait. The fact was he might have to take this news himself. Even if Helga were still able to travel to USA the level of this information was far too high to be trusted to a courier who may or may not pass the information to the Abwehr.

The source of the information was a scientist in the establishment of Peenemunde. A conversation overheard in a reception in Berlin had mentioned the V2 and a Doctor Wernher von Braun, a German scientist known to be involved in space rocket research, apparently in the Peenemunde research establishment. A third reference to von Braun was noted on another note in the documents. It was a copy of a transit order for house-hold effects to Rugen, in the name of Wernher von Braun.

Michael decided that there was sufficient information to make its transmission to London priority. In the meantime, he picked up the telephone and rang Mark's room. He made a note of the details of the rail movement on a separate sheet of paper.

Mark answered.

"Reichstag, 30 minutes." Michaele said and replaced the telephone.

Mark thought to himself, *Thursday. It will be Scheidmanstrasse entrance to Tiergarten.*

Each day there was a different meeting point in the Tiergarten.

He left the hotel and turned left along Unter den Linden to the Tiergarten. When he reached the gardens he turned right towards the Reichstag. As he reached the corner where Scheidmanstrasse entered the gardens, he stopped and put his foot on the low fence rail and retied his shoelace, he felt the close pass of another walker, and when he stood up he let his hand brush against his side pocket. He was aware of the crackle of paper. He continued along the footpath into the Gardens, then turned back toward Unter den Linden on the next walkway and strolled back to the hotel.

In his room he opened the note Michael had passed to him in the park.

There was a rail time and date with start date and time and destination. The instruction was: 'destroy the train before it reaches Peenemunde. M'

The schedule gave him four days to prepare.

Ewan had just arrived back in Berlin. Sarah should be back later in the week. It did mean that the entire team, now including Eric Rohm, excluding only Michael, would be available.

Mark set up a meet with Ewan. "You see, we only have three more days to arrange things." he finished.

Ewan thought about what he had been told. "We will need enough explosive to mine the train from end to end."

"Why?" Mark asked.

"Nothing useable must be left." Ewan said impatiently.

"But three of the carriages are going to be fuel tanks," Mark said. "Surely they will help the destruction anyway."

"I missed that," Ewan apologized. "Yes, of course. They will make an incredible bang. Ideally, we could do with a high bridge."

"Well, I believe we will be out of luck for bridge as such. But there is a causeway, and/or a tunnel."

The timetable for the line from Dresden to Greifswald for Peenemunde would allow for several breaks in service to let the saboteurs to work undisturbed.

"There would be enough time, provided we pre-packaged the explosives. A series for the tunnel roof, plus a second series for the rails. Hopefully an additional set for the trucks themselves, if we could get close enough to the train to hook them on. Mark concluded.

***

Alek used the car to run the roads nearest to the line to see if there was somewhere to destroy the train while it was in motion. There were places where the road paralleled the track, but not really suitable unless the train was stopped. Ideally, an air raid warning would cause the train to seek shelter in the tunnel. It would stop in those conditions. The problem was, time was against the team.

Ewan had everyone in the team working on the explosive packets. The roof sets all had hooks taped to them and were fewest in number. The track charges were heavier and were to be hidden in the ballast. They would be the first to blow, followed by the roof charges. Finally the truck charges, which, when combined with the fuel on the train, hopefully, would complete the destruction of the entire train and tunnel.

He looked ruefully at the pile of packages, wondering if they would manage to get them to the train on time, hating the hurried nature of the entire scheme.

A call came as the team was completing the work. The last set of track charges were being loaded in the vehicle they had acquired for the transport of the charges.

Ewan answered the telephone. "Alek, here. The timetable has altered. Track repair in Dresden marshalling yards has delayed departure, until the weekend. We have three days."

Ewan said, "How about the manual trolley?"

"It is with the overalls and tools in the service hut at the tunnel. I will meet you there, with two extra team members."

Ewan put the phone down. "Update: team ladies, drive the car to the rendezvous. Mark, drive your truck to the north end of the tunnel. I will drive the other to the south end. I will obtain the repair trolley and tools, and run the rail string of charges through for Eric and Alek to bury. The two extra men will be dressed in uniform as guards. Eric will be in charge of them. Once the track charges are laid, we will let the scheduled passenger train through. We then have a one-hour delay until the next is due. That is when we'll hang the roof charges.

"The worker signals will be at the southern entry to the tunnel. It will not stop the train but it should slow it down to a walking pace at best, a trot at worst. We will attach as many of the truck charges as we can. Mark will be at the northern end. As soon as the engine reaches the 20 metre mark. He will blow the track charges. Everyone should be out of the tunnel within 30 seconds of the guard van entering the tunnel. Otherwise…!" He shrugged.

"How about the guards on the train?" Marian asked.

Ewan smiled grimly. "The platoon of guards will be installed in a carriage, midway along the train, in front of the fuel trucks. There is a footway along the side of the tanks. Remember, these are not standard rail tanker trucks. These are low-loader flatbeds with wheeled, tanker trailers strapped to them. They are shipped that way, so that they can be towed from the train to whatever location they are needed." He smiled grimly. "The officers will be in the guards' van, which has a kitchen and bunks. Whatever else we do, it is essential that we dispose of the guards' van."

He looked around the group, Mark, Eric, Sarah, and Marian. He was in charge of this operation, but only for this occasion. Each of the people in front of him had taken the lead in other circumstances. "This could be the last time we are together like this. It has to be the most crack-brained operation we have been involved with. If we are going to succeed, it will be because of us. I have never worked with a better team to trust my life to." He looked and felt embarrassed saying it, but he meant every word.

The others shuffled and smiled. Mark said, "I think a small libation is indicated."

He took the bottle of scotch from the sideboard, and started pouring. Then they lifted their glasses, "To us all. 'The Team!'"

***

Ewan crouched by the track, his hand on the rail checking that the scheduled train was not about to arrive. He knew he would feel the vibrations of an approaching train, transmitted by the rails themselves. The servicing trolley was standing alongside the track ready to be lifted on so that they could run through the tunnel once the train was past. Margarethe had been roped in to drive the car, waiting to dash up the road to warn them that the target train was coming.

The scheduled passenger train arrived, and slowed down to pass through the tunnel. Ewan stood and waited. Dressed in the railway overalls, he was like a familiar piece of furniture, just part of the scenery beside the track, being highlighted by the flickering light from the windows of the train as it passed. The guard leaned out and shouted 'goodnight', as he entered the black cavernous mouth of the tunnel. Ewan waved and shouted a rude remark, as the red tail lamp of the train disappeared around the long bend in the tunnel.

"Right! let's get this thing on the track," he shouted and took his end of the trolley.

They started pumping the bars on the manual drive of the trolley. Alek ran alongside dropping off the charges at intervals as they progressed. At the northern end Eric joined Alek. They walked back down the tunnel with a lamp and shovels to cover the charges and to make sure the wires were still attached.

Meanwhile, Ewan and Mark mounted the platform on the trolley. It was needed, as the roof of the tunnel was too high for them to reach otherwise. At fifty metre intervals they screwed hooks in the roof, between the bricks. The wire, connecting the charges, was pulled as tight as possible so that it did not droop to get caught by the funnel of the train. They finished ahead of the walkers, and were waiting for them when Margarethe arrived with the news that the train was stopped, down the track.

"They are clearing an obstacle from the line, it seems a bomb fell and is buried where it might go off if the train passes. "

Eric and Alek appeared as Margarethe passed on the message. Ewan turned to Eric. He handed him the detonating box. "You know what to do. Connect the wires and twist the lever. Boom. We'll meet back at the house. Margarethe. Down the road. Keep your eyes open. Alek, Mark. Trolley on the track with the charges, please. Let's go and offer our assistance." The three men looked at each other and grinned.

***

They came to the train standing on the track, hissing, as it awaited the bomb disposal team to arrive from Dresden. The three agents, all in overalls, each carrying a bag and tools, walked down the side of the train, checking the trucks as they went. On each of the trucks they selected they placed a charge with the fuse, set at fifteen minutes. There were only ten charges for the eighteen trucks, but nine were placed on the trucks and the passenger carriage, the other on the second fuel truck. A small radio transmitter sent the signal and all the fifteen fuzes started counting down. The workmen returned to their trolley and started toiling back up the track, as the bomb disposal people arrived.

They were lifting the trolley off the track when the bomb apparently went off. The fifteen minutes were up by now and the truck charges went off, blasting the train and its contents. The fuel trucks both created a holocaust which enveloped the guards van and spread rapidly along the shattered carriage with the soldiers still within, trapped and screaming as they died. Those standing beside the train fared little better. The blast and the explosion of the high octane fuel, reacting with the liquid oxygen in the adjacent tank made a horrific circle of destruction and death.

Margarethe stopped on the road, and had turned the car to go back to the tunnel. She did not wait, but drove off as the unexploded bomb went off, so she did not see the destruction she left behind. But she heard it.

***

At the house, when all of those involved had returned, Michael turned up to congratulate them on a successful operation.

Ewan commented, "Like all planned operations, our plans did not survive beyond the first moves. Thank goodness plan B succeeded."

"Did we have plan B?" Mark asked.

"Plan B was to act according to the circumstances at the time," Ewan said blandly.

"So there was no plan B!" Sarah said with a grin.

Ewan shrugged his shoulders. "It turned out all right. We even managed to blow up the tunnel without the train inside.

***

The Office of the SD (Sicherheitsdienst), the security branch of the SS, was the civilian branch of the Intelligence service. The head of the SD, Obergruppenfuhrer Reinhard Heydrich, had been angling to take over the Abwehr, and all other intelligence operations since the early nineteen thirties. Up to now, things had been gradually moving his way, but his assassination in June 1942 had caused problems. He had not been replaced until Ernst Kaltenbrunner took over in January 1943. In the meantime, the office was in turmoil over the disastrous sabotage of the train north of Dresden. The main reason being, that the movement of the materials from Dresden to Peenemunde had been secret, and the secret had got out. There was a brief period when it was believed that it was a sneak bombing raid, but it was soon realised that such a raid would have been reported, and the signs at the scene indicated sabotage. The hunt was on for a group of men wearing rail maintenance overalls. Meanwhile, all rail traffic had to be diverted away from the direct line north, due to the complete collapse of the tunnel.

***

"The team," Michael reflected, "has thus far, borne a charmed life. Accepting the professionalism of you all, the element of luck must be taken into account for our survival. The loss of Klaus in the Regensburg operation was unfortunate and was the result of a lucky break on the side of the enemy."

They were all seated about the biggest room in the house in Potsdam. "You may be interested in the fact that you are all returning to London. Our role has been usurped by the operations set up by SOE and OSS. We, therefore, are now officially regarded as an embarrassment. In the words of Wild Bill Donovan, we are a 'loose cannon', choosing targets of opportunity, instead of following a directed program of activities, dictated by our lords and masters, as of now known as our 'betters'." He raised his hands at the chorus of protest rising from his assembled bunch of killers.

The latest addition to the group, Margarethe Froelich raised her hand. The others turned to see what she had to say. "When I was finishing training, the SOE agents were part-way through their own training course. Many of the things we learned were the same. I was offered the opportunity to join the SOE. I declined the offer as I was already committed to joining this collection of freebooters." This comment brought a murmur of approval. She continued, "One other reason I did not wish to join them was although they were using information from all sources, just as we do, the difference is they are working to a budget. When I was leaving, they had arranged to send out agents to three different destinations on the same aircraft. Apparently, the aircraft made it back safely. But what worries me, was the message we received, to look out for news of two captured agents in the area between Nancy and Liege.

"We, in the HQ, knew of the drop. So did all three of the dispatch teams. Instead of the individual team members being known to just one team, suddenly there were other team members who knew the secrets of all three agents.

"I guess, almost as soon as they landed, two of the agents were picked up by the SD."

She sat down, flushed and embarrassed, but her message was clear.

Michael took the floor once more. "I was aware of the information just divulged by Margarethe. I thought it better coming from her, than from me. I think you all have the message. Now, this is what I propose. First, Alek, if you wish to come with us to London you will be welcome as a part of our team. Otherwise, you may remain here to act as a focus for us when we return."

Alek smiled, "With everything going on the way Margarethe described, I believe I would be better remaining. I intend recruiting another partner and training him properly. Also, using the boss's resources, I am in a unique position. I am also flattered to be regarded as a member of this group. You say you will be returning. Then it is even more important that you have a team member here to make arrangements on the spot. I will have the radio for regular communication with you in London. In the meanwhile, I think in the interest of all, that I should not know how you plan to return to London, in case I am taken before you actually leave. However!" He held his hand up to stop interruptions. "If there is something to be done before you leave, I expect to play a part in it." He sat down once more.

Ewan broke in at that point, "Michael, as Alek puts it so aptly, you obviously have some parting task in mind. Let us discuss it in the morning. We have a lot to think about already."

There was a moments' pause, as they all looked at Michael expectantly. "Let's have a drink!" He said with a grin. "I feel the need to relax."

Chapter Twenty-seven

Prison break

The discussion started over breakfast. Edith had been thinking overnight about the capture of the two SOE agents, currently suffering interrogation by the SD. The capture of the people had been largely luck: good for the SD, bad for the SOE. She had been wondering about the third agent who had been part of the same drop.

Stolle looked at Edith fondly. Their relationship had been strengthened as they got to know each other better. "You believe that they are unaware as yet, of the third agent?"

"I am only guessing, but I cannot get over the fact that the plane did not turn back when it dropped the second agent. It actually turned north-east, and eventually crossed the North Sea having passed over the Netherlands. I cannot believe that it took such a dangerous route without real purpose"

"So you believe that there is another SOE agent between Liege and Arnhem?"

"That aircraft landed somewhere in that region. I suspect it to be nearer Liege than Arnhem. I think the aircraft would continue north to put us off."

"The SD have the two captured agents. They haven't killed them yet, as far we know. Shall we ask to speak with them?"

"We can try. I'll speak to the boss when we get in."

Admiral Canaris was deep in thought when the pair got into the office later that morning.

"They're going to kill me, you know. They cannot afford to let me live, The SS, the SD, the Gestapo. I know where the bodies are buried, you see. I cannot be allowed to live." He smiled, "The sad part is they would be doing me a favour. For you and Edith, however, I have made arrangements. I am considering replacing you during the next few months with an SD plant, named Schellenberg. Edith will be your wife by then so she will naturally go with you into retirement. I suggest Switzerland. I do not want either of you involved in my downfall"

Stolle shrugged. "I believe that they are stupid enough and vindictive enough. But why don't you and your wife come to Switzerland with us?"

"I know they will not touch Frau Canaris. And, to put it bluntly, they keep such a close watch on me, it would destroy any chance you and Edith would have of escaping." Canaris was adamant. So the subject was closed.

Stolle brought up the subject of the SOE agents. The Admiral picked up the telephone and spoke to the temporary commander in Prinz-Albrecht-Strasse. The Gruppenfuhrer, Herman Blucher, was cooperative. The two prisoners were transferred to the Abwehr office, and installed in one of the cells kept for the purpose.

Both of the agents were battered and looked the worse for wear. The man was French, nondescript but no fool. His hands were mutilated. The doctor was disgusted with the treatment the SD interrogators had given out. The woman was in better apparent condition, though it transpired she had been raped and otherwise abused by several of the SD interrogators.

She appeared surprised when Edith kept her company, while the doctor examined her and then treated her injuries.

On questioning, both refused to answer any questions about their activities. Between Stolle and Edith they kept their enquiries on a general level, and there was no real reaction until Edith casually mentioned the third agent. Both noticed the reaction to the mention of the third person, neither referred to man or woman. But it was apparent that a third person had been dropped, as Edith suggested. They both casually mentioned a sweep in the Low Countries which had captured most of the network that SOE had spent time to install. It was obvious that someone had misjudged the nature of the people in the Holland-Belgium area. The security forces had been warned of the new teams being inserted in advance. They had been waiting for them to drop straight into their hands. They had been rolled up and were currently being held in a temporary prison camp situated between Amiens and Liege.

***

Michael had been asked to try and collect several allied airmen and odd soldiers still hiding out, being sheltered by the resistance, in some cases since Dunkirk. He was to try and get them either to Spain, or across the channel. The beginning of an idea was stirring when he had been told of the capture of the network and their detention in the temporary prison north of Arras. He requested a landing of twenty commandos or Marines to help protect the men and assist in rescuing the SOE network.

The team discussed the assembly and movement of the people being sheltered by the resistance. From the information they had, there were at least fifteen and possibly as many as twenty in the immediate area of Pas de Calais.

The team was split up into pairs and sent to pre-arranged rendezvous, to link up with the resistance units in the area.

In Arras itself, Michael and Sarah had a meeting with the dentist, by appointment. The dentist was in fact also the leader of the local resistance organisation. Jules Portet was a short intense man, quick and intelligent. As soon as Michael identified himself, he was able to tell him that in the Arras area there were still fourteen allied airmen. "It is becoming increasingly difficult to hide them. The Germans are becoming more firmly entrenched in the area. Also, I am ashamed to say, the number of collaborators is increasing as the war drags on."

"Is it possible to arm these men?" Sarah asked.

"Of course. Many of them kept weapons. They have been hidden away. But I am sure we can provide, if needed."

"What do you know about the prison camp here near Arras?"

"We know all about it. Our local people built the place. It is the usual collection of huts, with a guard room and office complex. Why do you wish to know?"

"First, can you produce a plan of the layout, where the offices, the guard room and the telephones are? Is there a radio room, guard towers?"

Jules Portet looked intrigued. "You are thinking of a rescue, perhaps?"

Michael looked at Sarah, he shrugged. "We are looking at the possibilities."

"My people will help if you need them….."

"No, I think, in this case, if we can gather the men in the area, we will find trucks to transport them in. They can help in the rescue. Afterwards, we will arrange a pick-up for them all. What we need from you is the layout of the prison camp, and the assembly of the aircrews with weapons in a place where we can pick them up. Once we have achieved the breakout, many of the prisoners will need help. I leave it to your discretion to make any arrangements you can to disperse them. We will try to take any wounded with us, though it may not be possible."

Jules thought for a few minutes. "I will contact the other units in the region. I presume this is urgent?"

Michael nodded.

"Right, if we target three days time. I will gather all the soldiers I can locate. Can you keep in contact?"

"Yes, one of us will stay in the area to co-ordinate. They will have a radio to keep in touch with London, and our other units. Do you have a suggestion for where she should stay? The hotel perhaps?"

"If it is the lady, I suggest she cannot be French. Her French is very good and would fool a foreigner, but not a Frenchman."

Michael looked at Sarah. "I think you may have to be German, perhaps SD or Abwehr. What do you think?"

"I think, perhaps, I will be Abwehr. It will make it more believable without a uniform. Can we produce identity documents, and I will need a small Walther, 9mm if possible."

Jules smiled, "Allow me, madam. He reached under his dentist's chair and produced an automatic pistol. He expertly snapped out the magazine, racked back the slide and ejected the cartridge in the breech. He caught it and slipped it into the top of the magazine. He then presented the empty gun and the magazine to Sarah.

"Danke schone, Herr Portet," Sarah said quietly. Do you have any extra ammunition in your pocket perhaps?"

With a wry smile, the dentist reached under the seat once more. "I can provide another loaded magazine for madam. I will now have to restock from the armoury."

He passed the second loaded magazine to Sarah.

Having given them each his telephone number, and a dead letter box for messages, they departed, pleased that they had made a start on the project.

When Michael spoke to the other two teams, they confirmed that they also had been able to agree arrangements, and that the three day deadline could be met.

***

For Ewan another task had been set. Find proper transport for the operation, at least two serviceable trucks, preferably of military appearance.

Being Ewan, his immediate thought was the nearest army depot, then he thought of Alek. Alek was working on his own, since his zone of operation was always Germany/Austria.

When he heard from Ewan, Alek went into action. Travelling to Karlsruhe, he located the nearest army depot. Dieter Braun had contacts all over Germany. In Karlsruhe he found the man and immediately put the question, "Who is the fixer in the local army depot?"

Hans Weber was a sergeant in the Waffen SS, He was also involved in all the black market scams in the military base just outside the city.

The base was in the seized premises of the Jewish Oppenheimer Company. Repaired and refurbished after the infamous 'Kristallnacht', the premises now housed the base depot for the border area.

Alek sat opposite Weber. He had weighed him up. This was a man who would do anything for money. Judging by the office and the quality of the uniform the man wore he was not living off the income of a sergeant's pay.

"I want two army seven-ton troop carriers, the unit numbers suitable for operations in France. Drivers would be useful for delivery, so they will need warrants to return here. Do not expect the trucks back."

"Just like that. You want two troop carriers, not on loan or return, but on sale. I must remind you, sir, that this is the army. We do not buy and sell trucks. The trucks here are government property, not second-hand goods."

"So how much for the pair?" Alek said.

"I have just explained the situation…" The sergeant repeated.

"And I said 'cut the bullshit!' How much?"

"I cannot sell….." The sergeant began.

Alek leaned forward into the face of the crooked sergeant. "I am getting tired of your attempts to push the price up. Do I get the trucks or do I drop a hint to the army audit department about two armoured cars sold to the Russians when you were in Poland, or about the supply of army stores to the local black market?"

Weber drew back in shock. How did this man know about these things? He pushed the button under his desk. Then he heard the clack as Alek pulled back the hammer on his pistol under the desk. His stomach cringed at the sound. When the two military police walked in he waved them off. "False alarm, I'm afraid."

"What do you need them for?" Weber asked briskly.

"Personal business, my own personal business." Alek answered.

"It will be expensive." Weber ventured.

"The price is going down every minute I wait, while you try to bullshit me. Now, I will give you the message. I have been in business since before you were born. I could buy and sell this operation out of my own funds, today. But my boss does not work that way. He has a simple philosophy Place the order. Pay the money. Discounts for bullshit and. when that doesn't work, take over the business, with prejudice. Do you understand what I am saying?"

Weber seemed to have finally got the message. "How does five thousand sound?"

"Including drivers and expenses, with vouchers for fuel at army depots?"

"I'll throw in dispatch documents, open ended."

"When can I have them?"

Weber looked at his watch, "This afternoon. They will be fuelled and the drivers standing by at two pm. Will that be OK?"

"Perfect! Oh by the way, if it happens that the trucks are followed or that some accident happens involving police or sabotage in any way, don't look for me. I will be elsewhere, but someone will be calling to collect the penalty clause in the contract. You will only have to pay it once. It will be collectable at any time."

Weber looked into Alek's innocent face as he delivered this final comment. He knew at that point the promise was real. His idea of recovering the trucks and disposing of Alek was no longer an option. He picked up the telephone on his desk, and wound the handle. It was answered, he said, "Gunter, all off the team."

Gunter said, "But, chief, those trucks won't be easy to replace."

"So you had better get on with it then." Weber said angrily and slammed the phone down.

He hated getting beaten. He would have to think of a way of getting his own back.

***

Alek called Ewan, "I'm getting into uniform as I speak. We will be with you by tomorrow morning."

"All official?" asked Ewan.

"You would not believe it," said Alek.

The two trucks set off from Karlsruhe across the Rhine into France, heading for Amiens and Arras.

***

Sarah received the credentials for her cover as an Abwehr agent, by hand from Margarethe. She appeared and disappeared.

Sarah presented herself at the hotel in Arras and offered no information regarding her Abwehr status. The hotelier asked for nothing except standard I/D. It seemed that they need not have bothered. Then Sarah thought about the prison camp. Maybe the identity would be of use there.

The main problem when on an operation like this was boredom, waiting for the pieces to come together. It always took time. The action was fine, but normally it was all over in minutes. A big rush then nothing until the next time.

They had all discussed it. All concluded that they did not want to do any other job in the war, so they just had to put up with it.

***

Ewan, now the trucks were on the way, needed to find two drivers. The Germans would not be too keen to play along that far. He could not really expect them to blatantly betray their country. So, to be on the safe side, it made sense to get other drivers to take the German's place.

Eric had Gestapo papers. Using them he visited the commandant of the Prison Camp at Arras. He made enquiries about the situation of the network which had been rounded up in Holland. The Commandant made it clear that the people involved were all being kept separately, that no one had interrogated then as yet. No one, including Eric was allowed to see them without prior authorization from SD headquarters.

Eric left, having confirmed that no drastic alterations had taken place at the camp since it was first constructed. He also confirmed that the guards at the camp operated on a three shift system and their barracks were in two wooden buildings outside the wire. The six towers were manned by two men each, armed with mounted machine guns, while both men had MP3 semi-automatic personal weapons.

The office staff was a three man detail, one operating the switchboard of the telephone. There was no Radio set up. One female acted as the Commandant's secretary. The other was a paper pusher who kept the records. Eighteen guards on duty, six on the gate and standing by, twelve distributed around the guard towers. This information was passed to Michael to arrange for cover during the break out.

***

The trucks arrived at the Army depot in Arras. The drivers reported in and refueled their trucks. Alek ordered them to stand by until called, and left them at the depot. He reported to Michael, who was staying at the small hotel in the next village to Arras, on the road to the prison.

"I have arranged for a landing of troops at Merlimont Plage, just north of Le Touquet. I need a truck to collect them. I presume you will have a non-German driver in place?"

"The trucks can be brought to this village. There is a barn here where they can be stored on the farm at the end of this road." He indicated on the small local map. "The drivers can bring the trucks off the Army reservation and then leave and return to their unit. Our drivers will bring the trucks here, and drive to Merlimont Plage for the pick-up. The returning airmen will be here and we will have German uniforms for some of the men. I want you in charge of the German unit we will form. Are you happy with that?"

Alek looked sharply at Michael. "After all this time?"

Michael said hastily, "I was asking if you were comfortable dressing up as a German Officer. I never doubted you otherwise."

Alek relaxed. "Sorry, I'm getting sensitive in my old age. I miss my friend Klaus. He was an idiot in many ways, but he was my loyal friend."

"We all miss him, Alek. Don't ever doubt that. We have become a team, a family. Losing anyone in the family is a loss to us all." Michael's comment was heartfelt.

It was the truth, and Alek realised it and felt guilty for thinking that he may not have been trusted. All of them at one time or other had put their lives on the line for the others in the group, including him.

Nothing more was said on the subject. Michael arranged with Portet, the dentist, for two drivers to take over the trucks, and for Michael to accompany the truck to the beach pick-up point, 60 miles away. A uniform was provided for him to ensure their smooth passage to the coast.

***

Sarah took charge of the Arras end of the operation. Already the fugitive airmen were being delivered to the barn. There they were armed, and told what their role would be in the scheme of things. The enthusiasm to do something positive was infectious. There was one day left before they would act. Michael left that morning in the truck for the pick-up. They expected him back from the rendezvous, in early morning. Departure was scheduled for midday, lunchtime for the prison camp.

Chapter Twenty-eight

Turn left for England

Michael sat dozing in the cab of the truck as they drove across France on the D roads. Now approaching Montroix, there was traffic but not an excessive amount and it was mainly military of one sort or another. Their truck with its military markings was recognized. The German officer seated next to the driver ensured that not too much notice would be taken anyway.

They arrived at the rendezvous area and the driver hung a beach towel from his window, as he parked in the beachfront car park agreed upon. Though it was late in the year, there were people in the area. The beach itself was wired off. "Nobody is allowed to swim," the French driver commented. "Except the Germans." Michael indicated two men in uniform on the beach. Both wore the red flashes of the Engineers.

The two men strolled to the car park where their Kugelwagen was parked. Then one broke away and walked to the truck. He grabbed the towel and wiped his hands on it. "Early, are you not? If you follow my little wagon, we can collect the others and go for this jaunt you've arranged."

Michael poked his head out of the window, "Glad to see you are properly dressed at least. Lead on, MacDuff."

They followed the Kugelwagen out of the small village, and onto a farm track passing a wooded area.

The area was clear. When the officer in the small wagon ahead whistled, men poured out of the trees and vanished into the personnel carrier. All were dressed as German soldiers. With the small car leading they set off for Arras. The officer, who had introduced himself as Captain Billy Cameron RM, joined Michael in the cab of the truck.

"Better not be sitting with an SS officer. The guide would never live it down." He was joined by the French driver, and continued to lead the way. They arrived back at the barn at dusk. The two officers went straight into conference with a plate of sandwiches. The others sat down to stew and dumplings.

On the journey back, Michael had learned that the Captain had been to and from France on several occasions since the occupation. He guessed that the man was a commando, as he made reference to Achnacarry, the Cameron's home estate in Scotland. Michael knew that it was in use as the training base for the Commandos. Their completed mission had been accomplished without the Germans being aware that they were in France.

"With luck, they will never know we were here."

" Our plan is to take the airmen into the prison camp for the night. Take over the camp, rescue our people, and set all the others free. We will then take the airmen and the network people down to a rendezvous, and send them back to England, along with your people."

"What will your lot do?"

"Oh, we'll pop back to Germany, and find something to blow up there, I suppose."

Billy looked at Michael with different eyes. The casual relaxed attitude was deceptive. "How long have you been in Germany?"

"My team and I have been there since 1938 on and off, mostly on." Michael commented, "There are usually things we can find to do to upset the Fuhrer. It's an international team. We get on well together."

"But what do you do about security, the Gestapo, and the SD, and in fact, the Abwehr?"

"Well, we only interfere with them if they become a threat. Otherwise we leave them alone. I know they keep trying to catch us, but so far we have managed to keep one step ahead."

"Rather you than me," Billy commented. "These little excursions are enough to keep me entertained. Doing what you do would soon give me heartburn. Anyway, we'll be off in a minute. I will just have a quiet word with my lads first." Lifting the tommy gun he was armed with, he wandered through to other end of the barn where his men were chatting to the gathered aircrews, and squatted down to chat.

Michael watched him go.

They set out, led by the Kugelwagen. The troops followed in the first truck and the second contained the supposed prisoners. All had weapons concealed about their person."

***

Ewan spoke to the Sergeant. "What's it like to be a leatherneck? Different from the peacetime service, I guess?"

"Not really so different," the sergeant replied. "We get to shoot at people instead of targets."

"Where do you come from then? Are you one of the families that have served through generations?"

"No. I joined up in the thirties when I was out of work. Never expected this lot." He nodded at his sleeve."

"What about your boss? How do you get on with him? He looks a bit of a tarter to me."

"Oh, Billy's not bad. There's worse than him about, I can tell you."

"Are you based at Pompey then?" Ewan asked offhand.

"No, we're based in Portsmouth." The man hesitated, looking at Ewan and the silenced automatic. "I gave it away, didn't I."

"You were very good. But the boss suspected." Ewan called to Alek. "Give the boss a toot, Alek. In the cab Alec tooted the horn. In the lead the Kugelwagen stopped with the lead truck behind it. The order to debus was given. The twenty marines, in their German uniforms, lined up in the road. They were surrounded by the armed men from truck two.

Each man was disarmed and his uniform removed. They were then placed back in the truck under guard. When the convoy was ready to resume, Michael spoke to Billy. "Billy these are the options. Either you tell the guards all is well and you are in charge, or I shoot you, and shoot my way in. That way will end your career, and a lot of other careers. The other entails survival of you and several others who would otherwise die, all for the benefit of a few agents who know nothing.

Billy said, "There would have been a bonus for catching your team."

"They pay you a bonus for doing your job? What are you, mercenaries?"

"My boss is Otto Skorzeny. We are part of his special operation group."

"You are paratroopers? Is that what you are saying? You took part in the operation in Crete. Well, good on you, I presume you all speak English so that must count for something. I guess it is a shame you forgot that the British have a most irritating habit of giving nicknames to a lot of things. Leathernecks are US Marines. The British have another name. How did you know I was expecting help?"

Billy shrugged, "We picked up your message, it never reached its destination. Your SOE people used the same frequency so naturally we monitored the line and we acknowledged your message and arranged a reception for you."

"You have no idea what we were planning. That is why you tried to fool us into accepting you. Now you know what we're up to, you cannot warn the prison. So we go back to my first suggestion. We wish you to get us through the gate. We can take it from there. How about it?"

"Sorry, cannot do. You'll need to do it yourself."

"Well I gave you the chance. Now the gate guards will die."

***

The Kugelwagen led the three vehicles through the prison camp outer gates which were opened for them. The attitude of the guards was casual. They approached the small car with slung weapons. Both were thrust, tied and gagged, through into the back of the truck. The convoy entered through the second set of gates and parked within the compound, where an officer left the lead vehicle and entered the administration block.

He was taken to the Commandant's office,

Eric, now suitably clad in SS Uniform, was speaking to the Camp Commandant, Oberst (Colonel) Werner von Kramer,

"We have twenty-two prisoners of war here."

"I have plenty of space for them."

"You have? I've heard of a whole network of spies in the field, all trying speak at once." Eric took the opportunity to find out as much as possible.

The Oberst seemed quite happy to show this SS man that he was on the inside, as far as the operation was concerned. In fact, his participation was to provide the prison transport for the captives to be brought to the compound. The rest was based on gossip, and overheard by the bunch of disgruntled agents in the compound.

"That would be the spy-ring we captured in Holland. There are not too many of them, so we will, of course, have plenty of room in the camp. I will allocate a quarter for your prisoners. How long will you be here?"

"Just overnight if I may. I will then get them on to the POW camp at Düsseldorf."

"Perhaps you can join me for a drink a little later. I keep a pleasant hock chilled in the refrigerator, just for these occasions?"

Ewan appeared in the outer office. Eric watched him out of the corner of his eye as he approached the public address system and the operator seated at the desk beside it. The small telephone exchange was on the same desk. There was another man, a senior sergeant, otherwise the office was empty. Eric kept the attention of the Oberst, while observing Ewan through the window. Ewan was staggeringly fast, his actions difficult to follow.

His right hand lashed out with a small cosh. The Sergeant was down. The left hand clouted the operator with a second cosh, and the office was secured.

Something in Eric's face must have warned the Oberst, who turned in time to see what was happening. "What the......?" The feeling of frustration he felt as the barrel of the issue Luger pistol prodded his back was clear on his face.

Eric removed the Oberst's weapon from his holster saying, "Sorry, Colonel. We came to collect, not deliver."

The sound of the PA system operating was followed by an instruction to parade the prisoners. All guards to report to the parade square in the centre of the camp.

The Oberst was able to see the effect of the strict code of discipline through the window overlooking the parade ground. He saw the party of prisoners from the Dutch network standing apart from the other prisoners, political suspects, gypsies, and others lined up on the square. He watched the captured agents loaded into trucks.

An SS lieutenant strode out as he watched, and ordered the camp guards to board one of the camp troop carriers which had driven into the compound, unnoticed in the bustle before him.

The Oberst watched, with dismay as his guards boarded the trucks. each man was disarmed at that point."

He heard the PA inform the remaining prisoners that the gates would be opened when the trucks left the compound. They had the chance to leave the prison. The final comment, that the records held in the camp had been destroyed created a stir among the assembled prisoners who were now milling around talking, excited!

"Time to leave, Colonel," Eric said.

The Oberst, hands cuffed behind him, stepped down the stairs carefully and was ushered into his own car, with two escorts. Eric seated himself in front beside the driver. The entire column of vehicles, with the released agents, the allied escapees, two parties of captive German troops, and the group of rescuers, set off in convoy for Le Touquet area, where arrangements had now been made for collection. Led by the Kugelwagen, followed in turn by the Oberst's Mercedes, the prison troop carriers, and their own vehicles, the convoy was substantial.

"Where are you taking us?" The Oberst asked.

"Not quite sure yet. Though I do expect you will see the sea sometime in the not too distant future."

The Colonel had to be content with that. The convoy was stopping. Eric got out of the car to meet with one of the people from the lead vehicle.

Michael had a radio in the Kugelwagen and he had been advised by Jules Portet, the French dentist in Arras. "He said that we missed someone in the prison. Apparently he was a paid informer. He has given the alarm. Road blocks are up all around the area, looking for the convoy.

I'll rearrange our defensive set-up, and we can now get rid of the camp troops."

"I suggest we keep the Colonel. He might be useful." Eric said. "What about Skorzeny's commandos?"

"We will hang on to them for a while anyway. I really do not want them running loose, while we are trying to escape."

Michael went down the column detailing the new arrangements. The camp trucks with the guards drove off into a side road, where there was a large woodland area and wide fields beyond. There in a clearing the men were tied up and left. Two of the prison trucks were disabled by smashing the injectors. The third was used by their captors back to the main road. The Colonel's Mercedes was waiting and the party swiftly caught up with the rest of the convoy.

Progress was steady until they approached the town of Marconnelle, where a road block, including an armoured car, was at the crossroads, along with a platoon of soldiers. Occupation troops, probably. Not quite the obstacle front line troops would be. But nevertheless, twenty-eight armed men were still a problem.

Michael had a chat with the escapee's, mainly airmen of one sort or another. All were willing to assist in getting past the road block. Since all were already armed and had sworn that they were competent with their weapons, Michael decided that they might be able to distract the soldiers while his people dealt with the armoured car.

Meanwhile, Eric went to work on the Colonel. "I think, Colonel, that it would save the lives of the people seeking us if you smoothed the way."

"What are you suggesting, Major?" He used the rank Eric was wearing.

"We drive up to the barrier in the small vehicle. You tell them to open it, get angry and tell them you are co-coordinating the search. They open the barrier. You order their men out on parade to be inspected, including the armoured car."

"Then what happens?"

"Two things. We disarm them and pinch the armoured car. Keep you with us, and, either release you or take you on to England so that for you, the war would be over."

"Can I really believe this? Why me? I am just a camp commandant. I have no power, no information."

"If you stay they will probably hang you. But if you co-operate we will take you with us, beyond the reach of the Gestapo or the Schutzstaffl, What do you say, Colonel?"

Oberst Werner Schultz thought about it. He knew damn well that what the Englishman said was true. He had been duped, and as a result had lost political prisoners. Worse, he had lost the spy network prisoners as well. Nobody would be interested in how or why. He was in place, and would take the blame.

He sighed. He had never wanted to be a Colonel. He had been quite happy as assistant Governor in Nurnberg Prison. He was a loyal German, but this man Hitler and his cronies seemed to have gone mad.

He turned to Michael, "I will cooperate, provided you take me with you." With a rueful smile, he said, "I have the feeling that the man, Billy Cameron, might cooperate also. His fate as a Skorzeny man who failed will not be pleasant."

"Thank you, sir. Of course you realise that, as long as we are here, any sign of doing anything contrary to my orders…?"

"You may be reassured. Having given my word, I will not break it."

Chapter Twenty-nine

The Return

Normally, the direct route to the coast from their current position would have been straight to Montreuil on the main road. But in view of the fact there was a roadblock here, there would undoubtedly be others on the alternate routes.

Here, with the road block ahead and the convoy on the road, it was important to make sure that they got things right. With Ewan, Eric and the colonel in the Kugelwagen, and two trucks behind them, they approached the road-block. The men on duty were efficient enough. The colonel played his part without a flaw. The frustrations of the past few hours made it easier for the normally quiet man to become an angry martinet. With the Kugelwagen still standing, engine running, at the barrier, the Oberleutnant in charge of the block was informed that the colonel was not happy about commanding, and actually taking part in, a search on a cold night. Since he was leading a search party to look for escaped prisoners, and since, also, he and his men had driven down the road they were blocking and there was no sign of runaways or vehicles, he was not happy and someone was going to suffer.

The major, who was waiting for clearance from his superiors, stoically put up with the colonel's rant, until the colonel stuck his face in the major's line of sight, and ordered him to parade his detachment, then and there for inspection.

The unfortunate major had two options, continue to try to get through to his own superior officer and face the wrath from the colonel before him, or just bow to the fact that a superior officer had just given him direct orders.

The men on the rear truck, under cover of the darkness, had de-bussed and filtered through behind the men waiting, smoking and obviously not concerned about the tongue-lashing their major was receiving. The crew of the armoured car, were lounging about like the others. Nobody saw any danger from the small convoy.

The major appeared and shouted for the men to fall in, "At the double!" He did not sound happy. The sergeants pushed and shoved the slower men into place.

Colonel Schultz had many times endured the sly comments and disparaging remarks of line officers who regarded his bestowed rank as a joke in real terms. A normally mild-natured man, for the first time he decided to play the colonel. His initial private rant to the major had given him a thrill that he had not anticipated. Now, as he stepped forward to receive the salute of the major in front of the paraded ranks of soldiers including the crew of the armoured car, his back was straight. He became the colonel in fact and, returning the salute, he strutted along the men paraded before him, Eric one step behind, the major alongside him.

"The state of the weapons of these men is disgusting." The colonel snatched the weapon from the man in the rank in front of him. He operated the cocking lever of the machine pistol ejecting the round in the breech. "This man is on parade with a cocked weapon. Ground arms!" He screamed. The paraded soldiers reacted immediately. As one, they placed their weapon on the ground beside their right boot and straightened up as one.

The click of the cocking levers from the ambushers' weapons was the first indication that they had been duped.

The colonel stood back with a satisfied smile, as Eric drew the shocked major's own pistol from his holster.

The men were searched and loaded into the their vehicles, and when they drove away there was no sign of the road block remaining.

***

Ewan took over the armoured car and assumed the lead position. The convoy followed. He turned off at a point agreed with Michael, and drew to a halt at a heavily wooded area.

A light flashed from the car toward the woods. A light answered. The car and the convoy turned in through the trees following a dirt track used by the foresters who worked in the area.

The armoured car entered a clearing and circled around the open area to point back the way it had come.

The other trucks came into the clearing and parked. Finally, the Kugelwagen brought up the rear. As if at a signal, men and women of the local Resistance, armed with a variety of weapons, appeared out of the woods and surrounded the trucks. The trucks were unloaded one by one. As each set of prisoners was offloaded, they had their uniforms removed. All were bound and gagged and left in a long row. The prison guards, Skorzeny's men and the men from the road-block, all received the same treatment. The remainder of the party, the escapees, the agents from Holland, Michael and his party, arranged themselves between two trucks, while the colonel and Billy Cameron, alias Lieutenant Horst Nader, were kept in the Kugelwagen. Horst Nader was cuffed and well secured. The colonel was seated next to the driver.

Mark took over the armoured car with the two women, both of whom had received a swift course on serving the guns.

Ewan sat in the lead truck, with Alek in charge of the second truck. This time the convoy drove off with the Kugelwagen in the lead. It was driven by Michael, while Eric kept his weapon handy keeping an eye on the passengers.

The other trucks, and all the weapons recovered from the captured troops, were taken away by the French Resistance group.

The convoy headed south, until it finally turned north toward Calais, heading for a rendezvous near Wimereaux, where a pick-up had been scheduled.

The collection had been arranged in conjunction with a drop-off, and the arriving agents took over the vehicles. They would be dispersed at an arranged spot for the Resistance.

***

With all the team now aboard the big Fairmile Motor Launch which had collected them, Michael was able to relax for the first time in months. He was in someone else's hands until they reached land once more. The cabin was warm and he dozed. As he lay there his mind wandered over the past years. He could not ignore the fact that the team needed a break from the continual pressure of living in a country supervised by a megalomaniac.

Since he had the entire team, apart from the recently joined Margarethe—who was being watched over by Alek—was on the boat, this time they would get a proper break to let their hair down. Determined, Michael settled back on the cushions in the saloon and promptly fell asleep.

***

Sarah came into the saloon with Marian and Eric. Seeing Michael asleep, they exchanged looks, and each claimed another piece of the cushioned seat, where they collapsed to sleep. The boat made its way across the troubled waters of the English Channel. Off Cap Gris Blanc, four gunboats, showing signs of action, joined it without fuss, and watched over the ML for the remainder of on her passage home.

***

In a quiet tearoom in the Black Forest, Margarethe Froelich sat opposite a distinguished-looking, wounded officer. His Wehrmacht uniform was immaculate. The Iron Cross, with oak leaved clusters, conveyed to all present that this man was a decorated soldier. The artificial hand and his limp as he entered made it quite clear that his decorations were merited.

Margarethe sat talking to Richard von Stalheim. They had been girlfriend and boyfriend at school in Vienna and, though they had parted seven years ago, they had always been friends.

Richard lived in the Black Forest. He was on medical leave and unlikely to return to the front again. Margarethe had returned south briefly while the others were away to England and had called to Richard's home to see if there was news of her friend.

Her call was taken by Richard himself, who arranged to meet in the restaurant where they were enjoying their meal.

When they had eaten, the waiter left them with coffee and cognac. Richard spoke. "I am delighted to see you, my dear. It has been too long since we last talked." He reached out with his good hand and touched hers. "There was a time when I thought we might have been together, but it wasn't to be." He grinned, and Margarethe saw, briefly, the friend of years ago.

Margarethe said a trifle coyly, "I was never meant to become a Grafin. Your mother made that quite clear. And I am not designed as a bit on the side, I'm afraid, though it might have been fun for a while. Where is she by the way?"

"Berlin, of course. She has done her duty and produced Oscar, my son and heir. She has a title in her own right, of course. Staying here with damaged goods is a waste of time for a popular young blond, safely married. He paused, a little sadly. "I was surprised that you were able to travel here so freely. You were living in Austria when we last met. Living in Berlin is apparently exciting. "

Margarethe had been shocked at the change in her old friend. His drawn face was more handsome than ever, but the hidden scars had taken their toll. She tried to ignore this as she answered, "I live there because of my job, but the nightlife is not fun. Everybody around seems either wealthy, or grabbing wealth from others. The whole scene is based on excess. I see, when I am travelling, the problems of people making ends meet, while our leaders are living the high life. It sickens me."

Richard gripped her hand and leaned forward, "Keep these thoughts to yourself, for your own protection. There are ears everywhere. Comments like that have put people in concentration camps."

"Surely, I can talk to my friend freely?" Margarethe said a little plaintively.

"Of course you can. It is just that others may hear in a public place like this. Anyway, you may not have to suffer much longer." He looked at her intently. His look checked her instinctive question. "Perhaps you will join me for a stroll after our coffee. The weather is quite mild for this time of year."

***

Richard managed the path despite his limp. As they walked through the wide meadow, he talked. "I am dying."

His raised hand stopped her instinctive words. "I've been told categorically that my life is limited to the next few months. There is nothing to be done, and I am reconciled to the situation. I was wounded on the Russian front, and facilities there are non-existent. So, by the time I was brought to a hospital, things had gone too far. My leg came off at the knee, and the arm, of course. The head injury will finish me off." He chuckled, "All those teachers who clouted my ear and called me thick-headed." He shook his head from side to side. "It seems the reverse is the case. My thin skull did not survive so well."

Margarethe thought for a moment, then said. "You mentioned I would not have to wait too long for things to change in Berlin?"

"Margarethe, I wish to trust you as I always did. Can I still trust you?"

"You can always trust me. I work in the Reich museum. But I see things I cannot agree with, and I hear things also." She stopped, turned and faced him. I am engaged to an American." She did not say anything else, just waited for his response.

"He is a lucky man, and I do not wish to hear any more in case we do not succeed. But I have become part of a movement to end this bloody war. Stop the unnecessary killing. I am not alone, and we are all dedicated to that madman's removal." He looked at the face in front of him and thanked God that there was at last someone, out of the loop, that he could share his secret with. He did not feel quite so alone.

"Richard, if there is any way that my friends and I can assist, please contact me. We have resources and can help." She reached into her handbag and wrote down a number. "Call, if you need us."

Richard looked at the number for a few seconds then gave it back to her. "My memory is still the same. I won't forget."

She tore the paper up. When they returned to the restaurant she put the scraps in the fire and watched them burn.

When they parted they realised that it was for the last time. Margarethe had tears in her eyes, as the Mercedes carrying Richard went off through the trees. She stood for some time, all alone, looking into the forest, before departing herself.

Chapter-Thirty

Last Call

The sojourn in England for the majority of the group was a break they all appreciated, although Mark was missing Margarethe.

Sarah disappeared to Scotland for two weeks. She took Mark, Ewan and Marion with her. As she put it, "To see what real country looked like."

The therapy of the old house and the land soon worked on them all. For Sarah especially, there was time to consider her feelings for Michael. She admitted to herself that, being alone was no longer the fun it had once been. Over the months, years, she suddenly realised, working with Michael and the others, they had become a family despite the variety of backgrounds and upbringing. When her thoughts turned to Michael she felt warm throughout her body. He had promised to come and join them, here in Lochaber, as soon as he could, and for her it could not be soon enough.

***

Ewan Fitzgerald stood watching the skyline as the stag grazed. He smiled wryly. Just a little further along the hill another stag stood watchful, gazing around and sniffing the keen highland air. He carried a rifle, but he was not in the mood for shooting. He had been surprised at his reaction to Sarah's invitation. He had always been the wary one, looking for the angle, the reason why anyone ever did something for him. It was only now that he had realised that working with the team where everyone's life depended on each other, he trusted others; his feelings for Marian had contributed also. That was another thing, for both of them. The fact, that another person meant more to him than he had thought possible, took time to establish itself, mainly because the team was so close knit.

Marian had been quite cold and clinical at first. She didn't smile much, but when she did, he first pulled her leg about it, hardly realising that he was bothering to bring that smile to her face for the pleasure it gave him, personally. He turned. As Marion came into view, she turned toward him. He smiled across the twelve foot ditch between them.

"What?" She asked.

He opened his arms and breathed in, a big silly smile on his face as he took in the vista in front of them.

"You are an idiot!" Marian said laughing. "Just a big kid."

For Marian the shock of finding someone who cared nothing for her past, and was interested in her, just as Marian Smith, was unsought. Her associations with men had always been an almost clinical, 'use and cast aside' matter. She had never let anyone get close, until now.

The country was having its effect on her also. Whatever it was it had entranced them all. Perhaps, she thought, because they worked so closely together, they each shared the feelings of the others. She had never felt so relaxed, so happy. Even Eric, with whom she had become firm friends over the years, had relaxed, and, though like them all, was concerned that Margarethe was still in Germany without them, was showing the effects of his stay here in this beautiful place.

***

Michael arrived at the end of their first week. Eric left them to visit friends in the south. When he arrived Michael had been tempted to bring them up to date with events. Luckily, he had realised when Sarah met him, this was not the time or place. For a week he allowed himself to relax and enjoy it. His love for Sarah was returned. His work colleagues were all his friends. It was all he really needed.

***

They returned to the office refreshed and cheerful.

Michael had been thoroughly grilled about the exploits of his team. There was strong opposition to its continued existence. Not the least from the combined efforts of SOE and OSS, the US Intelligence agency operating in Europe.

"What does that mean to us?" Sarah asked.

Michael thought for a moment, "While I'm not quite sure, I think it means we are still in business. M I 6 gently pointed out that we had rescued the entire Dutch SOE network, apart from our other activities, many of which occurred before their departments existed in Europe."

"As you all know, Margarethe is still in Germany. She has a post in the Museum in Berlin. Alek is there keeping an eye on her as a back-up. He will, if it seems sensible, be her cousin from Bavaria.

"Now, she has some information, she can only pass on verbally, so I will be returning to Berlin myself. Ewan can re-establish the Potsdam house for the others, meanwhile, we work on the possibility that was proposed. Assassination!"

The others looked at each other. The idea had occurred before, but no one was really in favour. The objection was that it could make a martyr of Hitler which could lead to the wrong people gaining control of the country and the war.

"I know," he said, shaking his head, feeling among the others the disapproval he himself shared. "Now listen to this. We investigate. We can make a plan. But we do nothing without very careful consideration. If we find that there are other plans in being, we can either act in concert, stand back and see what the result is, or perhaps go in ourselves. Whatever happens, keep your eyes open for other possibilities."

Chapter Thirty-one

Finale

As the aircraft left the formation of Halifax bombers, it dropped rapidly to the height of one thousand feet. The team prepared for the rapid transit from the DC3 to the ground. All stood in a row. Each checked the gear of the person in front. Nobody took chances with the check, and when all were done. They each raised their left hand. The right was gripped around the shackle tethering the release for their parachute. As they reached the door they let the shackle go and dived out of the door, into the night.

***

The atmosphere in Germany was not as up-beat as it had been in the past. The parties among the upper echelon of the Berlin circle seemed more frenetic. The certainty of 1939 had somewhat diminished over the past three years. The losses in North Africa and Russia, were taking their toll. More and more, the atmosphere was reflecting the true effect nearly four years of war.

To Ewan, there was no doubt that the impact of the war was now really beginning to come home to the German people. He checked the Potsdam house, and was relieved to find that the tell tales he had left when he was last in the area were still in place.

He moved in with minimum fuss, and prepared for the arrival of the others.

***

Commander Stolle was getting worried about the Admiral. For the past few weeks Canaris had been preoccupied, leaving all the day-to-day, activities to Stolle and Edith.

The open, easy relationships within the Abwehr office were a thing of the past. Now there were private calls and the Admiral operating behind a closed door, and secret meetings with senior officers from all three services.

Edith mentioned her own misgivings about the matter Stolle found he had no real answers to her questions.

He caught the Admiral as he was leaving for yet another meeting. Sir, we really need your input. Things are falling behind, and we may be having a problem with the SS."

Canaris stopped and thought for a moment, "Sorry, Heinrich. I've been pre-occupied lately. We'll talk when I get back after lunch."

"Thank you, sir. Is there anything we can do to help?"

"Not at the moment. Make sure Edith is here with you when I return."

Stolle stepped, back relieved. The Admiral was aware. They would soon get things sorted out and back to normal once more.

***

He was talking quietly with Edith when the Admiral returned, going straight to his office. Thirty minutes later the office door opened, and the Admiral appeared. He looked at them silently, then waved them into his office.

Sitting behind his desk, he leaned forward in his chair and stroked his chin. Stolle looked at his chief anxiously. Edith stepped over to the coffee pot on the burner and poured three cups. She served them and seated herself next to Stolle, facing their mentor.

Canaris sipped his coffee. "What is the problem with the SS?" He asked. Despite his own problems, he went straight to the point.

Stolle knew him well and was ready. "The new man they have brought in, Schellenberg, is truly dangerous. I am convinced he is attempting to take us over before much longer. He is insisting on having a list of our agents with their locations. I have told him there is nothing I could do about it. He would need to contact you direct. What worried me was his attitude when I mentioned your name. I swear he said 'I expected that man to be sacked by now'. He was turning away as he said it, but I believe I have it right."

Edith spoke then. "I have noticed that the people I speak to over in their HQ are getting more demanding and arrogant in their dealings with us."

The Admiral thought this over for a while, then quietly he said, "As you are both aware, I believe in National Socialism, but I have been concerned about the way it has been run. After the business with the rescue of Mussolini, I was forced to intercede to prevent our leader's revenge operation. I am aware that I have many enemies within the regime. Our success in the field of intelligence has roused considerable envy among other organisations. The war is coming to the borders of our country. The Allies are gathering to invade from Britain, and the Russian front grows nearer daily."

Edith said, "Then sir, you and your wife should leave before things go too far."

Canaris smiled sympathetically. "I still have things to do, Edith. So, though I appreciate your concern, I cannot leave yet. Others also depend on me."

He turned to Stolle. "Heinrich, I mentioned to you before that the time would come for you to retire to

Switzerland. They are bound to try to kill me. How they go about it has not been revealed. In the circumstances I have posted you both abroad. You are both transferred to the Embassy in Lisbon. Our agent in place is already preparing to be replaced. You will probably arrive on site and find you have been made surplus to establishment. Consequently, you should clear out immediately. Under a different name, with the money you will have with you, disappear. That way, I will no longer feel guilty about you." He sat back and reached down to the drawer on his left. He retrieved a package, which he passed to Stolle. "Passports, money, and air tickets.

"Travel light and be prepared to run. With the Gestapo involved, nobody can feel safe. If you're suspicious at all, drop out. Tell no-one."

"But what about you, sir?" Stolle was concerned.

"There are things I must do, and with other plans ongoing, you need not worry too much. If things go right, I'll recall you, via the embassy in Lisbon. You will probably realise anyway. Do not accept a recall from anyone else. If all goes well I will still be in charge, If Schellenberg has taken over, my plans will have gone wrong and I will have failed. I will probably be dead." The Admiral stood up and came round the desk. He took Stolle's hand and shook it firmly. "Good luck to you both."

Stolle and Edith left the office by the special route known only to Canaris and Stolle. The exit, through the offices of the custodian of the gardens on the other side of the street, did have garage space for the van which was kept available at all times. The van itself was more than it seemed, apart from its nondescript look to allow it to blend with the background, it could provide protection from bullets, if needed. The identity plates were interchangeable, with several different combinations, depending on where in Germany the van was used.

When Heinrich Stolle and Edith Korder drove away from the park, they had made their decision. Portugal could well be their destination, but not in any official capacity.

When the Admiral noted the van had disappeared, he arranged for a replacement vehicle. He realised he would never hear from Stolle again under the current rule. He squared his shoulders, it was up to his colleagues and himself to set things right for Germany.

***

The gathering of agents at the Potsdam house was discreet and unobserved. The newly revitalized SD had still no more to go on than the vague descriptions of the bogus Gestapo agents, and the still unfound Grafin of the Peenemunde and Metz episodes. The link between them all was tenuous at best. The coup at the prison camp was not linked to the other events thus far, and was unlikely to be without further evidence.

The disclosure of the 'officer plot' to depose Hitler was the immediate topic of conversation. For Michael, it was a relief, since it pushed the Allies' plans for assassination onto the back burner. In Norway the raid on the heavy water plant had been enough to push back the German researches into the bomb almost to beyond their possibility of solution during the present conflict.

Michael addressed the team, "Listen everyone! For the present we are reverting to what we seem to do best. Sting the authorities here, there, wherever, and whenever, we can."

There was a general acceptance of this positive news from all present.

"What news is there of the forthcoming invasion." Mark asked from his seat on the sofa.

Michael shrugged. "You know as much as I do. It is the end of May already. It should be soon I think."

Ewan said, "Why so important to go now?"

Sarah smiled. "It's all about the weather. Starting in spring means reasonable weather, meaning no deep mud, no snow, no ice, at least for several months. Armies make a big mess, and in winter, the mess gets bigger." She sat back to the murmur of agreement from the others.

"Now we have that out of the way, I understand that we have plenty of explosives in the store. What I mean to do is use the cover of the increasing number of air raids to blow up any places which would merit the trouble of setting up." He looked around the people in front of him, "Any suggestions so far?"

"Gestapo HQ for one," Ewan said.

"Reich Chancellery, perhaps," Sarah put in.

Michael looked at Alek, any suggestions?

"The Luftwaffe HQ in Wilhelmstrasse, but also the Flak towers scattered round the city."

Michael smiled. "That sounds like a reasonable program to start off with, but keep thinking anyway. The war is not won yet."

***

Despite the fact that they were back here in Berlin together Michael knew the group were all on borrowed time. Regardless of their record, the established intelligence agencies were taking command of all the privateer groups, and the day of his small group was about over.

He had just received a pack of orders which would probably relate to the invasion of Europe whenever it happened. The one-time code used was tied to an announcement that would be made on the day of the invasion. It would require the entire team at that time. He was aware that, when these last orders were carried out, the team would be broken-up and returned to England, their place finally taken by the established security services.

Michael sighed wearily. There was a loose end that he would need to tidy up. Taking Alek as back-up, he left the house to the team busy planning, and visited the Adlon. There, using the private telephone of Karl Curnow, the concierge, he called Helga Berger.

"What a pleasant surprise." The sultry voice answered.

"Are you alone?" He enquired.

"As usual, I'm a little sad to say."

"Pack a bag and come to the Adlon. Karl has a room and we can meet."

"Thirty minutes." Helga was quick on the uptake and made her decision instantly.

Michael turned to Karl Curnow, eyebrow raised?

Karl smiled. "I will be here for her. Room X11. We have used it before."

***

Michael and Alek left the hotel and made their way to the gardens opposite SD headquarters. The brightly lit building went suddenly dark, as the air raid sirens started their wail across the darkening city. Michael looked on in wonder, thinking of London at night by comparison. Across the street, the still lit windows were finally covered as the blackout was completed. Only then did the two men cross the street and enter the alley behind the building, where the rear entrance to the premises was still established. The increased security, initiated after the earlier incursions before the rearrangements of the security set-up had been completed, though apparently still in force, were more dependent on the terror generated over the past years than the actual physical force that once maintained the security of the building.

Michael and Alek stood at the outer gate and Alek produced a key. He opened the door, still chatting with

Michael. As the door swung shut both waved I/D cards at the two SS uniformed men, who were on guard duty.

Neither soldier bothered to do more than glance at the cards. They waved the two men through, and carried on their conversation.

The two men walked swiftly along the lower corridor to the secure vaults area, where the cells and interrogation rooms lay, alongside the secure record rooms of the SD and the Gestapo were held.

Michael had rationalized that, when the invasion of Europe occurred, the security services would embark on a frenzy of activity, to cover tracks, and to wipe out all trace of their less than honorable activities. It meant people would die all over the continent, as the suspects recorded in SD files were eliminated. In addition, the prisoners held for interrogation would also disappear.

What the pair were doing was a one time opportunity. Over the past several years the location and the diagrams of the self-destruct system had been obtained. On three occasions when things had gone wrong, secure repair men were called to put things right.

The suborning of one of these engineers was not really difficult. 'Sigmund', the mob boss, for whom Ewan and Alek had worked, had provided a package that the engineer could not resist. The plans were made available. The Mob then, trusting no one, especially politicians, proceeded to insert a branch into the system. It allowed the control to be operated from elsewhere. The external control point had been compromised in an air raid. Thus the intrusion into the building was needed, with the addition of a receiver to the system which would respond to an external radio signal. They turned into the basement, greeting the overalled stoker there, in passing. He did not even reply to their greeting. He just carried on trudging between the coal and the furnace, his shovel dribbling coal dust on the way. Luckily, out of sight of the stoker, they traced the alternate wires for the self-destruct system. Alek attached the radio receiver, which would trigger the system if required.

All went well until they approached the rear exit once more. There, they found the guards rigidly at attention, being tongue-lashed by a short, plain clothed man who was obviously known to the guards.

"Ja. Herr Oberfuhrer!" The soldier turned to leave and spotted the two men approaching from within the building. "Here are two men, sir."

The short man turned spotted them and beckoned them to him. "Come with me, you two. We have a call to make. Alek looked at Michael. Michael shrugged. Alek said, "Zu befehl"(Yes Sir.) Herr Oberfuhrer". Outside in the alley was a Mercedes car, the driver leaning on the front wing, smoking.

At the sight of the small party he snapped upright. The cigarette, still alight, flicked across to the other side of the alley to strike the far wall in a scatter of burning tobacco. He had the door opened before the small man made it to the car. "Get in. I'll explain on the way." The irascible man said.

The car drove off with a squeal of rubber and swung into the main street.

"We are going to pull in Commander Heinrich Stolle of the Abwehr who is suspected of passing information to the enemy". He looked at each man keenly. "We have not worked together before, but you will find that, if you do your job, all will go well for you. I reward diligence and punish poor work. Do as I say. We'll have no conflict. Understand!"

The pair chorused. "Zu befehl."

At the offices of the Abwehr they followed their leader into the HQ and encountered a smart young woman, who demanded their reason for being there." I am Oberfuhrer Karl Stich SD. I have come to see Commander Stolle."

"Well Oberfuhrer Stich you will need a long telescope. The Commander is posted to the Embassy in Lisbon, and has been gone now for most of a week. Shall I ask the Admiral to speak to you. The Commander was one of his men."

The small man snarled, "No. It was the commander I wanted. Lisbon, you said?". Turning to Michael and Alek, he said, "Fancy a trip to Lisbon, lads?"

On the way back to the SD offices, Michael produced his Walther, and told the driver to pull over. The Oberfuhrer looked sharply over at Michael and reached for his gun. Alek tapped him with his pistol. The Oberfuhrer sat back looking angrily at the two agents.

The driver swerved sharply and tried to destabilize the two agents. The tyres squealed, Michael shot the driver and the car lunged toward a tree beside the road. In the struggle for the gun, Alek shot the Oberfuhrer in the head. The driver, already wounded, finished up through the broken windscreen, his head at an odd angle. Waiting only to grab the briefcase that was in the car, the pair made their slightly unsteady way to their own car. Such was the tension in the night city of Berlin, any night walkers avoided contact with the wrecked car, hurrying past on the other side of the road. The wreck ticked and steamed in the cool night air.

As a police vehicle approached, a small flicker of flame appeared. It crawled along the body of the car and reached the puddle of gasoline, from the ruptured fuel tank.

The burned out wreck was just another reminder of an active night in war-torn Berlin.

***

There was an announcement on the radio, the voice clear through the crackle of static created by the inadequate aerial system. As the announcer told the world that the invasion of Europe was underway, the key words were spoken.

Michael was in the safe house in Potsdam. The entire team was present. All had taken part in the activities during the first few days of June. When the sirens wailed, they departed through the late twilight, casually delivering packages of explosives to places where they could cause the maximum disruption. Now all were seated around the room, waiting to hear what the orders contained.

In the resulting let down, Michael could read the secret fingers of the established Intelligence organizations. The orders were not target directed. They stated that it was time to wrap-up the operation, and concentrate on recovery of personnel back to England. In a separate envelope, sealed and coded, was a warrant for the arrest of Ewan Fitzgerald, for anti-British activities pre-war. That he put into his pocket for further thought,

"Ladies and gentlemen, having seen these orders, it appears our lives have become precious to the Government." He hesitated for a few moments, and then continued in the face of the dismayed looks of the team. "It seems that, despite the huge conflict taking place in Normandy, we are too important to risk." He looked at the members of the team who had without question undertaken hideous risks, and created mayhem wherever they had struck.

To say the team was disappointed may stretch the truth slightly, but there was no doubt of the surprise, followed by the resentment, at being dismissed so arbitrarily.

"That's it then?" Ewan said bitterly. "Not even thanks for the past four years. Go home?"

Mark smiled grimly. "Ewan, look at our leader. Cool it! I can hear his brain working from here."

All three women were deep in thought. Sarah said, "I was thinking of Peenemunde. Not the research centre, the operation centre. Think of all that liquid oxygen, the jet fuel, not to mention the warheads for the V1 and the V2."

Marion interjected, "Yes, I have never understood why the commandos have not paid it a visit by now. Especially, since the top rocket and weapons scientists are all grouped there."

"Are there many troops there?" Margarethe put in.

"There should be. But that can be an advantage. Since we have not really thought about it." Sarah turned, "Michael, is it possible to still hook up with our friend with the powerboat in the Baltic?"

"Maybe, not sure," Michael said thoughtfully. He looked around the room. "Am I to assume that you are not happy with the orders to fold up our tents, and disappear into the night?"

"Damn right, you are." Ewan and Mark both spoke together. The three women all nodded in agreement."

"First, I will gain us time from London. Mark, gather all the explosives together. By the way we will need explosive made from common cleaning materials, especially those that will benefit from association with liquid oxygen and or nitrogen.

"Alek and Ewan, take the small radio with you and set up in the locality. Spy out the land. As the others reach the area, we will use the Reinberg Ferry as a contact point. How does that sound for starters?"

At the nod from the others they started the process of planning.

Chapter Thirty-two

Peenemunde

Ewan nodded to Alek and adjusted his high collar. The Luftwaffe Hauptmann uniform was form-fitting and the small ribbon supporting the Knight's cross with Oak leaves and swords was an important part of the outfit for a Nachtjagdgeschwader (Night fighter) pilot, wounded in the service of his country.

Across the room, Alek was completing his ensemble as a Luftwaffe Lieutenant, also decorated with an Iron Cross, though of lower degree.

Once both had completed their dress, they checked each other for errors. Ewan collected his stick. He had fitted a false dressing to his right leg, to maintain his image of a wounded officer.

The visit to the establishment was a courtesy, apparently arranged by Oberst Hans Heindorf, present Commodore of the Nachtjagdgeschwader division of the Luftwaffe.

The Mercedes swept up to the gates of the Operation base at Peenemunde. The sentries did their job, checking the passes of the two men. The driver showed his pass, but was of little interest the guards who were seeing a Knight's Cross on a genuine hero; a Captain, a man who had earned his decoration the hard way. Their actions reflected their admiration, as they flung the gates open. One man stepped onto the running board to direct them to the administration building. Mark, who was driving, followed directions. The car coughed twice as it made the journey. Mark observed to the guard, holding on by the windscreen frame, "Bloody car started running badly, yesterday, I still haven't found out what is wrong."

From the rear seat Ewan called good humouredly, "Put it into the garage in the morning, Helmut." They all thought that was a marvelous idea, since the nearest garage, still open, was probably in Poland.

The guard said, "I'm sure our engineer will sort it out, while you are here at the plant."

"That sounds good to me, Ewan said. "See to it, Helmut!"

"Yes, sir. I will see to it, sir."

The guard glanced at him in surprise, hearing a sergeant speaking to an officer like that.

Mark was still muttering, "I'm a bloody air gunner, not a driver. Nor am I a bloody mechanic."

They reached their immediate destination, the administration offices for the site. The car drew up and coughed. When the sooty smoke cleared. Ewan stepped out of the car followed by Alek, both came to attention and saluted the people who came to meet them.

"Welcome to the establishment, our name for the current setup here." The tall man in the white coat had a slight lisp.

Ewan looked at the building which seemed to grow out of the low hill. "Impressive!" He said.

Alek kept his mouth shut and listened.

The guard spoke to the Warrant Officer, who stood to one side watching the proceedings. And when the party went in through the door, the warrant officer beckoned Mark to drive the car into a tunnel entry in the face of the hill, hidden from view by the building itself. He drove the car in gingerly, carefully avoiding any projections from the tunnel walls. The tunnel opened out and Mark was directed into a room at the side, where there was a ramp and a pit, though both were currently in use. He could see further within the hill. In a cavern a tall rocket, was standing there, being attended to by a team of overalled and hooded technicians. It was fifty yards away at least from the repair shop.

Too far, to be confident that it could be damaged from here. Mark thought, *At least without a bazooka or some such weapon.*

***

Ewan and Alek were being given the tour of the clean part of the area, the operations room and the accommodation, and administration area. At the luncheon that followed, the assembled officers and scientists were entertained by stories of the night fighters in action and sneak bombing raids over southern England. Stories carefully researched for the role with this situation in mind. When the subject of 'Radio Location' came up, both became secretive. Ewan commented that the same secrecy surrounding what was going on here, prevailed elsewhere.

"I must say that given the fact that we are entrusted with secrets which still preserve the lives of our friends and ourselves, it does seem silly that we are not trusted with secrets elsewhere." He shrugged. "I really thought we might have been shown the operation scheme for your super-weapons. It was that aspect of things I hoped to see. Sadly, we have all been on the sort of tour we have seen so far." With a sigh, he raised his glass. "I will not waste any more of your time, gentlemen. We shall depart forthwith." He paused with a chuckle. "Provided your mechanic has been able to repair the car." He joined in to the general laughter that followed his remark.

Their guide had been put-out by the comment about ultra secrecy. They were comments he himself had made during research. Justified, after all, the heroes of the Reich created the time and freedom to allow the scientists to work.

***

Michael Wallace was chatting with an old fisherman on the quay at Stralsund. Michael was dressed, as was his companion, in waterproof leggings and sea boots, their braces in view, as with jackets off they were stacking fish boxes ready for filling. Three of the boxes were filled with weapons and explosives. The old fisherman was Major Paddy Flynn, on detachment from no 2, Commando. He currently commanded an orphaned platoon of Marines, appointed to, but unable to join, the destroyer HMS Martlet, which had been allocated to the Normandy beach operation before she had time to collect her additional Marine contingent. The link-up of the major, the Marine lieutenant and his men had occurred in Portsmouth. The major with his Special Operations Motor Launch had been allocated to carry out diversionary operations, at the time the invasion was scheduled. With the delays, the components of the plan fell apart, the men allocated to the major were now part of the landing force. The Marines were all fitted out with nowhere to go.

Michael had been in touch with naval intelligence direct, on the old pal's network. His request for amphibious support in the Baltic brought everything together for the harassed Naval Ops Captain, Major Flynn and the Marine contingent. The ML was loaded with fuel and a promise of a further fuel drop by air at the Skagerrak. Michael was now discussing the type of operation the major was born for. The ML now had black crosses on her superstructure, and flew a German ensign at her stern. The crew all appeared to be the usual Kriegsmarine men for all who came within view, though few saw them at the moment, the boat having been moored behind Rugen Island.

Paddy Flynn and Michael conferred on the quay.

Margarethe and Marian, dressed in the uniform of the 'Lightning Girls', (Radio operators, RDF and electrical assistants.) the lightning flash on their uniform, were reporting to the local defence unit, who knew nothing about them. It appeared that the invasion had thrown the communication set up into confusion. Orders were going astray on a regular basis. In the confusion the appearance of the two girls was welcomed and they were flung straight into the confusion to help sort it out.

Sarah was located in a small cottage, where she was pivotal for the entire operation. The extra weapons were stored with her, and all information and reports were routed through her.

The tour of the V1 base and facilities had been a success. A private reveal had been given to Ewan alone after lunch, and the car had to be left awaiting spare parts. Alternative transport returned the two officers to their hotel accommodation. Mark had stayed with the car in the camp, the strategic dispersal of the sack of prepared charges was accomplished without fuss. Each of the small technical-looking metal boxes were placed where cables met. Twice he was nearly caught, each time he was able to talk himself out of trouble. There was no chance for him to place the charges within the restricted area. Interference in that region was down to Ewan, Alek and the raiding platoon from the ML

Preparations for the final move from Berlin had been made whilst the planning for the Baltic escape was being made. The placement of explosive packages in the various selected areas of the city was completed, and merely required a signal on the correct radio frequency to set them off at staggered intervals. The return trip was undertaken by train. Michael decided it was his prerogative, and, as the train arrived at the Hauptbahnhof in Berlin, he boarded the train to return north. He set the signal as they passed the junction just on the city boundary. The tracks to the rear of the train blew up. The other explosions scattered throughout the city were accompanied by the explosions of the bombs falling from the sky.

Michael was picked up by the Station Security Police in Stralsund. An alert was out for any suspected people, and the answer to the alert was to gather all strangers arriving at the Port for further examination. Held in the local police station with fourteen others, Michael had full confidence in his papers passing the test, but it would be inconvenient if his picture was broadcast, around the country, a possible result of the check-up.

Marian was on duty for the local police forces, handling the switchboard and the teleprinter operations. Aware of the problem she stood by and kept an eye on things. When a message came through to hold Michael for the Berlin authorities, she 'lost' it. It was found soon after Michael had been released out of detention.

The subsequent hunt for Michael prompted the advancement of the operation. Parts for the car arrived the day Michael was released. The repair was carried out and Mark was instructed to remove the vehicle from the underground garage.

A detachment of armed Kriegsmarine, under the command of their Lieutenant, arrived at the gate of the Rocket Base. At the same time, an irate Naval Captain appeared, demanding to know what emergency had prompted the call out of his men. As the guard tried to sort things out, there was an explosion from within the complex. This coincided with several others. The guard panicked and opened the gate. The naval party ran through the gate at double time and the gate closed behind them.

Within the complex, Mark had driven the car out of the garage the way it had gone in. It was therefore pointing downhill toward the rocket chamber. Making to reverse back into the garage, Mark drove past the entry. But where he should have stopped and reversed back, there seemed to be a problem with the brakes. The car rolled on down the slope. The hand brake did not work. Mark shouted out in alarm, opened the door of the accelerating car and rolled out apparently in panic. As he did, he activated the explosive charges in the doors of the car. As he lay on the ground, he watched the car roll steadily down to the chamber at the foot of the slope. He was passed by running men who ignored his damaged body, while they tried to stop the escaping car.

Back on his feet, he turned uphill and ran to the double door leading to the surface. The guard at the door opened it. "What the devil is going on down there?"

"I gave up trying to fathom the military mind years ago," Mark said, with a sigh. "It's always a panic. No one ever gets things organized in time." He passed through the door, and, since the guard was peering through the open door, he said, "Well, close it again, I don't want to be the excuse for you failing your duty."

The door was firmly closed when the explosion occurred , but Mark was already at the entrance to the tunnel by that time. The initial explosion—the noise suppressed by the closed doors—was followed by a massive explosion which the doors could not contain.

Mark met the Naval Marine party at the tunnel entrance. They were there to perform if Mark's effort went wrong. His appearance was in time to wave them to one side to avoid the blast from the tunnel.

When it came, it brought the wreckage of the car, the doorway, and bits and pieces of the guards. The hill behind the office complex erupted, flinging rock and earth and the wreckage of the doors high into the air. Windows in the offices cracked and shattered, with the stresses imposed on them. People poured out of the offices in the confusion; the Marines moved in. Their targets, the offices and safes of the scientists. Ewan and Alek had made their effort at the gate of the V2 ramps running parallel to the sea shore.

The uproar and the noise of the explosion had created certain panic among the guards of the establishment, none of whom were front line troops. The arrival of two officers, driven by a Senior Warrant Officer, was enough for them to allow the vehicle through.

Michael, driving, took the car direct to the control booth. Alek leaned out and placed the satchel charge against the wall where the transmission cables were bunched. They drove on through the running, men who appeared to be at a loss in the panic. There was little the saboteurs could do to the launch rails for the V1 flying bombs, so the main effort was directed at the actual stock piles of the weapons themselves, and the tunnel leading to the assembly plant inside the hill.

There was no way of knowing as yet. Michael stopped the car Alek grabbed a running man. "What is happening down there." He pointed at the tunnel. "Tunnel is still open, but the assembly roof collapsed. It's hell in there."

Michael drove into the tunnel entrance. there were fewer people running out now. there was a Warrant officer lurching along, exhausted. "Get out. The whole place will blow in a minute."

The three men looked at each other. Between them they dumped most of the satchel charges in a heap beside the wall of the tunnel, where an alcove was formed. He retained two and leapt back into the car, grinning at the dirty faces of the others. He said, "Shall we?" Not waiting for a reply, he reversed the car out of the tunnel and into the open area beside the stack of weapons awaiting launch. The last two satchels were tossed into the stack. He turned the car to the gates once more. The tunnel charges blew and the collapse of the tunnel was signaled by the cloud of dust and rubbish coughing out of the tunnel mouth.

At the gate, the guards were creating mayhem , not allowing any one out, saying that the saboteurs were still inside. The earth shook to the explosion of the weapon stack. The guards were overrun. The gates opened. The assembled men and women flooded out. The car continued, moving in the middle of the stream of people. There were several more sympathetic shocks following. The hill at the rear of the establishment had virtually gone. There were dusty, dirty people everywhere, the unaffected troops working to try and sort things out. Shocked men and women walked looking for friends. The general attitude seemed to be that the first explosions were caused within the factory itself.

***

The group assembled in the town square. Sarah was already there, waiting as the others came in, Mark first, then the two other women, and finally the three, Michael, Ewan and Alek, all covered in dust and dirt. The naval Marines arrived and assembled around the group. They proceeded to escort them along to the town quay. The sleek grey ML slid in, to come alongside and collect the raiding party. By this time the relief forces were flooding into town. The straggle of people and vehicles from Peenemunde itself was tailing off. The firefighters and local troops were still struggling to get the damage into some sort of control.

***

It was several hours later that the grey painted launch motored quietly through the Kattegat. There was no panic and so far no pursuit. In the main cabin below, the team was assembled. Michael spoke to them all, quietly explaining the situation as he saw it. "I will be returning to the office and I do not expect to be allowed out again. My arrangement for you all was to transfer all of you, with the exception of Sarah, to the US forces of OSS. The arrangement has taken into account the different nationalities of the non-Americans. After this final action against orders, I am worried that things may not be as simple as they seemed. He turned to Ewan. "There is a warrant for your arrest, current for you, in England."

Ewan grinned. "I would have been surprised if that had gone away. What will you do about it?"

"I will do nothing. Whatever problems you have had with my government, as far as I am concerned, your past five years have more than cleared the slate. Alek and Margarethe, both of you are technically enemy aliens. I will not risk your freedom to the mercy of the other agencies in Britain. I have spoken to our friend in charge of this boat. He is willing to drop you all at Cork, where there should be no political repercussions."

Ewan looked around at the others of the group. The smile on his face said it all. "I have a pleasant place in the country. You are all welcome to stay. There is plenty of room for you all, and that includes Sarah and you, Michael, if you wish. When we began this journey, it was the fact that you, Michael, had the foresight to collect us together and set us off. It's been a blast for me and, I know, for all of you. We collectively showed the establishment the way. Whatever they do now they cannot take our victory away from us.

Chapter Thirty-three

Loose Ends

Michael walked into the office in Whitehall, his uniform a little looser than he was accustomed to, his hair a little shorter. Sarah greeted him, with a bunch of letters and a kiss.

"Good to have you back, boss." She said, a little breathlessly.

"Good to be back, and out of the hands of the vultures."

"That bad?" Sarah said.

"Could have been. But the fact, that Churchill found out about the final operation put a full stop to the whole matter. The decorations I suggested have all been approved when I was asked to explain how we managed to get the entire operation under way. He saw for himself the documented series of operations that we undertook, with the support of Naval Intelligence only." He paused and grinned. "I watched him tear up some papers on his desk. His only comment was, "Bring them home, if they would like to come. The King will be happy to decorate them, personally."

***

The beach house in Sea Point, Capetown, was comfortable. The couple, who were renting it, were well pleased with the arrangement. It was not where they were planning on settling, just a waypoint on their journey to California. Henry and Edith were a quiet, easy going couple, who had been accepted in the community since their arrival three months ago. His artificial leg was not really inconvenient for most situations. It was rumoured that the loss of his leg had forced him out of the navy. He and his wife, Edith, were planning to emigrate to USA when the war came to an end.

~*~**~*~

Meet our Author
David O'Neil

Frequently compared favorably to noted author, W.E.B. Griffin, O'Neil is an avid student of military history, especially during the time of sea battles and political uprisings. A native of the United Kingdom, artist and photographer David O'Neil started writing seriously with a series of Highland guide books. His boyhood ambitions were to fly an airplane, and sail a boat. As a boy he and his family were bombed out of their home in London. He learned to fly with the Royal Air Force during his National Service. He started sailing boats while serving in the Colonial Police, in Nyasaland (Malawi). He spent 8 years there, before returning to UK. Since then he lived in southern England where he became a management consultant, for over twenty years. He returned to live in Scotland in 1980, and became a tour guide in1986. He started writing in 2006, the first guide book being published in 2007. A further two have been published since He started writing fiction in 2007 and has now written five full length novels. A student of history and formerly military, O'Neil has been compared favorably with the UK's Ian Fleming and is frequently referred to as the "W.E.B. Griffin of the United Kingdom" due in a large part to his insightful recounting of exciting military exploits and his unique ability to develop credible characters.

Also by David O'Neil

Action/Adventure/Thriller series
Counterstroke # 1

Exciting, Isn't It?

O'Neil's initial entry into the world of action adventure romance thriller is filled with mystery and suspense, thrills and chills as *Counterstroke* finds it seeds of Genesis, and springs full blown onto the scene with action, adventure and romance galore.

John Murray, ex-Police, ex-MI6, ex management consultant, 49 and widowed, is ready to make a new start. Having sold off everything, he sets out on a lazy journey by barge through the waterways of France to collect his yacht at a yard in Grasse. En route he will decide what to do with the rest of his life

He picks up a female hitch-hiker Gabrielle, a frustrated author running from Paris after a confrontation with a lascivious would-be publisher Mathieu. She had unknowingly picked up some of Mathieu's secret documents with her manuscript. Although not looking for action, adventure or romance, still a connection is made.

An encounter with Pierre, an unpleasant former acquaintance from Paris who is chasing Gabrielle, is followed by a series of events that make John call on all his old skills of survival to keep them both alive over the next few days. Mystery and suspense shroud the secret documents that disclose the real background of the so called publisher who is in fact a high level international crook.

To survive, the pair become convinced they must take the fight to the enemy but they have no illusions; their chances of survival are slim. But with the help of some of John's old contacts, things start to become... exciting.

Counterstroke # 2....

Market Forces

Market Forces, Volume Two of the Counterstroke action adventure romance thriller series by David O'Neil introduces Katherine (Katt) Percival, tasked with the assassination of Mark Parnell in a hurried, last-minute attempt to stop his interference with the success of the Organization in Europe. As a skilled terminator for the CIA, Katt is accustomed to proper briefing. On this occasion she disobeys her orders, convinced it's a mistake. She joins forces with Mark to foil an attempt on his life.

Parnell works for John Murray, who created Secure Inc that caused the collapse of an International US criminal organisation's operation in Europe, forcing the disbanding of the US Company COMCO. Set up as a cover for money-laundering and other operations designed to control from within the political and financial administration, they had already been partially successful. Especially within the administrative sectors of the EU.

Katt goes on the run, she has been targeted and her Director sidelined by rogue interests in the CIA. She finds proof of conspiracy. She passes it on to Secure Inc who can use it to attack the Organization. She joins forces with Mark Parnell and Secure Inc. Mark and Katt and their colleagues risk their lives as they set out to foil the Organization once again.

Counterstroke # 3....

When Needs Must...

The latest action adventure thriller in the Counterstroke series opens with a new character Major Teddy Robertson–Steel fighting for survival in Africa. Mark Parnell and Katt Percival now working together for Secure Inc. are joined by Captain Libby 'Carter' Barr, now in plain clothes, well mostly, and her new partner James Wallace. They are tasked with locating and thwarting the efforts of three separate menaces from the European scene that threaten the separation of the United Kingdom from the political clutches of Brussels, by using terrorism to create wealth by a group of billionaires, and the continuing presence of the Mob, bankrolled from USA. An action adventure thriller filled with romance, mystery and suspense. With the appearance of a much needed new team, Dan and Reba, and the welcome return of Peter Maddox, Dublo Bond and Tiny Lewis, there is action and adventure throughout. Change will happen, it just takes the right people, at the right time, in the right place.

Young adult action/adventure/ romance thriller series
Donny Weston & Abby Marshall # 1

Fatal Meeting

A captivating new series of young adult action, romance, adventure and mystery.

For two young teens, Donny and Abby, who have just found each other, sailing the 40 ft ketch across the English Channel to Cherbourg is supposed to be a light-hearted adventure.

The third member of the crew turns out to be a smuggler, and he attempts to kill them both before they reach France. The romance adventure. now filled with action, mystery and suspense, suddenly becomes deadly serious when the man's employers try to recover smuggled items from the boat. The action gets more and more hectic as the motive becomes personal

Donny and Abby are plunged into a series of events that force them to protect themselves. Donny's parents become involved so with the help of a friend of the family, Jonathon Glynn, they take the offensive against the gang who are trying to kill them.

The action adventure thriller ranges from the Mediterranean to Paris and the final scene is played out in the shadow of the Eiffel Tower in the city of romance and lights; Paris France..

Donny Weston & Abby Marshall # 2

Lethal Complications

Eighteen year olds Donny and Abby take a year out from their studies to clear up problems that had escalated over the past three years. They succeed in closing the book on the past during the first months of the year, now they are looking forward to nine months relaxation, romance and fun, when old friend of the family, mystery man Jonathon Glynn, drops in to visit as they moor at Boulogne, bringing action and adventure into their lives once again.

Jonathon was followed and an attempt to kill them happens immediately after his visit. They leave their boat and pick up the RV they have left in France, hoping to avoid further conflict. They are attacked in the Camargue, but fast and accurate shooting keeps them alive. They find themselves mixed up in a treacherous scheme by a rogue Chinese gang to defame a Chinese moderate, in an attempt to stall the Democratic process in China.

The two young lovers, becoming addicted to action and adventure, link up with Isobel, a person of mystery who has acquired a reputation without earning it. Between them they manage to keep the Chinese target and his girlfriend out of the rogue Chinese group's hands.

Tired of reacting to attack, and now looking for action and adventure, they set up an ambush of their own, effectively checkmating the rogue Chinese plans. The leader of the rogues, having lost face and position in the Chinese hierarchy, plans a personal coup using former Spetsnaz mercenaries. With the help of a former SBS man Adam, who had worked with and against Spetsnaz forces, the friends survive and Lin Hang the Chinese leader suffers defeat.

Donny Weston & Abby Marshall # 3....

A Thrill A Minute

They are back! Fresh from their drama-filled action adventure excursion to the United States, Abby Marshall and Donny Weston look forward to once again taking up their studies at the University. Each of them is looking forward to the calm life of a University student without the threat of being murdered. Ah, the serene life.... that is the thing. But that doesn't last long. It is only a few weeks before our adventuresome young lovers find that the calm, quiet routine of University life is boring beyond belief and both are filled with yearning for the fast-paced action adventure of their prior experiences. It isn't long before trouble finds the couple and they welcome it with open arms, but perhaps this time they have underestimated the opposition. Feeling excitement once again, the two youths arm themselves and leapt into the fray. The fight was on and no holds barred!

Once again O'Neil takes us into the action filled world of mystery and suspense, action and adventure, romance and peril.

Donny Weston & Abby Marshall # 4....

It's Just One Thing After Another

Fresh from their victory over the European Mafia, our two young adults in love, Abby Marshall and Donny Weston, are rewarded with an all-expense-paid trip to the United States. But, as our young couple discover, there is no free lunch and the price they will have to pay for their "free" tour may be more than they can afford to pay, in this action adventure thriller. Even so, with the help of a few friends and some former enemies, the valiant young duo face danger once again with firm resolve and iron spirit, but will that be sufficient in face of the odds that are stacked against them?

And is their friend and benefactor actually a friend or is he on the other side? The two young adults look at this man of mystery and suspense with a bit of caution. Action, adventure and romance abound in this, the latest escapades of Britain's dynamic young couple.

Donny Weston & Abby Marshall # 5

What Goes Around...

Just when it seems that our two young heroes, Donny Weston and Abby Marshall are able to return to the University to complete their studies, fate decides to play another turn as once again the two young lovers come under attack, this time from a most unsuspected source. It appears that not even the majestic powers of the British Intelligence Service will be enough to rescue the beleaguered duo and they will have to survive through their own skills. In the continuing action adventure thriller, two young adults must solve the mystery that faces them to determine who is trying to kill them. The suspense is chilling, the action and adventure stimulating. Finding togetherness even among the onslaughts, Donny and Abby also find remarkable friends who offer their assistance; but will even that be enough to overcome the determined enemy?

Donny Weston & Abby Marshall # 6

Without Prejudice

Donny Weston and Abby Marshall, on their way to park their beloved boat *Swallow* in Malta to be ready for the summer, encounter the schooner *Speedwell* at La Rochelle, where problems arise for Commander Will and his wife Mary Pleasance. Tom Hardy and Lotte Compton, both from the *Speedwell* join forces with Donny and Abby to oppose the threats to the Commander. From Valetta the four follow up the threat, only to find themselves faced with a plot to use a famous mercenary in an assassination that will rock the foundations of the Euro community, and the western world. Backed by Russia and with the tacit approval of the head of MI6, a rogue CIA operative has set things up for a public shooting at a Euro summit.

The four foil the plot and the assassination fails, but ironically the CIA agent, is credited with foiling the coup and promoted. He wants revenge, and comes after the four with blood in his eye and his guns loaded. The outcome is decided in a action-packed shoot-out in high speed boats in the cold waters of the Thames estuary.

Sea Adventures

Better The Day

From the W.E.B. Griffin of the United Kingdom, David O'Neil, a exciting saga of romance, action, adventure, mystery and suspense as Peter Murray and his brother officers in Coastal Forces face overwhelming odds fighting German E-boats, the German Navy and the Luftwaffe in action in the Channel, the Mediterranean, Norway and the Baltic – where there is conflict with the Soviet Allies. This action-packed story of daring and adventure finally follows Peter Murray to the Pacific where he faces Kamikaze action with the U.S. Fleet.

Distant Gunfire

"Boarder s Away!" Serving as an officer on a British frigate at the time of the French Emperor Napoleon is not the safest occupation, but could be a most profitable one. Robert Graham, rising from the ranks to become the Captain of a British battleship by virtue of his dauntless leadership, displayed under enemy fire, finds himself a wealthy man as the capture of enemy ships resulted in rich rewards. Action and adventure is the word of the day, as battle after battle rages across the turbulent waters and seas as the valiant British Royal Navy fights to stem the onslaught of the mighty French Army and Navy. Mystery and suspense abound as inserting and collecting spy agent after spy agent is executed. The threat of imminent death makes romance and romantic interludes all the sweeter, and the suspense of waiting for a love one to return even more traumatic. Captain Graham, with his loyal following of sailors and marines, takes prize ship after prize ship, thwart plot after diabolical plot, and finds romance when he least expects it. To his amazement and joy, he finds himself being knighted by the King of England. The good life is his, now all he has to do is to live long enough to enjoy it. A rollicking good tale of sea action and swashbuckling adventures.

Sailing Orders

For those awaiting another naval story of the 18/19th century, then this is it. Following the life of an abandoned 13 year old who by chance is instrumental in saving a family from robbery and worse. Taken in by the naval Captain Bowers he is placed as a midshipman in his benefactor's ship. From that time onward with the increasing demands of the conflict with France, Martin Forrest grows up fast. The relationship with his benefactors family is formalised when he is adopted by them and has a home once more. Romance with Jennifer the Captains ward links him ever closer to the family.

Meanwhile he serves in the West Indies where good fortune results in his gaining considerable wealth personally. With promotion and command he is able to marry and reclaim his birth-right, stolen from him by his step-mother and her lover.

The mysterious (call me merely Mr Smith) involves Martin in more activity in the shadowy world of the secret agents. Mainly a question of lifting and placing of people, his involvement becomes more complex as time goes on. A cruise to India consolidates his position and rank with the successful capture of prizes when returning convoying East-Indiamen. His rise to Post rank is followed by a series of events, that sadly culminate in family tragedy.

While still young Martin Forrest-Bowers faces and empty future, though merely Mr Smith has requested his services????

Quarterdeck

Following the highly successful introduction of Martin Forrest-Bowers into the Royal Navy in the best-selling sea adventure, ***Sailing Orders***, David O'Neil, the UK's hottest selling author, presents another daring tale of Martin and his valiant men in a stirring story of war and sea, romance and action, valour and courage.

Now married and a decorated Captain himself, Martin returns home to find his wife Jennifer at death's door. Prompted by his safe return, her recovery is assured and is followed by the necessity of returning to work for 'plain Mr. Smith' with clandestine excursions and undercover trips to France. . At sea once more, he is involved not only with preventing treasure ships from falling into French hands, but also with events on the east coast of America in the run-up to the war of 1812.

Action, battle, romance, adventure and thrills abound in O'Neil's latest venture into the world of sea battles with France, Spain and American pirates.

Winning

Continuing the dynamic series of Captain Sir Martin Forest-Bowers RN and the unconquerable crew of the Royal Navy are once more in the thick of the action, with the task of upsetting the Maritime life of the Newly Independent Republic of America. The war of 1812 has been declared and combined with the French war it puts the Royal Navy into the position of possibly fighting on two fronts. Fortuitously the American navy is small and spread wide. The new ships are being built but are slow to come into service. In fact apart from one inconclusive action Martin fights most of his actions against pirates and the French. To his astonishment, the major action Martin fought was on land alongside Americans against a man setting up his own kingdom. Returning after a final sea battle with a renegade French flotilla and its prize, Martin finds that the war was over,

Part Two: With Admiral Bowers retiring, and the fleet shrinking rapidly, fewer commands are available. Martin finds himself on the beach. With his friend Antonio Ramos and many of his former officers and men, He forms a trading company and with two discarded frigates and an East-Indiaman, crewed by investors in the company they undertake a voyage to South America, with an undercover role to remove two renegade ships from the Pacific shores of Chile. Their travels take them around the world. The voyage is financially successful. But there are still no naval commands available, accustomed to winning, it seems this time it is Jennifer his wife who is winning this final battle.

Adventure thrillers

Minding the Store

O'Neil scores again! Often favourably compared to America's W.E.B. Griffin and to U.K.'s Ian Fleming, and fresh from his best-selling action adventure, "Distant Gunfire," O'Neil finds excitement and action in the New York garment district. The department store industry becomes the target of take-over by organized crime in their quest for money-laundering outlets. It would seem that no department store executive is a match for vicious criminals, however, David Freemantle, heir to the Freemantle fortune and Managing Director of America's most prestigious department store is no ordinary department store executive and the team of ex-military specialists he has assembled contains no ordinary store security personnel. Armed invasions are met with swift retaliation; kidnapping and rape attempts are met with fatal consequences as the Mafia and their foreign cohorts learn that not all ordinary citizens are helpless, and that evil force can be met with superior force in O'Neil's latest thriller of adventure and action, romance and suspense, mystery and mayhem that will have the reader on the edge of his seat until the last breath-taking word.

The Hunted

David O'Neal, UK's answer to W.E.B. Griffin and Dean Koontz strikes again with his newest suspense thriller filled with action, adventure, romance and danger. When the Russian Mafia joins forces with other European and Asian gangsters to take over a noted world-wide charity organization to smuggle guns and drugs into unsuspecting nations and begins to kill innocent people, one man – Tarquin Gilmore – Quin to his friends – declares war on the Mafia. To achieve his goal of total destruction of the criminal gangs, he surrounds himself with a few dangerous men and beautiful women. But don't be fooled by their beauty, the girls are easily as deadly as any man. On the other hand, there are a lot more gangsters than Quin and his friends and it's a battle to the finish. A stirring tale of crime and murder, mystery and suspense, passion and romance, guns and drugs… but that is war!

The Mercy Run

O'Neil's thrilling action adventure saga of Africa: the story of Tom Merrick, Charlie Hammond and Brenda Cox; a man and two women who fight and risk their lives to keep supplies rolling into the U.N. refugee camps in Ethiopia. Their adversaries: the scorching heat, the dirt roads and the ever present hazards of bandit gangs and corrupt government officials. Despite tragedy and treachery, mystery and suspense while combating the efforts of Colonel Gonbera, who hopes to turn the province into his personal domain, Merrick and his friends manage to block the diabolical Colonel at every turn.

Frustrated by Merrick's success against him, there seems to be no depths to which the Colonel would not descend to achieve his aim.

The prospect of a lucrative diamond strike comes into the game, and so do the Russians and Chinese. But, as Merrick knows, there will be no peace while the Colonel remains the greatest threat to success and peace.

Romance

Seasons

Life and Death, Love and Hate in the Luscious Vineyards of France
Take one French Mademoiselle. Add one recently jilted English stone-mason. Put in a dash of a French one-legged ex-paratrooper. Stir in one inquisitive French priest. Blend in a crooked French businessman, a lawyer without a conscience and several strong-arm Serbian gangsters willing to do anything if the price is right, and you have the makings of a first-class brawl.

Top that with blatant attempts to steal valuable crops of grapes and olives and you will have the latest masterpiece from David O'Neil.

And More to Come

CPSIA information can be obtained
at www.ICGtesting.com
Printed in the USA
FSOW04n1941160616
21665FS